THE
FLOAT
TEST

The Kenner siblings are at odds. Jenn is a harried mom struggling under the weight of family obligations. Fred is a novelist who can't write—maybe because she's lost faith in storytelling itself. Jude is a recovering corporate lawyer with her own story to tell, and a grudge against her former favorite sister, Fred. George, the baby, is estranged from his wife and harboring both a secret about his former employer and an ill-advised crush on one of his sisters' friends. Gathered after a major loss, each sibling needs the others more than ever—if only they could trust one another.

A family story is, of course, only as honest as the person telling it. This family story in particular is fraught with secrets about kids and sex and jobs and why the Kenner matriarch had a gun in her underwear drawer. The biggest secret of all, though, is the secret of what happened between Jude and Fred to create such a rift between the two once-close middle sisters. Over the course of a sweltering Florida summer, the Kenner siblings will revisit what it means to be a family and, if they are smart and kind and lucky, will come out on the other side better for having one another.

A rich exploration of family, ambition, secrets, and love, *The Float Test* is an elegant and gripping testament to the power that family has to both nurture and destroy us, from a critically acclaimed writer working at the top of her craft.

THE FLOAT TEST

ALSO BY LYNN STEGER STRONG

Flight
Want
Hold Still

THE
FLOAT
TEST

A Novel

LYNN STEGER STRONG

MARINER BOOKS
New York   Boston

THE FLOAT TEST. Copyright © 2025 by LLS Writing & Editing. All rights reserved. Printed in the United States of America. No part of this book may be used or reproduced in any manner whatsoever without written permission except in the case of brief quotations embodied in critical articles and reviews. For information, address HarperCollins Publishers, 195 Broadway, New York, NY 10007.

HarperCollins books may be purchased for educational, business, or sales promotional use. For information, please email the Special Markets Department at SPsales@harpercollins.com.

FIRST EDITION

Designed by Emily Snyder

Library of Congress Cataloging-in-Publication Data has been applied for.

ISBN 978-0-06-339073-7

$PrintCode

Dedication TK

And would it have been worth it, after all,
Would it have been worth while,
After the sunsets and the dooryards and the sprinkled streets,
After the novels, after the teacups, after the skirts that trail along
the floor—
And this, and so much more?—
It is impossible to say just what I mean!
But as if a magic lantern threw the nerves in patterns on a screen:
Would it have been worth while
If one, settling a pillow or throwing off a shawl,
And turning toward the window, should say:
"That is not it at all,
That is not what I meant, at all."
—T. S. ELIOT, "The Love Song of J. Alfred Prufrock"

And with all of this, I am still allowed to miss it so.
—JOY WILLIAMS, "One Acre"

Once, when we were little—I was eight, and Fred was almost ten; Jenn was twelve but she felt teenage; George was almost three—Fred and I ran away from home. It was summer. Our favorite nanny had just quit. Mom, a lawyer, had court and she'd left Jenn in charge, and Jenn was busy looking after toddler George, yelling upstairs to us not to get our rooms too messy. *Jude*, Fred said, she whispered, coming into my room, her hair pulled back. She climbed onto my bed, blue Umbros loose on her long spindly legs, a two-sizes-too-big Shane Matthews jersey falling off one shoulder. *We're leaving*, she said. I was still under the covers, reading *Anne of Avonlea*. Fred took the book and grabbed my hand. *We aren't ever coming back*, she said. Her face, her voice: I sat up, got out of bed. Fred packed a pint of strawberries, half a pound of presliced Boar's Head honey maple turkey, a quarter pound of provolone, two Snickers bars, four bags of potato chips. The garage had years of Christmas-present bikes that we mostly didn't ride but got new every year. We lived four miles from the beach but hardly ever went. Mom got antsy: all that sitting. Dad despised the mess of sand.

Fred and I never made it to the beach that day. We had to scale three bridges, two rivers, and the inlet, and on the second, steepest bridge Fred's bike flipped. We weren't wearing helmets. It was 1991. She ducked her head just shy of making contact with the concrete, scraped her lower back and ass instead. *Freddy! Freddy!* I said, running toward her. She looked shocked and scared but wasn't crying. *Jude*, she said. I helped her up. We wore no sunscreen, and her face was bright red, sweating. I went to get her bike down at the bottom of the bridge, and we walked back. A storm rolled through and soaked us, and when we got home Jenn made us strip off all our clothes in the backyard. We were, she said, *too wet, disgusting*; Dad would *lose his shit* if we dripped on his floors. She threw towels at us out on the porch and only let us in once she was sure we were dried off.

I'm guessing Jenn told Mom and Dad, and Mom got mad, and Dad sulked and said he didn't know why we had to scare him like that. I know for sure Fred lied and said we'd only meant to swim.

Nothing ever came of it.

But still, that day, brand new tires bouncing on cracked sidewalk, hands sweating on the rubber handlebars, panting as we climbed that first steep bridge, Fred in front of me, her backpack lumping past her bike seat, her dark hair up tight in a bun, I felt so lucky that she'd chosen me to leave with her like that.

By last summer—the summer Mom died, the same summer Fred would find the gun—whatever lived between us had been corrupted, shifted. It was more than thirty years after I watched her body tumble; Fred had become *a writer*. All three of us siblings, Jenn and me and George, none of us much liked or trusted Fred by then.

JULY

1

It was the hottest summer in the history of Florida summers, and while out running in the gummy stick of the late-July morning heat, Mom had a stroke. A blood vessel in her brain burst, and she fell over, legs and elbows, ass and shoulders skidding on cracked concrete. Another runner stopped and called an ambulance. Dad sat with her in the hospital the whole time, not even going home to sleep. I bought a flight, but Dad put me off. They told him she'd be fine, *only superficial damage*, all those scrapes and bruises. Mom died two days after that.

Jenn, who lived close by, came to sit with Mom both days and stayed to help Dad fill out the paperwork. She took the bag with all Mom's clothes, her three rings, diamond studded earrings, and fifteen-karat tennis bracelet that she wore even when she ran. Jenn drove Dad home and threw the plastic bag containing Mom's shorts and shirt and bra straight in the trash. She put each piece of jewelry back in its place in Mom's custom closet drawers. Dad padded barefoot, quiet, around that house that he'd never spent a night inside alone. For the next few days, while I was making plans to come down from New York, he mumbled inaudibly to me each night on the phone. Jenn made sure he had food and rum, Diet Dr Pepper, and new, clean sheets. She organized the funeral: invites, flowers, speakers, casket, meeting with the minister. Fred was living two miles from Mom and Dad's, and although she hadn't ever been inside that house, she drove over to see Dad every day.

George's and my flights arrived minutes apart: his from Houston, mine from New York. Dad picked us up in his big hulking SUV, shoulders hunched and eyes flitting past us twice outside Arrivals, his face too flat and absent to look sad. I brought Cass, my teenage daughter, who was technically with me that week on summer break, her dad, Brian, and I divorced eight years by then. Cass was hardly talking to me and had been staying with a friend upstate; I'd had to meet the mom in a Bronxville Dunkin' Donuts parking lot to get to JFK on time.

We had a mostly silent dinner at the Cheesecake Factory (Dad's favorite). George asked Cass questions more appropriate for someone half her age. Dad had a third drink, and I had to grab for his keys four times before he begrudgingly handed them to me.

That first morning, around sunrise, Fred walked up to Mom and Dad's front door, wearing shorts and an oversize black T-shirt. From far away, my contacts not yet in, she looked exactly as she had at sixteen.

"I invited her, Mom," Cass said, coming down the hall behind me. She wore sneakers, shorts, her legs long like Mom's and Fred's. "We're going for a run."

Fred stood staring at us through the pineapple-etched glass door. She grasped her elbows, arms over her head, leaning to one side and then the other. I realized I hadn't heard her car pull up because she'd run here.

I clutched tightly to the warmed-up frozen waffle I'd found in the freezer, my just-poured cup of coffee. I wore no bra and an old John Prine T-shirt of Brian's that I'd managed to keep in the divorce.

"Don't worry," I said, as Cass opened the door, and I turned my head so Fred's eyes couldn't catch mine. "I won't ask to come."

George and Dad and I spent two days fielding calls from Jenn about the service, caterers, the invitations for the gathering that Jenn said we weren't allowed to call a party. (*Have more respect for yourself, Jude,* she said, when I suggested that we send the invites via text).

Each morning, Fred came by to pick up Cass to run. "It's for soccer, Mom," Cass said to me—she'd made varsity at her boarding school for the first time that last spring—"not some conspiracy against you." I nodded, did my best to be outside with my coffee and my breakfast. I stalked the concrete deck around the pool, the man-made beach along the river, feet bare and burning on the shipped-in sand. I climbed the sea wall, the long stretch of dock, and stood a long time staring at the water, until I felt sure that they'd gone.

At the service, Fred sat next to Dad in the family pew and cried quietly, her hands and shoulders shaking. She wore a black dress that Jenn had complimented in the parking lot beforehand.

"You look thin," Jenn said. This was also an accusation. Jenn wore a black silk shell and three-hundred-dollar slacks.

"It's from Target," Fred said about her dress.

Jenn's face got tight and hard.

I sat on Dad's other side, sandwiched between him and George. Jenn was beside Fred on the aisle so she could exit easily to give the eulogy. Cass sat behind us with Jenn's six kids, teenager to toddler.

When it was time for Jenn to speak, she stood and brushed her slacks straight, walked up to the podium. She said a bunch of stuff about Mom that was at least half made-up.

I watched Fred's shoulders shake. Unthinking, I reached over Dad, squeezed her hand, turned back twice to look at Cass.

Cass and I drove with George and Dad back to the house. Fred drove by herself. Jenn's husband, Adam, drove their three-row Escalade with all the kids. The house Mom and Dad had been living in when Mom died was even bigger (Fred would say *obscene*) than the one in which we grew up. Seven thousand square feet on the wide water, the beach, the dock; Dad had had the (*futile*, Fred said) seawall built before construction started. Big windows and high ceilings, too much empty, open space and lots of glass. White walls with blurry, beige-based beach and boat paintings; gray couches, cleanly lined wood-and-marble countertops and coffee tables, that fake plastic wood for floors that Dad's architect promised him wouldn't ever creak or rot. The place was not quite three years old and perfectly pristine. Dad built everything, first and always, as an investment, and whole rooms in this house—the billiards room, for instance—went mostly unused.

At the party that was not a party, people milled around the kitchen and the living room, trickled out onto the deck around the pool: a smattering of both Mom's and Dad's clients (Mom a lawyer, Dad a CPA), secretaries, paralegals, moms and some (fewer) dads of friends of ours from elementary school. It was early afternoon and thickly humid, 93 degrees. People pulled at shirts and waistbands; wicked away the sweat across the bridges of their noses, underneath their eyes. A woman in a long black sheath and a cardigan rolled a cold bottle of Heineken along her neck and face.

Fanny Boaz, mother to a friend of Jenn's and real estate agent turned college counselor—hoop earrings and embroidered leather pink-and-orange flip-flops, an understated knee-length dark-green-and-blue shift—cornered Fred out on the porch, asking Fred if she wanted to work with her, help kids with college essays. Warm, damp hand cupping Fred's bare elbow, wine and chicken on her breath, she offered Fred her card. Fred picked at a caprese salad, a small bowl of fruit, and nodded, smiled, looked grave-faced when it seemed like she should be looking grave-faced, clutched Fanny's card into a tight fist and felt it crumple wetly in her hand.

I stood and sipped a glass of too-sweet wine close to the table filled with food, searching every quarter hour or so for Cass—with her cousins, talking to Fred, holding Jenn's youngest up in front of her face and squishing her lips against that soft baby belly skin. Tanned and carefully preserved women pinched the stems of wine-glasses, took the tops off deli sandwiches. They huddled in anxious clusters. The husbands' faces were all wet and red. I took a brownie from the still-wrapped dessert tray in the walk-in pantry, ate it in three quick bites, and went outside in search of Dad.

"Judy," he said as I walked toward him, halfway down the path to the dock. Dad was by nature quiet and observant, but the more rum he drank, the more I heard him laugh. The group to whom he was talking nodded kindly at me, looked confusedly, bemusedly at him.

He put an arm over my shoulders as I leaned toward him. When I was growing up, he'd never liked me much, but now he did.

"You hanging in?" I said to him.

I watched him grimace and sip from his fourth rum drink. I'd been watching, counting each time he called a waiter over. He looked small, his limbs thinner than ever; even his potbelly looked less forceful beneath his crisp, white, slightly sweaty button-up.

"Not much choice," Dad said.

Fred snuck away from Fanny at the first lull, escaping down the long hall to Mom and Dad's room. Early on, when they moved into the house, our parents had a small fridge and a coffeemaker installed in the hallway, so that they hardly left that wing when it was just the two of them, and as a result their bedroom always smelled of coffee beans. Fred wanted to smell Mom, maybe, be close to her. The coffee but also her overpriced French lotion, the rows and rows of button-ups and dresses, sweaters on a rack above the dresses, blazers (organized by color) with their matching skirts or slacks beneath; tennis shirts, bras, shorts, underwear, and shapewear, all organized and sorted and tucked neatly in her drawers.

Mom and Fred had texted, tersely, once a month or so over the past year but hadn't been in the same space in close to two. A few weeks before Mom died, they'd made a plan to meet somewhere for dinner, but then the Supreme Court had upended affirmative action and Dad had texted Fred celebratorily about what he called *a more level playing field* and Fred had canceled in order not to have to fight with him up close. A few days later, after the first July days turned out to be the hottest days ever recorded on Earth, Fred had emailed them (and George) a string of articles, and Mom had responded, *we know it's hot out Fred*.

Jenn would say that Fred had probably gone to Mom's closet to steal something, to pawn it. But I knew that was unfair. Fred hadn't been broke like she was once broke in years.

The gun, when Fred came upon it, must have been a shock. Mom was not at all the type to own one: less that she was squeamish, more that she trusted too much in her own power. But standing in that perfect, color-coded closet, the gun's hard weight and cold, sharp edges must have felt, to Fred, like Mom. (I knew about the gun, its origins, because I talked to Mom and Dad, I *listened*; Fred did not.) She slipped it in her canvas bag and left.

At a stoplight, gun in her bag in the seat beside her, Fred took off her calf-length, short-sleeved Target dress. In only bra and underwear, with Sinéad O'Connor on the car's stereo (Sinéad had died one day after Mom, and Fred had been listening to "Nothing Compares 2 U" on loop), Fred undid her seat belt and reached into the backseat to get a sports bra and a pair of already sweaty shorts she kept in the car for runs. The guy in the truck next to her gawked at her bare legs and arms and belly as she unhooked and slipped her bra out from under her sports bra and pulled on her shorts and an old T-shirt, also from the floor.

Though she'd run that morning with Cass, Fred went another hour barefoot on the beach, the tide low, sand hard-packed. When she finished she stripped off her shirt, dove into the water, and swam out. Florida summer ocean: warm and easy, glassy, a light greenish-blue with dark patches where clouds hovered. About a hundred feet offshore, she hit a sandbar, then a drop-off, this time deeper.

Once she'd swum well past the drop—the beach was mostly empty, a fisherman just barely visible a quarter mile south—Fred flipped over, arms out, feet still churning, late-afternoon July sun still hot and unrelenting. That rare summer day without a storm. At the private swim classes Mom had brought us to when we were kids, we'd all passed everything except the float test: head back, arms outstretched. All of us were too obsessed with forward movement, with beating one another to some random destination. None of us had had the patience, the ability, to lie back and be still like that. *Who gives a shit about floating anyway?* Mom said. *That woman has to pass you because I paid for you to pass.*

Fred dipped her head back, but her bottom half started to sink if she stopped churning, her ears filled up. She turned back onto her stomach and swam farther out.

2

George was already drunk, out by the pool, rum in hand, when Fred left with the gun. Everyone pretended they didn't notice that Fred left early, that it wasn't rude that she hadn't said goodbye or told anybody where she was going, hadn't even talked to Dad. She'd known well enough at least to avoid me, who hadn't spoken to her or answered any of her texts or phone calls in almost nine months.

Nobody knew yet that George's wife had left him. We had all, over the years, told him she would leave him, which was probably why he hadn't told us yet. He'd brought the Lhasa apso—*not a shih tzu*, he and his almost-ex-wife, Allie, were both quick to remind us when they got her. Her name was Libby, *as in*, George explained, *leveraged buyouts*. (George traded oil and gas equities. Fred hated George's job, called it *sad and shameful, craven*, when he wasn't in the room.) Four years before at Christmas, when he'd introduced the dog, Fred had winced at me, eyebrows raised.

He's tall, George is, which Mom would say made it even more offensive *how fat*, in recent years, he'd let himself become. All us girls, and also Mom, are almost a foot shorter, and we still managed to stay thin. Though I had, the past year, begun to allow myself more often to indulge. My face and body were both lusher, fuller; for the first time in my grown-up life, I managed, at least once a week, to not hate the way I looked.

Out by the pool, Libby cradled in an arm held against his chest, George moved from group to group, made bad jokes, grabbed hold of women's wrists. Something rustled in the mangroves by the dock, and Libby leapt out of his arms. He watched her run and sidled up close to Cass and Jenn's older kids and tried to make them laugh.

"Not a good look, Uncle Georgie," Anelise said, when he asked them if they TikTokked. They left him there alone.

George got a second plate of food, a third drink; he went outside to entice Libby back with a piece of chicken tender. When he found her he scooped her up and went into the largest upstairs guest room with his food. He'd checked his texts all night—hopeful, maybe, that Mom's dying might compel Allie to call, to beg him to forgive her—but he had none.

"Where's George?" Jenn asked, as we cleaned up.

"I think he's sleeping," Anelise said.

"*Of course* he is," Jenn said.

Jenn had organized and hired the caterers, checked in with them, scolded them when we were too long without passed food out by the pool. She had then tipped them (not well) before they left, taking everything they came with just as Jenn had asked. Dad couldn't stand disorder, any sign of mess or other people's presence, so Jenn and I vacuumed, mopped, wiped the furniture with the special spray cloths Mom kept in the second pantry. We loaded, ran, and emptied both the dishwashers, cleaned the guest bathroom sinks and toilets, made sure Dad had breakfast foods.

Dad sat on the couch with CNBC on, staring blankly past it to the pool.

Jenn called in her kids to go.

"Your mom died," Cass said, as she stood next to me by the dessert tray I'd kept hidden from Jenn's cleaning. The sun was setting. Jenn and her kids had just left.

I broke the brownie I'd picked up and handed her half, looked past her to the river and watched a heron glide a foot above the slate-gray surface of the water.

"You should talk to Fred," Cass said.

The year after Cass was born was the closest Fred and I ever were. Twenty-three and terrified, I'd just finished law school, and both Fred and I lived in New York. Brian was still working weekends; he was—he is—a horse trainer (briefly, in my twenties, he'd been mine) and had to be at a show in Topsfield, Massachusetts, twelve hours after Cass was born. Thirty hours of labor and then a frantic, scary C-section. Cass's heart rate had dropped briefly. The OB had had to use her elbow to help dislodge her; a big, splotchy blue-and-purple bruise had already begun to spread across my abdomen, the stitches angry, oozing, the skin around them red. Fred had driven our car from Brooklyn with Mom to bring Cass and me home from New York-Presbyterian. Mom and Fred weren't really talking, though, so Fred had left not long after they got there.

At the hospital, Fred had held Cass, kissed her, her eyes welling, then left so Mom could change Cass into the pink-and-white-striped Ralph Lauren outfit she'd brought, take a thousand pictures, drive us home. My stitches stung each time I sat or stood, and nursing wasn't working. *I don't know why you're doing that,* Mom said, making a face, when I began to cry again while trying to get Cass to latch before we loaded her into the car. Mom had never driven in the city, any city, and on the West Side Highway she began to panic. *Fuck, fuck, fuck*, she started yelling. Cars around us honked. Cass cried, her face scrunched. I sat in the backseat with her and tried to angle my bare breast into her mouth. *It's okay. It's okay*, I said to both of them. Mom continued to come undone, like so many times before, hard-won steel turned to grasping slop and mush. She ran two red lights and had to cross three lanes at the last minute to make the turn for the tunnel. Cass finally passed out. I held Mom's shoulders briefly, thumbs kneading the knots on either side of her neck. *Jude, don't*, she said. I sat back again and stared at Cass. By the time we got to Brooklyn, Mom was desperate for a drink, and Dad, who'd stayed at the hotel to work while Mom came to the hospital, had made a reservation at a restaurant in Manhattan Mom had read about on-line. Mom pulled over close to our apartment, and I took over the driving even though, technically, I was not supposed to be driving. She ordered herself a car as I searched for a parking spot. Alone, I took Cass up to our apartment, whispering, *It's okay, it's okay* again, though she was still passed out. Twenty minutes later, Fred showed up with Thai food and my favorite gummy candies. *I had a feeling*, she said. She walked Cass up and down the long hall of our apartment while I stood under the shower a long time and sobbed.

"I know, Mouse," I said, turning toward Cass now. Her face was still the face I'd stared at that day, though more angular, less mottled. I'd thought when she was born—I was so young and dumb—that we'd be better, different. I didn't think so much as hope and want, and then time passed. I'd gotten too much of it wrong.

I brushed a brownie crumb off Cass's chin, and she stiffened. "I will," I said. "For you, Mouse, I'll talk to her."

3

The gun was still in the bag on the floor when Fred got back to the car, salty and wet.

She drove back to the house where she was staying, which was not her house but the house of her soon-to-be-ex-husband's parents' friends—not as big as our parents' house but still massive: one story, three bedrooms and four bathrooms, art on the walls and lots of mirrors in the hallways, slippery tiled floors and new and shining steel appliances, bigger than any place Fred had lived since childhood. For all the intervening years, she'd lived in New York, in the tiny studio apartment she had had since she was twenty-one, alone the first five years and then with David for the next fifteen.

Fred walked barefoot around the back of the house to the pool. A chain-link fence spanned half the yard, which was lush and overgrown, three palm trees in the south corner, a few now-defunct lemon and orange trees, a large Bismarck palm, round and thick and greenish-silver, by the pool's steps. The fronds' sharp edges scraped Fred's skin as she walked past it, stripped off her clothes, and dove into the pool.

She swam back and forth, then set out a towel on one of the metal-framed thatched plastic chairs and lay a long time with her eyes closed, her head back.

Around five thirty, Fred's friend Maeve and her three-year-old,

Tallulah, showed up, as they had near every night for the past six months. Maeve had been Fred's closest friend in high school, after which they hadn't spoken in years. Months after moving back with David, Fred had climbed out of the ocean post-run to find Maeve playing with Tallulah in the sand. Barefoot, hugging—Fred forty-two, Maeve forty-three—they laughed, disbelieving. Like most all kids, Tallulah'd taken immediately to Fred. Their feet in the sand, Tallulah running back and forth from the shore break with a big pink mermaid bucket, Maeve told Fred she'd finally got free of the opioid addiction she'd been stuck in for most of their lives. Fred believed her, the way Maeve's eyes landed, the way her limbs all had the steady confidence they hadn't had since they were kids.

Often, Fred had food ready for them, but this day, hours after Mom's funeral, Fred was still outside, naked in the sun.

"Freddy, Fred, Fred, Fred," Tallulah said.

"Tallulah, Lu, Lu, Lu," said Fred, tying her towel tightly at her chest.

Tallulah had big brown eyes just like her mother; she was towheaded and nut-brown from the too-hot Florida sun. Fred picked her up.

"How was it?" Maeve said. She had offered at least once a day, as had David, to go with Fred to the funeral, but Fred had declined.

"It was," said Fred, Tallulah's legs now wrapped around her, her heft a comfort, a bolster.

"How was what?" asked Tallulah.

"Pizza?" Fred said, knocking her forehead against Tallulah's. "My phone's still in the car."

"I can go," Maeve said, turning toward the driveway.

"I've got it," Fred said, still holding Tallulah, grabbing at Maeve's arm.

She saw Maeve blanch, maybe thinking that Fred didn't trust her not to steal something to sell later, thinking of those years when Maeve still used, when she'd stolen from Fred. But Fred had left the bag with the gun on the floor and didn't want Maeve to find it, ask where it was from or why she had it.

"Lu and I need a swim before the pizza anyway," said Maeve.

"And I need clothes," Fred said, making a face at Tallulah, who laughed and knocked her forehead into Fred's again.

Tallulah squirmed out of Fred's arms and followed Maeve into the pool as Fred went inside to dry off. Outside, dressed, her wet hair up in a bun, Fred opened the unlocked car. She clocked the shape of the gun in the canvas bag but left it, grabbed the phone, and ordered a large pizza. She answered the texts from David, from two friends in New York who'd heard about our mother's death.

Fine, fine, fine, she told them.

Please call me later, David texted back.

Fred held the bubble with her thumb and highlighted the thumbs-up.

Like Fred and Maeve, David and Fred had met in high school, but unlike Fred and Maeve, they were not friends then. He was three years older, cool, and handsome; Fred's only friend was Maeve, and they often showed up drunk to class. For years, Jenn had been guessing, offering to take bets from George and me, on how long it would take David to smarten up, see *what Fred really is*, and leave her. Except it had been Fred who left.

The year after I had Cassie, when Fred was almost a decade out of high school, she'd run into David at a bar. She was still, then, coming to our apartment every weekend. Brian had cut back on work and was home with Cass while I worked weekdays; as an associate at a midsize corporate firm, I seldom got to see her before he put her down at night. Brian taught lessons in Westchester on Saturdays, some Sundays, traveled to horse shows once a month with the kids he taught.

We never talked about it. Fred just showed up, often running from her apartment in Manhattan, stopping on the way to pick up two big coffees, egg and cheese sandwiches on whole wheat bagels. Cass sometimes waited for her by the door. (Brian sometimes said, when we fought back then, *It's like you're scared to just be with her on your own.*)

"I hid in the bathroom when I saw him," Fred said, the weekend after she ran into David. It was January. Cass was in the stroller, pulling off her socks and shoes as we walked toward the park. "Like, I thought that I might hug him if I got too close. He had no idea who I was." She grabbed at the shoe that Cass tried to drop out of the stroller and shoved it in the diaper bag. "He was wearing a pink shirt."

Fred was tutoring, applying to grad schools. Some weeks, on the Saturdays we spent together, Cass and I took her to the Whole Foods in Union Square and put two hundred dollars in prepared foods on the credit card that I still had from Mom and Dad.

Fred had never had a boyfriend, only drunken one-night stands that sometimes lingered. She tutored, waited tables, talked about *being a writer*, mostly walked around the city for hours on her own. "I know you," she'd said, walking up to David. I stopped the stroller to hand Cass a pouch of applesauce to hide my shock. They went back to his apartment; he had roommates, but his place was closer. He had stacks of books on the floor next to his bed. "What does he do?" I asked. Fred shook her head. I laughed at her; of course she hadn't asked. They'd talked about the strange place that we were from, about the amorphous, odd sensation of now living in New York. They talked about the stack of books. "He was an art major," she said. She opened the playground gate as I pushed Cass through it. "He has a job."

I must have looked concerned.

She pulled Cass out of the stroller and put her in the swing she liked best. "The next morning he put on a nice shirt and pants, and I walked him to the train on my way home."

She'd gone back the night after. She'd cleaned her apartment, and he'd come to her place, the night after that. He was a project manager for an interior design firm. He'd studied art in college, but his dad had been a carpenter, his mom a painter. He was the first person in his family to finish college.

Cass and Brian and I met him a month later. He was kind and funny, steady; tall to Brian's not-tall; slim and sinewy to Brian's broad-shouldered sturdiness. I watched his hand on Fred's knee—easy, careful—underneath the table, watched her brush the back of her hand along his ass as we walked out of the restaurant. I wondered when or if I had ever touched my own husband quite like that.

David moved into Fred's apartment. She got in to grad school. His job was good but not great, it was a small, family-owned design firm where he'd gotten promoted as much as it was possible for him to be promoted by the time he and Fred met. Fred's apartment was rent stabilized. Their whole lives together, David sent his parents five hundred dollars a month. Some years Fred and David barely scraped by; some years Fred sold a book or got a better adjunct gig and they went to Paris for two weeks. They went out to dinner, were members of museums, went to plays and movies. Fred spent three weeks alone in Prague the year her third book came out.

And then, in December 2020, David got laid off. His boss had died the first month of the pandemic; his son panicked and sold the business. David had, by then, worked there twenty years. That same week they got a notice in the mail that their place was being converted to condos. Fred's fourth novel had come out that summer, and no one seemed to notice. Another writer had written mean things about her on his blog. David's parents' friends offered them this house, and they put near everything they owned in storage and drove down. Signs from the election still stood in more than half the yards. On January 6, Fred called me, scared (that first year, we were still talking; Mom was texting me, complaining—She's right here, she said, except she doesn't even make an effort to reach out). She'd gone running, and big trucks with flags rigged up in their beds had revved past her, honking, twenty-something men with half their bodies out the window yelling expletives.

I can't stay here, she said. But she did.

It's temporary, she kept saying. It was the thick of the pandemic. All those years of asking students to situate their characters in time and space, and now both felt murky, lost. She taught three classes at three different universities, remotely. They spent outside time with David's parents. A few weeks in, Fred decided that she'd write a Florida book.

She'd never written anything that was *really true*, she told me— having not spent more than a few days in our hometown since high school, still not having seen Mom and Dad since she'd returned— because she'd never written honestly about this place that we're all from. (To my first-ever friend in college, from Potomac, Maryland, swapping stories the way people swap stories those first days of college, I had only told a few, and mostly they were Fred's, but her reaction was, *You know, that place sounds really fucked*.)

Fred started reading nonfiction tomes on early Florida settlements, the Everglades. Almost everything that we were taught in school about state history was made up, she said. Ponce de Léon's fountain of youth—even though in fourth grade we all went on field trips to St. Augustine, stayed the night at a hotel named after him—

was just a myth; we all knew vaguely it had been embellished but not that, actually, not even a shred of it was true. Andrew Jackson: so much plunder and destruction, so many stories suggesting he acted in the name of safety, in the name of protection, when really it was greed. The powerful and vaunted Chief Osceola's given name was William Powell Jr.; not Seminole at all, child of a Muscogee mother and Scots-Irish father, he allied with the Seminoles because few forces were more galvanizing than coming together against the ravaging white man. Over and over all sorts of different stories from our lives, from our "educations"—*myth as violently inscripted over truth*, Fred said to me.

But also: What did it matter the myths were a lie, if they were how and why the place was built?

In Florida, as elsewhere, wildness attracted wildness, attracted people with an unrelenting impulse to make new. European settlers arrived, refusing to believe the land couldn't be cultivated (it mostly couldn't be); that there wasn't gold or silver, some metal, to be found (there never was). Later: New Englanders, Michiganders, people from Long Island, came down for vacation and thought to themselves, said to their families, *Why should our vacation ever stop?* Tech bros, billionaires came, escaping income taxes. The land low and flat, the greens and greens, the heat and water everywhere; rushing lapping waves and rivers swampland estuaries bays: before the territory was yoked to the already-formed United States, it had been a sanctuary for escaped slaves, anarchists, queer people, a place to hide, to feel more free.

The wildness attracted and excited, right up until it got in humans' way. As in other places, whole tribes and populations, ecosystems, were destroyed. Swamplands were filled in, replaced by landscaped lawns; lakes dammed up, estuaries drained. And now: neighborhood associations policing how often lawns got mowed and trees got trimmed, house after house and treeless, sun-bleached roads, pastel concrete big box stores, laws restricting books and women's bodies—no interest in preserving all that wildness once the need to own and lay claim won out.

(And here, of course, I thought, *Oh Freddy, poor, sweet Freddy*—I'm sure she thought she was part of the wildness that had been destroyed—*not everything is about you.*)

She spent two months with a notebook labeled *Limestone*. She'd text me screenshots, email links. Porous limestone had formed across the state's hard platform when water still covered large portions of the land, before the glaciers froze—that flooding, too, a portent for all the flooding still to come. Coral, shells, tiny skeletons, microscopic stores of calcium collected and accumulated into a hard, carbonated sponge. The porousness double-edged, a boon but also a threat, a naturally built water filter, sucking out the salt from the sea, the water pooling into freshwater aquifers to provide hydration, and then irrigation, to the many millions who would eventually come.

It was a spongy, malleable foundation; both too much water and not enough could cause the land to fold in on itself. If the state extracted too much (and it would, of course; by 2020, its twenty million and counting residents would make Florida the third most populous of all the states), the sponge would dry out, and the land would collapse: stretches of street, parking lots and big box stores, front yards and houses, a thirty-six-year-old man named Josh, could sink all of a sudden twenty feet beneath the earth.

That whole first year, the second of the pandemic, Fred read and read, took notes, drove and drove. Outside of teaching, she talked to almost no one besides David and his parents; she texted, DMed, but spent most days silent, reading, driving by herself: down to the Keys, up to St. Augustine, to all the beaches and the forts. She was rediscovering something, I think, something maybe we had never wholly understood. Florida but not the politics, the lies, not the sponge it sat atop, not the big, growling trucks and boats. Florida the way the water felt, the way the heat was unrelenting, stifling—but also how much she loved to sweat, how the air smelled just before a storm, the slick and pat of wet concrete beneath bare feet once the rain stopped. The coco palms, the mangrove knees, the herons, pelicans, ospreys, hawks. The lizards early in the morning, just like the lizards early in the morning every day when we were kids.

Fred had only ever wanted to get out. She yearned daily, desperately for New York—but also, all that time out at the beach, the way the light came up over the early-morning ocean, the crackle, rustle, creak of palm fronds in piles in front of coco plums; everything that wasn't lie or empty, fraud or concrete: Fred fell hopelessly in love. She kept reading, kept swimming, running, driving, writing—she wrote and published one short story that was not about Florida at all—but she couldn't get the love to translate into story, into language, into book. She began to feel less able to stomach the destruction, razed land, concrete, strip malls, asphalt, F-350s, so many massive houses, David's little sister's kid sent home from school for bringing *Maus* to class. The more she read and drove, the more impossible it felt to try to write about it. Her writing had destroyed too much already. She became paralyzed by the idea she'd get it wrong. She started searching online late at night, David asleep beside her, for apartments for rent in their old neighborhood. David had found a job, with his father's help, as a project manager, accruing hours to become a licensed contractor. Fred emailed her former bosses, looked for more work in New York.

David, who read more news than anyone Fred knew, didn't care about the politics. He was glad to be close to his family, his sister raising her kids half an hour north in Vero, parents down the street. To David, Fred must have seemed happy—all the swimming and the running, reading, driving. Fred loved Florida now, he kept saying. (*But not like this*, she thought again and again.)

Interest rates were down to almost nothing but threatening to rise soon. It was *financial profligacy*, David said, not to buy a house. *We don't have any money*, Fred said. But they'd just gotten the last payment for the paperback of her most recent novel, an FHA loan with only 3.5 percent down. (*Your work bought this*, David would say at the closing, grabbing hold of her hand, and Fred would have to work hard not to cry or scream.)

Fred found one listing she liked in her own searching: two acres, half swampland, west of town, a one-room, unairconditioned cabin that she'd tried to convince David had *charm*. The place was cheap because it was nearly uninhabitable. *Freddy*, David said, after agreeing to walk the property. Mosquitoes swarmed up from the standing water; three big banyans hung over the drive; clumps of cypress trees, some of which looked half-dead, keeled over the edges of the roof. *If we do this, I say we really do this*, Fred said. David shook his head. It would take years of work, more money than they had. (Fredlike, she'd forwarded him Joy Williams's 1997 *Harper's* essay about her own plot of land in Florida, but she knew almost nothing of their finances.)

A month later, she'd stood outside with David in the backyard of the house they'd buy (because their agent told them that people sometimes bugged the kitchens, bedrooms): a light-blue concrete box with not nearly enough windows, arid, too clean, whites and beiges. Just like our parents' except not huge. Enough space in the backyard, the agent said, to put in a pool. Fred ignored the wailing, screaming in her body that said, *Stop this*. David talked. She nodded, went along. (If we had been talking, if she had called and told me, asked me, I could have told her that this sort of self-sacrifice had not ever been her thing; I could have told her she was too old for new tricks.)

The offer they made on the house was accepted only because the house had not yet hit the Market. *Perks of being locals!* David said, and Fred could hardly look at him.

One night not long before move-in, David asked her to help him start to think about the furniture they'd get. He'd gone up to New York to load their storage unit into a U-Haul, driven it all down, but they only had the one couch, one bed, an old futon he'd brought from the place he'd lived in Williamsburg before they met. Furniture for a studio apartment.

It's time, he'd said—a little too glad, Fred thought, a little too enamored of all this bullshit bougie stuff—*to get a little more grown-up*.

Fred was anxious, lonely, itchy. She loved Florida but didn't want whatever life this was that David suddenly felt so sure of; she loved Florida, but she'd only ever felt safe, like she made any kind of sense, when she lived in New York. *I don't think I can do this*, she said.

She saw the anger in him then, the hard line of his lips and quick twitch of his chin. She'd known he wouldn't hit her but had wanted him to hit her, to yell with his face, his hot wet breath, up close to hers. She knew he had it inside him, had seen it when they were younger: a tight fist under the table, yelling expletives at other drivers, flat palm against the doorframe when he came into the apartment after a long hard day at work. She'd seen him once out at the beach, when she was thirteen and he was sixteen, at least a couple of shotgunned beers in: he and three of his friends had hit another kid with closed fists after he'd taken too many of their waves out in the good offshore tropical-storm surf.

Okay, fine, he said instead. *Don't do it. I should have known already how hard it is for you to want the same sort of life as me.*

Years before, I'd just left Brian, and I was two gin drinks in, and we were sitting on my new apartment deck (Mom and Dad had helped me buy it, and when Fred heard, she'd texted me an excerpt from Dante's *Inferno*: All hope abandon ye who enter here; I sent her a cry-laugh emoji and replied that she could bunk with me if and when she was broke again.) She said that sometimes when she and David fucked, it helped for her to think about the anger that she used to see inside him, that knowing he was more than just a nice, kind guy had been imperative for her to love him all these years. She seemed to worry, after she had said this, that I might not get it. *As terrible as that sounds*, she said. But I thought her need to know the shape and texture of her husband's violence, when so much of our lives had been shot through with a low boil of formless, unknown threats, made perfect sense.

So David had moved into that big, empty house, and Fred had stayed in this house that belonged to Monty, a contract doctor and David's parents' friend. He and his husband spent months-long stints at different high-need rural hospitals where they were put up, given a rental car, and paid obscenely well to fill the gaps that other burned-out employees often left. They came back sometimes for a few days, a weekend, but had stayed away since David had moved out.

The plan had been, still was, for Fred to go back to New York. But Fred and David had spent their savings on the down payment for the house. She wasn't writing. The universities where she used to work were back in person. She felt too worn down, out of control, to teach. She didn't think that she could stay in Florida, but what would she do in New York? We weren't talking. She felt untethered from her friends, had failed to keep in touch. She'd lost her best, her closest friend, Tess, five years before. Maeve was the only person she talked to now. For all that anybody from her old life knew, she might as well have disappeared.

4

"It was okay?" Maeve said about Mom's funeral, looking at Fred.

Tallulah swam, and Fred and Maeve sat watching, their feet in the pool. The sound of sloshing, splashing, Tallulah's tiny body shimmery as she dove down and up again.

"It was what it was," Fred said.

Fred and Maeve in high school: Ours was not the sort of house where you had people over; ours were not the sort of parents who encouraged friendships, parties, fun. But one time, Mom and Dad in Winston-Salem to see Jenn in her first year of college, Fred's drinking not yet bad enough that they knew better than to leave her in charge of me and George: Pizza ordered in for dinner; Maeve came over with a half-gallon bottle of Sutter Home white wine. I slipped out of my room and down the stairs to watch them, by the pool with that big bottle, smoking cigarettes and drinking, laughing, talking; knees and ankles touching; slipping off their shorts and shirts and going swimming in their bras and underwear. I'd never had a sip of alcohol, felt scared even watching them—only two years older, a thousand miles away.

Three times in their early twenties, Maeve stopped returning

Fred's, her mother's, any of their mutual friends' phone calls, texts, or emails. She left with money she had taken from her mother; once, with a thousand dollars she'd borrowed from Fred. Fred on the phone with Maeve's mother saying, over and over, the only source of comfort she could think of: *If she were dead, someone would have called.*

The last time, Maeve resurfaced in Arizona, where she spent three more years with some guy, sometimes responding to texts or phone calls. She claimed, though it was not confirmed, to have been to rehab twice while she was in Scottsdale. Fred had seen her once, the last year of their twenties, at Maeve's mom's house, when she was trying to detox. The way she'd writhed and yelled, scratched her skin so hard, nails dug in so deep, Fred worried that she'd break through straight down to bone.

But Maeve was clean now. Said she was and had no choice but to stay that way for Tallulah. She went to weekly, sometimes daily, meetings by the river, talked to Fred a lot about surrender. Tallulah had no dad as far as Fred could tell.

Another thing: when Fred was still a writer, she wrote about Maeve in all four of her novels. (*Exploitation and extraction*, Fred said about what George did, his work with oil and gas, making so much money. It was different, of course—opioid addiction was *topical*, a *crisis*—but not as different as Fred liked to claim it was.) Maeve hadn't read the books as far as we knew, and Fred had also written about us—Mom and Dad, me and Jenn and George. Dad had called me, crying, after the second book and whispered over and over, his words slurring, *What the fuck?* In interviews Fred said these people weren't us, weren't her. She wrote *fiction. It's reductive of the formal choices necessary to make art*, blah blah. But none of us were idiots.

The pizza came, and Tallulah got out of the pool, and they all sat on the porch around the table where they ate most nights, oversize thatched-bottomed chairs with waterproof cushions that swallowed up nearly all of Tallulah's lower half.

"How's Georgie?" Maeve said. George had always been Maeve's favorite of us siblings. He'd been Fred's favorite, too, when we were kids. More recently, Fred had ruined at least three family dinners (and she didn't often go to family dinners) by asking George how and why he continued to be *complicit in the destruction of the world*. Dad would then say something canned about how if it wasn't George, it would be someone else, and Fred would force her upper lip under her lower teeth and bite down hard, her arms crossed, and Mom would change the subject, and everyone would talk awkwardly about nothing through dessert. And then Mom, an hour later, in the kitchen, Fred gone or upstairs: *She's a writer, for Christ's sake. It's not like she's helping anyone.*

"He looked sad," Fred said.

"Well," Maeve started.

"But, like, body-sad," said Fred. "Sadder than just Mom."

Maeve looked at Fred, and Fred looked past her to the water. Wind blew; the heavy crackle of the palm trees' leaves, the creak of their branches.

"Was the wife there?" Maeve said.

Fred shook her head. "Mom hated her."

Tallulah got up out of her chair and walked slowly toward the porch screen. She squatted down, silent, sharp knees bent up to her chin. Fred followed the angle of Tallulah's body as she leaned toward a small lizard, light green and still on the screen's ledge.

"She hated Mom," Fred said. She dipped her head closer to Maeve. "You know Mom got sick at his wedding."

"Freddy," Maeve said.

"He might as well have killed her," Fred said.

"You said it was Allie."

Maeve watched Tallulah, who still watched the lizard. Thin skin stuck to its vertebrae as it breathed in; the outlines of its tiny, fragile bones popped out.

Fred when we were kids: chasing after, picking up the lizards in the screened-in porch in both the houses we grew up in, placing them—silent, careful—on Jenn's head, my head; those padded feet pat-patting, the stick and pull of their legs stuck in our hair. Also Fred: "dissecting" the dead, dried-out lizards she found on the drive-way and in the crevices of doors, prying off their skin with screws she found in the garage; *Look, Jude!* she'd say to me—Jenn behind her, pretend-puking—*want to feel the crinkle of its guts?!* (I did.)

"It was August 2020," Fred said to Maeve about the wedding. Mom had pushed for George and Allie to get married at the height of the pandemic. Fred had said she wasn't coming, and Mom had used Fred's absence as further proof of how unwilling Fred had always been to do what Mom wanted Fred to do. *We're all healthy*, Mom said. Most of their friends canceled the week before. I'd used Brian as my excuse not to bring Cassie but had gone myself. Mom had gotten sick, as had I, as had two of Jenn's kids. For four days, Mom was in the ICU. Mom and Dad didn't tell Fred because to admit that Mom was sick was to admit that Fred was right and therefore that Fred had won.

I was still talking to Fred then. I called and texted, sent her up-dates. She walked to me in Brooklyn from her place in Manhattan— Cass was with her dad that month while I stayed isolated from them post infection. Fred sat masked with me on my stoop as we waited, silent, knees and shoulders close to one another but not touching, to see if our mother would live. There was talk one awful night about a ventilator, but then they'd rolled her over on her stomach, given her the remdesivir. She'd been discharged complaining that the drugs had made her bloat.

How are you? we all asked over and over in the days and weeks that followed. *Two hundred percent better*, she said. *Stop treating me like I'm some invalid.* But Jenn claimed she wasn't the same. Her words slurred sometimes even before her nightly three to four drinks. The doctors assured us, thirty-five months later, that Covid hadn't killed her, but could they really know that?

By the time she died, Fred and I weren't talking. I sat out silent on my stoop alone. I called Brian (who had never liked my mother), who called Cass and the mom with whom Cass was staying, who promised to come water my plants while I was gone.

Tallulah slid her hand slowly toward the lizard, placed her thumb and finger on each side of its jaw. The lizard's tiny body wriggled, but Tallulah's hand stayed steady. She walked toward Fred, grinning. Fred matched her grin and leaned forward so Lu could fasten the lizard's mouth to the bare lobule of Fred's ear.

"I liked her," Maeve said.

"Really?" Fred said.

"I'd never met a mom like her before."

"She was . . ." Fred couldn't think of what to say. The lizard's tail brushed her neck, quick flicks beneath her chin then back along her shoulders, and Fred raised her eyebrows at Tallulah, who stood between her and Maeve watching the lizard carefully.

Maeve put her hands over her daughter's ears and looked past her to Fred. "She didn't let anybody fuck with her," she said.

Fred thought of arguing against this. She'd seen Mom cry plenty, lash out and dissemble, most often because of something that Fred did. "She would have loved to know you thought that."

Maeve wrapped her arm around Tallulah's waist and pulled her in, nuzzled her nose into her neck and kissed her. Head still bent into her daughter's neck, she smiled at Fred. "Oh, she *for sure* hated me," she said.

Fred laughed and shook her head. "She didn't."

"Who?" Tallulah said.

"My mom," Fred said.

"Why?" Tallulah said.

"You didn't make sense to her," Fred said. She reached up to touch her neck, and the lizard leapt onto her shoulder, the chair, the ground. "She had a hard time with anyone who didn't want and hate the same things she did."

Tallulah looked back and forth between them.

Maeve scrunched up her nose and pressed her lips together, looking over her daughter's head toward Fred. She knew Fred was thinking that Fred also hadn't wanted, had very seldom hated, the same things as Mom.

They watched the lizard run through a hole in the porch screen.

"She was nuts," Fred said.

Maeve pulled Tallulah farther up on her lap. "More like both of us than she'd have liked to think."

Fred carried Tallulah to the car after dinner. She liked the weight and smell of her, her warm head against Fred's chest. (A thousand years ago, Cassie fast asleep, me to Fred: *Put her down already so we can eat lunch.* Fred to me: *I still have one hand free.*) She buckled Tallulah into her car seat, grabbed and squeezed her warm, bare foot. She stood a long time, barefoot in the driveway, after Maeve pulled out, her hair still smelling like chlorine, skin itchy from the salt.

Back in the house, under the hot shower, Fred tried to convince herself she wouldn't go to David's. And then, as she did near every night Tallulah didn't sleep over, Fred walked barefoot the ten minutes to the house she'd bought but never moved into.

David was a deep, sound sleeper. Their whole marriage, Fred would be up all night, wandering the box of their apartment, or next to him on her computer, watching hours of TV, while he slept the deep sleep of the innocent. Now, Fred walked around the side of the house. She didn't ever use the front door and couldn't remember what any of the rest of the house looked like. Instead, she climbed onto the humming air conditioner and through the unlocked, screenless window. She took off all her clothes, fisted her hands a couple of times to warm them, slipped them under David's shirt.

He started and then opened his eyes wide. She pushed his shoulders down against the bed and straddled him. He picked her up from the waist, and she held his hips and guided him in.

He was a full foot taller than her, and they fucked standing, his hands cupping her ass, her legs wrapped around him. In the fifteen years they were married, they had never fucked like this. *I've got you*, he would say, but she would shake her head, afraid of falling, scared of hurting him. Now, she wrapped both arms around him, her ankles locked around his lower back. She closed her eyes and let him hold her and rock into her. Neither of them spoke more than assent—a *not like that*, a *just like that*, the guttural sounds of pleasure, a short inhale as bodies turned and shifted. He dropped her back onto the bed, and she came from the relief of it.

Fred used the bathroom quickly, peed and cleaned herself. She got dressed as David watched her, climbed back out through the window onto the air conditioner, walked back to the house she didn't own but where she lived, grabbed the car keys off the hook next to the door and drove. Parked at the beach, car off and windows down, Fred took the gun out of her canvas bag and held it in her hand. She turned it upside down and over, looked out the window at the moon and stars, a mass of sea grapes, shoved it back into her bag, and crossed the boardwalk to the sand. She swam another hour before driving home, where, without rinsing off the sand or salt, Fred finally fell into bed.

5

The day after Mom's funeral, George drove Cass and me to the airport in Mom's bright-red Porsche convertible, windows up, top not down, the nondescript Top 40 station Mom used to listen to playing on low. Cass sat in the back, curly hair up in a bun, staring at and scrolling through her phone. George (thirty-four) looked more childlike to me than Cass (sixteen)—his smattering of grown-up acne along the bottom of his chin, his heft all smooshed into the sleekness of the car. Cass looked happier, more engaged, typing and then staring and then typing and then staring, than she had the whole three days we'd spent together on this trip. (We'd had a sort of breakthrough during the pandemic. After my bout of Covid, we'd agreed on one summer month with me, and one with Brian, and we'd sat and talked like we had maybe never sat and talked. But then she'd gone back to school, and then she'd felt betrayed by me—because of Fred—and I was still grasping, desperate, for that brief glimpse of intimacy that we'd been able to settle into those few months.)

George had been my closest friend when we were kids: we shared the third row of Mom's van, separate from our older sisters; when we were older, we called and texted more than any other sibling pairing. But we weren't friends on this drive to the airport. He did not ask a single thing about my life; he had not asked in years. When I called him, he'd talk at me, thirty minutes about some slight Mom and Dad had made him suffer, some car he bought, the garish hyper-modern fire pit he and Allie had installed in their backyard. I'd hang up angry. *He did not ask a single question*, I would say to Fred. *Has anybody told him how human interaction is supposed to work?*

Once, a therapist I saw for three weeks told me that I was aban-doned. *I was not abandoned,* I said, quickly as I could. *No one left you in a way that anyone could see or call out,* she said. *But your whole life, when you needed someone, the people who might have felt obligated to show up did not.* This felt absurd to me, and I never went back. *Aban-donment* was loud and sad and awful. It was the culture, everybody grasping at any claim that they might make to the word *trauma,* so that someone might listen to them, pay attention to them, read their long screed on the internet and comment with yellow hearts and *sending so much love.* If I'd called Fred and told her what the therapist had said, used the word *abandoned,* she would have nod-ded earnestly, and I would have known that she was nodding even though I couldn't see her. She would have said, *That feels true to me,* and I would have thrown up in my mouth.

"What will happen to the car?" George said. Dad hated convert-ibles. When I was six, Fred eight, Jenn ten, George still a baby, Mom had bought Dad a sports car as a birthday present—a gift he hated for its profligacy in addition to the car's smallness and im-practicality, a gift he drove begrudgingly while she continued to cart all of us around in her conversion van. When Jenn was old enough to drive herself, Mom started getting herself a new convertible every two years.

"I guess it's ours until the lease is up next year," I said to George.

Jenn had tried to turn the car in early, no doubt yelling, threatening—Jenn-like, Mom-like—but she'd been denied.

We didn't know then that George didn't want to go back to his two-million-dollar Houston house because Allie had left. (A lot of what I'm saying here I found out later; the rest, as Fred would say, I've *imagined my way into*, because why not). He had found explicit text messages one day when her phone was vibrating on the counter when he arrived home from work. Some of them were nude photos of Allie, and he had vomited up his lunch in the backyard. He hadn't told us she'd said mean and awful things when he'd confronted her, had laughed at him, said loudly, brashly, *You don't even* fuck *me anymore*.

He'd told us the day before the funeral that he wanted to spend more time with Dad, and Jenn had scoffed because that just meant, for her, another person in the house to be cleaned up after, fed. *Dad will just work*, I said. *I'll work next to him*, said George. Dad was a CPA, and much of his work, as well as George's, had gone remote the past three years. Nobody loved our father like women over seventy. He was an obsessive, careful cataloguer of their money, sometimes even eloquent on the topics of margins, ebbs and flows, and debt curves. They'd all become accustomed, some addicted, to talking to him *on the Zoom*.

Mom had been a litigator, marital and family law and white-collar criminals. She worked longer hours and still had to put on a suit, go to court and mediations, had complained often the last year that she had to go out into the world while Dad continued to refuse. This was not entirely fair: they'd gone to Portugal, to Iceland, on a Mediterranean cruise; he'd come with her to visit me and Cass, George's new house. But when Mom got home from work to find Dad still in his shorts and flip-flops, on the couch with his computer, she had to walk outside with her vodka soda, sip it quickly, stare a long time at the water, so as not to ask him why he hadn't thought to leave the house.

"Dad's going to come get us," Cass said from the backseat.

I felt George watch me. "Perfect," I said, eyes fixed straight ahead.

"Are you annoyed?" Cass said.

"Of course not."

"Your dad's great," George said.

I caught Cass's eye in the rearview mirror. She winced at me.

"Posey's going to stay with the baby," Cass said. (*She's so rich she doesn't even have to have a real name*, Fred said when we found out Brian was marrying one of the women whose horses he took care of; I was grateful for her willingness to not force me to acknowledge that I was the one who left Brian, that likely, because Brian was very kind, Posey was also.)

"That's nice of her," I said. Unclear how watching her own kid was a favor.

"I wish we could have kept him to help with Christmas dinners," George said, smiling at me.

All three of us laughed.

Brian and my family, the second to last Christmas before we split: Jenn did Christmas Eve and Mom did Christmas, both massive, over-the-top meals. Jenn was starting to make more money; Adam had just made partner at his firm. She'd seen Cornish game hens in some magazine and thought them cute—their tiny legs, the soft, curved breasts. *The kids can give each of theirs names!* Cass and Anelise were five and six. Jenn's two youngest were four and one, the baby not yet born. The year before had been the second year she'd made the hens, and they'd been dry as dust, near impossible to chew— cute, flavorless husks. *I want to help this year!* Said Brian, when we were all out to dinner, long past Cass's bedtime, the day that we flew in. *I'd love that!* Jenn said. *What a catch you found, Jude!* She smiled, holding her then-youngest. *A man who cooks!*

We went to Jenn's after breakfast. Brian had stayed up late on his phone googling the hens and taking notes. Careful and exacting, he'd researched cook times, seasonings and stuffings, hen placement on the pan. Cass came with us, and the kids played. Jenn had a massive playroom: more than one toddler-size dollhouse, a huge flatscreen TV. Brian and Jenn jostled, mixed, taste tested, braised, and seasoned. I'd brought a novel, some work; I sat on the couch and scrolled emails and read. I listened as Brian and Jenn planned and joked and laughed. Adam came out from the ensuite office of their bedroom and offered me a golf cart tour of the neighborhood. They lived west of town, where land was cheaper because the lots were mostly swampland filled in with shipped-in sand. The houses were all massive, three or four variations on the same look, same plan, lots of white and gray. We saw an alligator in a ditch half a mile from their house. When we came back, we took the kids out to the pool. It was almost fun, those first few hours. We opened a second bottle of wine. The kids had a dance party. I wondered why and how we hadn't done this more.

Mom came a little after five.

Mom and Dad and George showed up as promised, dressed up, George flown in the night before from college. They made two trips from the car with platters. *You all were here together?* Mom said. We were laughing when she walked in, Adam and I on stools talking to Brian and Jenn as they cooked. The kids ran down from upstairs and greeted everyone. The whole morning, Brian had looked proud. He'd convinced Jenn to let him make the brussels sprouts and do the salad; we'd stopped at Publix for balsamic vinegar and spices on our way. Three times, Jenn came up to me to say how great she thought he was. Until then, my family's most common comment about Brian was that he mucked stalls for a living. His mom had immigrated from Guatemala, groomed and taken care of other people's horses in Hialeah and then Ocala; he'd gone with her to work often and fallen in love. I'd met him at the barn where I'd started riding when I was in law school. I hated law school, and he'd given me dressage lessons once a week, with his hand resting sometimes too long on me as he shifted my hands on the reins and told me once again to put my shoulders back.

Cooking, Brian? Mom said, but in a wholly different tone than Jenn had used earlier. He nodded, maybe sensing something. *We're having a great time*, he said. Mom opened the Carr's crackers, unwrapped her Publix cheeses and shrimp cocktail, the still-warm pigs in a blanket she'd cooked at her house. Jenn had two ovens, and Brian kept checking the hens as Mom and Dad made their own drinks. The kids came back inside, and Adam turned on a movie for them. I had a glass of wine. Brian stuck with seltzer the whole time to *keep a focused eye* on his hens. I'm not sure I ever loved him like I loved him that night.

The hens took longer than expected. The kids were exhausted. It was seven and then seven thirty. I held Jenn's smallest baby and walked her back and forth while also holding my full glass of wine until she fell asleep against my chest. Brian came up behind me, cheeks flushed, hot from all that cooking. He stared down at the baby. *You want another one?* he said. I set down my wine and shifted the baby's weight and grinned at him, thinking maybe, not so long from now, I would.

Finally, at eight, we all sat. It was an hour past Cass's bedtime. Brian had finally opened his first beer. I was three glasses of wine in. George was playing with the kids, on his phone, watching football with Dad, sipping his rum and Diet Coke.

Only six of the hens were out and on plates when Mom screeched. Everybody stared at her. *All of you stop right now!* she said. *These hens are raw!*

Cass was sitting between us, so I couldn't immediately grab hold of Brian, who stood up. *What do you mean?* he said.

Mom had cut open her hen. She pointed to a vein she'd found inside. *It's red!* she said. *They all have to go back in the oven!* George looked at her, uncertain. Brian stayed quiet. Mom rushed from person to person, retrieving the hens.

"Mom," said Jenn, but it was clear she knew this was futile.

Brian kept his and cut into it. "They're cooked," he said. "Mine's cooked."

"You feel free," Mom said, "to get yourself sick."

Oh, fuck you, my brain muttered.

"The kids aren't eating this," Mom said.

When I was six and Fred was eight, Fred used to set up obstacle courses in the driveway to dribble a basketball around: all the bikes from all the Christmases, old board games, Dad's yard tools, whatever she could find. We'd had the same babysitter for years, but then she'd quit, and Mom paid the woman who cleaned the house to watch us while she worked, and the woman never really talked, just picked us up from school, made sure we had food, then left us to ourselves. Fred would dribble out there on her driveway obstacle course for hours. She was too short for basketball, played on the fourth- and fifth-grade teams and never made a shot. But she loved the method and the repetition, over and over around that course she made. One day, Mom was mad and in a rush, had been stuck in court—a massive judgment for the other side—and Fred had left the basketball out in the driveway, and Mom ran right over that basketball with the big van she had to drive all us kids around in when she wasn't working, and the basketball went splat, flat and irretrievable, and Fred cried.

Brian, that night: walked out of the dining room while Mom collected all the hens, took what remained of his meal—the salad and the brussels sprouts he'd made, the Pillsbury rolls Mom brought, the mac and cheese. He poured himself a single thumb of whiskey and sat out on Jenn's back porch, Cass on his lap with a cookie fisted to her lips. When I looked at him, he looked just like that basketball Mom had flattened going too fast up the driveway in her huge conversion van.

As we pulled into the airport drop-off area, George stared at me, looking anxious, right glasses lens smudged and scratched. He stared and smiled as Cass and I pulled our matching black rolling suitcases from the trunk. "See you later, Uncle George," said Cassie, one hand on her suitcase handle, the other still clutching her phone. She had been mad at me for months by then, disappointed; she felt lied to (again: Fred's doing), but when I reached for her shoulder outside the airport, she didn't push me off.

"Take care of yourselves," George said, playing at being grown-up, sitting up a little straighter, both hands on the wheel.

6

When he got home, George went on the internet in search of Allie, in search of her boss, whom he knew now that she'd begun to fuck. It was George's fault. He'd told her, months ago, that she had to get a job even though she didn't want to. She'd been laid off during the pandemic; they'd bought that house. She'd wanted to spend the next year or two, she said, *making it a home.* (Jenn, on this, when it was briefly, accidentally, mentioned: *Can you imagine—all the* Live, Laugh, Love *pillows she has to buy?*)

Allie was from Louisiana, but not Baton Rouge and not New Orleans, some tiny town that none of us had heard of. She'd gone to a small Southern Baptist college, had been working in HR when she and George met on an app. She was small and pert and pretty, dark hair, light eyes; she wore bright-red lipstick that she picked at, reached her thumb and forefinger between her wide, plump lips and brushed away invisible lines as she talked. None of us had ever liked her, though Fred often argued that we needed to be kinder. What Fred didn't know was that the Christmas after her second book came out, one of the Christmases during which Fred and Mom and Dad weren't talking, Allie had walked around to everybody as we ate hors d'oeuvres together in the kitchen before dinner with the Wikipedia page for narcissistic personality disorder open, saying it explained all the many obvious things that were wrong with Fred.

Being honest: we all thought Allie was craven, in it for the money. Our parents' but also George's. *Gold digger*, Mom said, though none of us kids would actually use that term. We thought Allie loved the life she had with George, that he was nicer than most of the other guys—almost certainly the other guys in Texas, anyway—who were rich like that. He was our baby brother, and we felt allowed to point out and discuss his flaws with one another, but we also wanted her to feel lucky to be with him, with us.

Since their first date, he had liked to watch men watch her. He liked to let them skulk up to her when they were at a bar, flirt and talk, liked to watch the way their faces worked to please and charm her, her head swiveling left and right in search of him. He liked to wait a beat, then bound through the crowd, a few mumbled *excuse me*s and then his arm around her—a quick kiss if the guy was taller than him, an ass slap if he'd watched the guy make her laugh.

He liked her feet up on his lap after dinner, each of them with a big glass of wine; college football, *Selling Sunset*, any of the House-wives; the smooth sinew of her calves, the soft press-push of her lips. Neither of them was particularly good at cooking but both tried it. He did Mom's salmon in a nonstick pan with brown sugar and soy sauce. She did her mom's triple-meat lasagna, homemade mac and cheese with bacon and sausage, shepherd's pie with cream of mushroom soup out of the can.

She got him fat to keep him, Mom said. George wasn't thin be-fore he met Allie, but he was definitely less fat. After our parents went to visit them before the wedding, to help with planning and picking venues (all mid-pandemic), Mom mentioned how Allie force-fed George. *Okay, not force-fed him, but she encouraged all this greasy, cheesy shit*, Mom said. Not long after the wedding, there was a fight—Jenn picking at Allie, Mom saying that she wasn't helping in the kitchen and then, when she did, complaining that she was do-ing it all wrong. George and Allie left early, and then George wrote

Mom and Dad an email, bcc'ing all of us sisters. *She is my wife*, he wrote. He was demanding that we all love her and treat her better. *She is my wife*, he wrote again, *full stop*.

Allie had three sisters, and one of them had almost lost a baby during labor, months after George and Allie's wedding: cord around the neck, the baby halfway down the birth canal before they realized; her sister cut open and the baby yanked out, all blue and silent; chaos and horror and the nurses rushing, whispering, working; the anxious, tangy taste of fear. Allie's sister had a catheter for months because her bladder had been damaged by the yanking, and the baby stayed in the ICU for a long while.

Allie had been at the hospital in Louisiana with her sister, had stood with her (the baby's dad a blubbering mess out in the hall with Allie's mom and other older sister) as she'd asked and asked and asked to hold her baby, as Allie, too, had cried. *I don't think—* Allie said to George when she got home. *I'm too scared*, she finally said, *to try for babies yet*. Libby, then, as consolation in the meantime. George stayed late at work, and Allie got home early and waited. He encouraged her to *take more initiative* at work. She started to push to do more recruitment; recruitment meant more travel. One of those trips ended with her sitting with her boss at the hotel bar, George texting to say he was off to bed and would call her in the morning, Allie's boss following her—both of them a little drunk but not so drunk as to not know what they were doing—into her hotel room, the door closed and locked, up against the wall, then on the floor.

It was true, too, that George didn't often fuck her. This wasn't because of her. He didn't like his body; he didn't like the mess and sweat of it. He liked to stay all cozy and covered up on the couch with her. He liked blowjobs, with his shirt on. Again, this wasn't about Allie. When he jerked off alone in the house when she was visiting her sisters, out with friends, working out or grocery shopping, it was often her he thought about. But her hands moving freely on his heft and the smooth, hard curves of her above as he jiggled below was its own indictment of his lack of self-control.

Back at the house, George made himself a rum and Diet Coke. He'd started intermittent fasting two months before, after Allie'd emailed three links about it over a few days, and his hunger always snuck up on him; now, he realized that he was starving. He knocked on Dad's door. "I thought I'd order food," he said. Whenever George came down to visit, he and Dad ordered from the same place, which had been around forever. Dad would call in burgers, fries, a steak salad with blue cheese and walnuts and dried cranberries that George asked for when he was feeling good (as in well-behaved and chaste) instead of the buttermilk fried chicken with garlic smashed potatoes and sometimes, too, a side of fries.

"A burger, I guess," Dad said. Our parents had a sitting room off their bedroom with a large flatscreen TV propped up in front of the big windows that looked out on the river, beach, and dock, looked out on the sprawling landscaped lawn that was Dad's greatest joy. George thought briefly of sitting next to him, of asking him what to do about Allie. He looked so small though, hair thinning in the front, pops of sweat along his temples and his chin, his spindly ankles crossed. "Great," George said. "I'll order now."

He brought Libby out back to pee and used Dad's iPad, which had Dad's payment information saved, to order the food. He got the chicken, the smashed potatoes, and the French fries. At the last minute, he added a salad to share. While he waited, he opened his phone, sipped his drink, and retrieved one of the bags of Doritos Jenn had stocked the pantry with. He fed bits to Libby as she sat with him on the couch. Allie had been pissed he took her, but he had always done the morning and the evening walks, had thought to pick up treats on his way home from work. Libby always slept on his side of the bed.

On the internet, George saw that Allie's boss had three kids and a wife. Their house was not as nice as George's—it was not as big, which was what George thought of as nice. George was richer, he felt sure, looking at Allie's boss's wife's Instagram, based on the vacations that they took, their appliances, the house's size, their cars. He scrolled through picture after picture: children swimming, laughing, dressed up for Easter in matching pastel floral prints; this asshole holding them and laughing, his arm around his wife, smiling like he wasn't also fucking George's wife in his spare time.

George thought briefly of DMing the wife and offering to love her, move her and her three kids in with him instead. He thought he'd send her a picture of the fireplace, the pool, the custom-designed backsplash in the kitchen. It was all he'd ever wanted, someone who would promise always to stay with him, proof, in the form of other people, that he was right and strong and good.

7

The next morning, Maeve dropped Tallulah at Fred's early so she could work a day shift at the Bonefish Grill, a corporate chain and the busiest restaurant within twenty miles. Maeve had been triumphant, it had felt life-changing, when, not long after she'd moved out of her mother's, a friend of a friend had helped her get this job.

Fred wasn't working, as has been mentioned, not writing nor teaching. She had not, before this, ever had fewer than four jobs at once. She still had notebooks full of bits and images she couldn't help but try to capture, lists of invasive species. A new batch of giant snails was once again infiltrating large swathes of Miami. She still drove out sometimes to that cabin David said didn't make sense. She'd begun to research native plants and spent time walking around plant nurseries, taking pictures of those that attracted pollinators, writing down the names of flowers that she liked.

She had, in the end, texted Mom's friend Fanny from the funeral about helping kids with their college essays, because she knew too well the feeling in one's chest and teeth and shoulders when there was no money left. Senior year of college, she'd cut up her credit cards from Mom and Dad. Very like Fred: petulant, performative, absurd. She had, of course, almost immediately wanted to ask for them back. But she'd said so showily, that Christmas, *I don't need your fucking money*, that there had been no clear route back through the mess. She loved so much to feel self-righteous, to nod knowingly when Mom and Dad decided to keep the place they bought me and Cass in their name.

Fanny immediately responded to Fred's text. Send a resume and you're hired! she wrote, seemingly forgetting the drunk mess that Fred had been in high school (four different visits to the hospital after being found unconscious from too much sweet liquor; she'd also crashed her car three times), confusing her perhaps with me or Jenn. Just to send to parents!! A famous writer!!! ("Fame" here obviously a small pond/big fish thing.) We're going to kill it!!!! This was followed by a string of heart emojis intermixed with money and fire emojis and a final melting smiley face that did not make sense to Fred.

Fred packed lunches, made Tallulah breakfast.

"I fed her," Maeve said, as she kissed Tallulah once more on the forehead, as she watched Fred put brown sugar and chopped walnuts into the pan of oatmeal.

"Just in case!" Fred said.

"Second breakfast!" Tallulah said.

They each ate a bowl, and Fred packed the car and drove the half hour to Busch Wildlife Sanctuary, Tallulah in back, humming to herself, strapped into the car seat Fred had bought online.

Fred was not a good driver, often got distracted. David had once said to her—loving, sorry, likely slightly patronizing: *It is so totally your family's MO that you got a brand-new car when you turned sixteen, but no one ever taught you how to drive the fucking thing.*

Fred had found Busch Wildlife in her year of research. It had started as an illegal, home-run sanctuary founded by some guy with lots of land who took in hurt animals: Alligators that kids had taken home as babies, kept in bathtubs or tanks until they grew too much, the kids got scared, parents found out. Opossums hit by cars, picked up by some concerned driver stopping traffic. Panthers, bears, victims of hunters misfiring then feeling bad; skunks who could not spray and therefore had no recourse to protect themselves. More and more people came to see the animals, gave money, volunteered. A swathe of land was donated. The grounds were moved, expanded, revamped, expanded again. So, now: gift shop, parking lot, dirt-and-pine-needle paths, a handful of boardwalks over swamp and sand, employees, volunteers, an animal education show in the late morning and a second after lunch.

Fred took Tallulah when she had her, at least once a week. Tallulah liked the panthers and the bears best, their big, thick, rippling limbs. A large lone alligator, also named Fred, also female, circled the swamp below one of the raised boardwalks. Our Fred was Winnifred, named after a favorite aunt of Dad's, in a rare and never-again-seen moment in which Mom didn't get her way. The alligator Fred had been misgendered when first found; months later, she'd laid a bunch of eggs. She had—Alligator Fred—a limited range of motion with her jaw. *No telling*, one of the volunteers stage-whispered to Fred and Tallulah, *how she survived in the wild*. Tallulah and Fred liked to watch as one of the workers slipped fish into Alligator Fred's mouth with a long stick—the way her jaw set, the bottom of her mouth got big.

Human Fred and Tallulah walked the wooden path over a long stretch of swamp, a thin layer of dark water, mangrove knees popping up out of black soil. It was late July and so hot they sweated through their clothes—an excessive heat advisory on Fred's phone near every day—and Fred and Tallulah both wore long sleeves and hats because sunscreen would only melt right off. On the boardwalk close to the swamp, mosquitoes swarmed and left itchy welts on the bare tops of Fred's flip-flop laden feet.

Once, in summer, Fred had driven George and me down to Florida City to try to search for alligators. She was often drunk then, often hiding in her room, and always very sad. But this day, Mom and Dad were at work, Jenn had taken summer courses at college to avoid coming home, and the rest of us were too old for camp or babysitters. We wore shorts and T-shirts, packed lunches and sunscreen, and all of us got sunburnt because Fred drove a convertible, top always down like Mom. When we got there, the mosquitoes were so thick—swarms so dense they looked like clouds—that we didn't see a single alligator, had to leave not long after we got out of the car.

There were fewer people at the park with Fred and Tallulah because it was summer; the visitors were mostly locals and regulars like them. They walked the boardwalk path to visit Alligator Fred, watched the panthers and the cougars and the black bears, all sleeping in the shade out of the heat, the slow up-down of their bellies. One of the panthers rolled over, and they watched the heavy, easy shifting of her legs and body. Tallulah squealed, grabbed at Fred's arm to pull her closer, as the panther yawned a gape of teeth and tongue and dark red roof of mouth.

Fred had packed water bottles filled with ice, and they each poured cold water over their heads. Drops fell onto Tallulah's nose and down her chin, and she squealed with glee again, and Fred laughed. They climbed another set of wooden stairs right past the cages filled with squawking birds and looked down in a wooden barrel where a whole pile of baby alligators—greens and browns and small black speckles—lay.

"If they were with their mom, they'd still be attached to her, crawling on her face and body," said Tallulah.

This was something Fred had told her weeks ago.

"The babies are my favorite," Fred said.

"I like the way they're squirmy," Tallulah said.

Near the exit was a large, round cage of injured eagles—one of them missing a wing, another missing a leg, a chunk cut out from another eagle's shoulder, a corner of a beak chipped off. Tallulah and Fred watched as a boy dumped out a large bucket of what looked like carcass, blood and meat. The birds swarmed, beaks pecking at the pink-and-red and fat and sinew. The cage had no top, and a group of vultures, smaller than the eagles but jet black, sleeker, swooped in too. They were spat at by the eagles, but they all ate, sometimes making hissing noises but never getting close enough to touch each other's wings or beaks.

Tallulah's hand wrapped tight around Fred's wrist. "They're stealing," said Tallulah.

The boy turned to her—twenty-something, big straw hat and bright-red face. "They're starving," he said. "There's very little food for them."

"They eat carrion?" Fred said.

The kid nodded. "The land where they'd live and hunt is all developed now."

"What's carrion?" Tallulah asked.

A few weeks, before a biological conservationist from the University of South Florida had come to Busch Wildlife to give a talk about Florida panthers, how the highways hindered their migration patterns and the endless unfurling of developments kept them trapped in smaller and smaller bits of land, how many of them starved and failed to mate because they got separated, cordoned off, pushed out. But just last year, the woman in her khaki pants and green collared volunteer shirt had said to them, a female had crossed some major highway for the first time in a decade; there was a small sliver of hope that she might find a male and mate. *It would be huge*, the woman said, one of the few new panthers born outside captivity in the past decade. Tallulah and some of the other kids had cheered.

Fred had backed away—left Tallulah hanging on the fence with two older girls on each side of her—afraid that she'd start crying. It felt so desperate. One female maybe making contact with one male, which meant what? Maybe, maybe one shred of something other than extinction, death. This woman was now offering it to these kids as some great win.

"I hate that," Tallulah said about the vultures, their beaks still pecking at and piercing the quickly disappearing mass of meat and blood.

"Me too, Lu," Fred said.

They went back to the car, engine on and air on high, to eat their lunch, the peanut butter and jelly on whole wheat that Fred had packed them, the long thin slices of mango that she'd peeled and cut the night before. Maeve texted to say the restaurant was dead and she was getting cut, and Fred felt briefly sad for less time with Tallulah by herself.

"Your mom's off early," she said.

Tallulah wiped a drop of jelly from her mouth and licked it. "Great," she said, a shred of mango trapped between her right front teeth.

Fred texted back and asked Maeve if they wanted to stay for dinner. *I'll make pasta*, she offered. David had always been the cook when they lived together, but the past few months, she'd finally found her footing with it. She'd come to look forward to all the chopping: carrots, onions, peppers. She'd put her AirPods in and listen to her favorite long, old books on audio.

Right after Maeve confirmed her late-afternoon arrival, Fred texted George and Dad: *You guys hanging in?* She felt obligated, maybe, though it seems to me she seldom felt any sort of obligation, any care, concern, responsibility, when it came to us. But Mom was dead. Every morning, Fred woke up and thought of Dad and George in that big house by themselves. What is the feeling that tells any of us, even after we're grown-up and know better—know it's likely that they'll hurt us, maim us, leave us flayed open—to check in with the people with whom we share DNA?

Just fine, Dad texted back.

Plans for dinner?

Fred didn't want to have them over, make all that awkward conversation, share Maeve and Tallulah, see all or any of them through the eyes of the others, but she still had that queasy feeling from those starving vultures. The word *starving* had begun to run over and over in her head.

Probably takeout. George this time.

Want to come have pasta by the pool at mine?

Fred had been having, the past two and a half decades, a hard time interacting with our father, though she had once been his clear favorite, until everything she did became abhorrent to him: the drinking and the skipping school, but also failing classes, not showing up to track or cross country meets, dropping all the classes he'd advised she take in college, choosing a whole life that made no sense to him. Sometime around Fred's fifteenth birthday, Dad had stopped being able to be in the same room with her without looking viscerally, physically upset and afraid. Like it was awful, painful—all that love, investment; how she'd wasted it.

He can't be in the same room with me, she said. *He's scared,* I said. *Of what?*

Before, though, Dad and Fred on beach vacations: we lived twenty minutes from the beach but only spent time as a family near the ocean in other places—different parts of Florida, Georgia—when *vacation* was the purpose, plan. When the house we tracked our sand back into wasn't Dad's. Dad would rent a surfboard; he'd grown up surfing. *Ready, Freddy?* he'd say. He always asked her first, because she was most willing maybe. He rented long boards, and Fred stretched out; at six and seven, her arms barely reached the water, and she'd splash her hands, and Dad would paddle far out past the breaking waves. We'd all stay on shore with Mom, jumping and laughing in the shore break as the glide and swoop of Vs of pelicans flew past. Dad and Fred would drift so far out they'd turn to specks, just the flash of Fred's favorite fluorescent bathing suit, Dad's blue trunks and his already bright-red burning skin. They'd stay out an hour, paddling, then sit up on the board and float and watch for waves that they could catch, the slap and clunk of water against fiberglass, wet skin drying, salt sticking, crystallizing, in the heat. Once or twice, they'd catch a wave and laugh, cheer, coming close to shore; maybe George or I would run toward them.

This night, George and Dad agreed to come to dinner, and Fred put down her phone and immediately began to rap her knuckles on her bare crossed ankle, set down her peanut butter sandwich, took two

bites of mango. Her stomach twisted. She put the window down
and held her face out toward the heat.

"You okay, Freddy?" said Tallulah.

"Fine, Lu Lu Lu," said Fred.

Fred texted Maeve to tell her Dad and George were coming.
Seriously? Maeve texted back.

I'm going to need you to be here too.

Will it be appropriate, Maeve texted, followed almost immediately by: for children? And then a laugh-crying emoji.

Fred sent back a laugh-crying emoji of her own. We'll see!?!?

8

The storm that day—because late summer in Florida means storms every day—was quick and loud and violent. The sky was already dark by the time Fred and Tallulah rolled onto the highway. Fred put the windows down until the wet came, let in the sweet pre-storm smell while the darker sheets of rain in front of them got closer and closer.

"Big storm!" Fred said.

"Big storm!" Tallulah yelled.

One moment, the car was dry, you could feel the heat still; then the thunder cracked, a flash of lightning, and hard, heavy drops came crashing down at once. Fred leaned forward, trying to get purchase on the lights of the car in front of her. Clenching arms and neck and shoulders. Tallulah sang a song about the storm, and Fred's windshield wipers whooshed fast but not fast enough.

"Lu, Lu, Lu," Fred said as she finally pulled into the driveway and turned off the car.

"Storm, storm, storm," Tallulah sang back.

Fred unbuckled her and lifted her up out of the car. Within seconds, they were both soaked through, shirt and shorts and hair dripping, the air and rain both warm. Fred twirled Tallulah, legs swinging out, then set her down, and they both twirled and twirled some more. They stayed outside just long enough for Fred to wonder if it was irresponsible, both of them wet and laughing, heads tilted back and mouths open, and Fred figured what was a few more minutes. When thunder cracked again, she picked up Tallulah and let her legs fly out.

Fred ran Tallulah a hot bath, stripped down and changed into a dry shirt and shorts while it filled, then bathed her, got her dressed— Tallulah had a whole drawer of clothes at Fred's by then. She let Tallulah sit in front of the TV while she showered, dressed herself, knotted up her hair. Maeve let herself in through the back sliding glass door, still in the corporate-issued chef's coat she wore at work. Ten minutes later, Dad and George pulled up.

Fred put on music, S. G. Goodman—the house had three well-placed Bluetooth speakers—and cooked pasta: sweet tofu sausage (Fred hadn't eaten meat since she was twenty), orzo, spinach, onions, garlic, parmesan on top and extra on the table.

The first thing Dad asked Fred to do when he and George arrived was turn off the music. Fred shrugged and shook her head. Our father was the only person any of us had ever known who drove with the radio off. Also, if it was after dark, he always had a drink with him—one rum and Diet Dr Pepper, or two, before he left the house, and then another for the road in a red Solo cup.

Fred once, when she was ten and I was eight, a few weeks after that day we ran away: up to Dad in the driveway as he was getting in the car to pick up dinner, knocked one of those red Solo cups out of his hand with the flat of her palm. Diet Dr Peper spilled onto his shirt and pants, and Dad swore, and Mom stared. Jenn said, *Fred, what the fuck?* Dad went into his room, wouldn't come out. In the end, dinner was turkey sandwiches on stale bread made by Jenn, who yelled at Fred another couple times, after which we all went to bed. (Worth noting: lots of parents we knew drove with rum in red Solo cups. *That place sounds really fucked*, said that girl from Potomac. It was. It is. It's also just the place that we are from.)

Dad and George both held those same red Solo cups when they walked through the door.

Maeve went into Fred's room to change out of her chef's coat.

The gun had, in the past day, been moved to the room where Fred slept. She'd put it in her underwear drawer, just like Mom.

George wore a T-shirt that was too small, because when he'd started to gain weight years ago, he had refused to buy new clothes.

Dad wore his collared shirt tucked in.

The rain had passed. The sun was still up but covered by the clouds. That perfect post-rain not-quite-cool seeped sweetly, wetly, into everybody's skin.

Fred directed everybody to the screened-in outside table, where she'd set out plates and glasses. Maeve brought out the pasta as Tallulah heaped piles of Parmesan straight from the bowl into her mouth.

"Lu Lu," Maeve said, setting down the pasta, reaching for her, but Tallulah and Fred both laughed, and Tallulah kept spooning in the cheese in heaping scoops.

"When did you learn to cook?" George said.

"Twenty years ago," said Fred, trying to make him feel bad. Really it had only been these past few months.

"Pretty sure this is the first time you've cooked for us," said Dad.

Dad was right. Fred was often kinder to people who were not our family. She was also much better at the sort of caring, loving, that one didn't have to do up close. She donated money to abortion funds, grassroots campaigns in other states, climate actions (money,

Dad would say, that she didn't have to give away); she felt so sure of her opinions, got high, likely, on the pulsing, coursing rush of her own rightness. She teared up, in the morning, listening to NPR, diligently composted and then, week after week, forgot to bring it to the drop-off in Union Square. Mom would call after spending any time in Fred and David's tiny apartment: *The smell, though!* But Fred got antsy, anxious, when she was asked to perform that same caring up close.

"Fred's always been embarrassed by us," Dad said to Maeve.

Maeve swallowed her bite of pasta, sat up straighter.

Fred shook her head, looked down.

"You read any of her books?" asked Dad.

George stood up, picked up Dad's glass. "You want another one?" he said.

Dad nodded.

"She's never said she was embarrassed," Maeve said.

"Probably told you how wonderful I am," said Dad.

Fred laughed, and Dad laughed too, and whatever had begun to sharpen became softer.

"Best dad I've ever had," said Fred.

"And you're my favorite second child of mine named Winnifred," said Dad.

No one talked about Mom that whole evening. No one mentioned that she'd died, that Dad was all alone for the first time in his grown-up life (George staying there didn't count). Our parents had met in their second year of college, got married the summer after senior year. Mom had gone to law school straight through the summers, finished in two years. Fifty-two years married, they would have been, that winter. As far as we knew, Dad had never made himself a meal.

Dad had a bad heart, took two pills every day for blood pressure and cholesterol, ate much worse and exercised much less than Mom had. His dad had died at forty-four. No one had figured, thought to plan for, the possibility that he'd be the one left alone. Fifty years of rhythms, grooved so deep they felt like steel, all now missing: Dad looked wobbly, not sure how to act or talk, what to think or feel, without her there.

Worth noting: when we were kids, it was Fred's job—and then George's, though George was less good at it than Fred—to convince Dad not to disappear into his room all the times that he got sad, his feelings hurt. Once, an arborist had cut down the wrong string of trees in the backyard, trees Dad had loved, and he'd stayed in bed the whole weekend. Sometimes, if we were driving home from a restaurant, after Mom and Dad had had one drink each at home, another in the car in those red Solo cups, their third and fourth at dinner, he'd have Mom drop him off on the side of the road so that he could walk home, one of us kids having made some off-handed comment that he took as a slight, or Mom having directed some fury at him about his stinginess, his sensitivity.

One time, we were all in bed but Mom and Dad and Fred. Jenn might have been awake but she'd long since gone upstairs. A fight had happened. Again, the specifics of the grievances feel irretrievable, all so incidental and petty—so much misperception, desperation, someone saying something and Dad capable of hearing only *blah blah blah, we hate you; blah blah blah, we wish that you were dead.* (This was not ever what we said.) Mom's response was, more often than not, yelling, more often than not angry accusations that she hurled and hurled until Dad would finally crack, give in.

That night, though, Dad went outside, and Mom chased after him. Fred followed.

You stupid motherfucker, Mom said. She often said this. *You pathetic piece of fucking shit*. She was desperate. She was furious.

Dad went into the three-car garage that held only Mom's convertible; Dad only ever parked his SUV outside. The garage held all those bikes we got for holidays, scooters and old toys, a wall for hanging tools, though Dad was not ever handy. Dad locked the door to the garage behind him. The garage door had a window in it, so Mom and Fred could watch as he leaned into her center console, where she kept the keys, and turned on her car.

Sometimes, Mom would talk about Dad's childhood, about his mother. His dad died when he was very young; his mom would live—the last fifteen years with dementia—until she was eighty-five. But Mom agreed to see her only at alternating Christmases—December twenty-sixth or twenty-seventh, never on the day. When we went to Dad's mom's house—only a couple of hours north, in central Florida—Mom would remind us not to accept any food, to sit on the edge of the couch, to try not to touch anything. Grandma smoked, and the house smelled, and more than once Mom made us throw out our clothes in the hotel dumpster if we had lingered in there for too long.

About Dad's childhood, Mom would only say, *Who knows what awful things must have happened in that house?*

We liked Dad's mom—Fred and I did. Jenn only ever said that she was gross. But she seemed to love us—as well as her son, our dad, as well as our aunt, her daughter—very much. Her house was small and dark, and she always had a lot of animals. Dried-out cat or dog shit was caked sometimes to the floor. Once, I dug my fingers in the corner crevice of the couch, and dog shit crusted underneath my nails, and I tried to keep my face still and not look at Mom as Grandma and Dad talked. But Grandma held us very close to her when we walked into the house and when we left. She asked us probing, careful questions. Once, she gave me a picture from when she was young in which she looked just like me: same nose and eyes, same close-lipped, awkward smile. I'd thanked her, hugged her, breathing through my mouth because of the smoke and dog smells, slipped the picture quickly into the back pocket of my jeans so Mom wouldn't see.

Anyway.

That day in the garage: Dad locked the door and turned the car on. We all had TVs in our rooms, and Fred watched a lot of Lifetime movies late at night, and she knew that people killed themselves by turning cars on in their garage. She knew, too, that Dad had done it wrong. In the show she'd watched, the woman taped a tube to the exhaust pipe and then pulled it through the cracked car window and taped that up as well.

Dad leaned into the car, the convertible top down, to turn it on and then stood up. He walked to stand behind the back fender.

Mom threw Dad's shoe at the garage-door window. She threw Fred's shoe, three rocks, yelled more expletives. Fred stood frozen, anxious, looking on.

Fred said later that she knew Dad wouldn't die, not then, like that, not on any of the nights he got down and she was sent to make it stop. But one of the reasons she always remembered that night— him standing barefoot in his tucked-in shirt, his sad, sad face behind Mom's bright-red convertible, Fred picking up all the shoes off the driveway while Mom yelled and yelled—was because it was that night Fred realized that for all the ways we loved our father, all the other times he was fun and funny, this roiling undercurrent of begging, pleading, yelling, threatening—and the feeling it engendered in our jaws and bellies—wouldn't ever go away.

So, then, Dad and George, Tallulah and Fred and Maeve, at dinner in Fred's borrowed house in Florida: everybody ate and drank, and

Tallulah asked George to swim, and George agreed, jumping in the water in the shorts he was already wearing. Maeve felt an unfamiliar sensation, an almost pleasurable itch or bristle, hearing Tallulah squeal as George threw her, followed almost immediately by *again! Again!* Watching George's floppy body holding Lulah, something structural or chemical unfurled in her body or brain: how safe her daughter looked in his big arms.

Fred watched him notice Maeve watch him. Her jaw and shoulders tightened.

"I'm not sure I have anything you could change into," she said, once George got out of the pool. She handed him a towel.

"I'll drip dry," George said, unbothered. "Dad, do you want another drink?"

"Sure," Dad said. Turning to Maeve, he asked, "How're your parents?"

George went inside to make another drink for himself and Dad.

"Tallulah, want me to toss the rings for you?" Fred called, moving toward the pool.

"We don't talk much," Maeve said.

"Fred does that to us," Dad said.

George reemerged and handed him his fresh drink.

"Your family will get past it," Dad said to Maeve. "It helps if someone dies."

Maeve laughed. "It might," she said. Tallulah pulled herself from the pool and ran over, dripping. Maeve picked up the towel Fred had left out and wrapped Tallulah in it, settled her daughter onto her lap.

Fred went inside and came back out with bowls of mint chip ice cream.

"My favorite," Dad said, a little shocked by the small kindness.

What Fred didn't say was that it was her favorite too.

9

Fred got up early the next morning even though she'd walked over to David's for sex late the night before. She'd been freaked out by that dinner. She'd wanted to talk to David, wanted him to have been there with her so they could have stayed up late after and talked about us all. If they'd still been together, Fred would have poured them each a sip or two of whiskey. They'd have sat close together on the couch and talked and talked, and slowly she'd have felt better, more hopeful. She'd have begun to talk in longer sentences and felt more sure, felt her chest and shoulders settle, widen. She would have kissed him, let him pull her to him as they walked together to their room.

But this was part of him she knew she didn't have a right to anymore—the extra store of patience, long slow sitting, talking, listening. It was the part of Brian that I missed the most too. Someone to talk about it all with after.

Instead, Fred climbed onto the air conditioner and through David's open window, took off her clothes, and crawled slowly up from the bottom of his bed. She felt him start. She did not touch his dick but ran her hands slowly over nearly every other part of him, let her shoulders settle onto his chest while her toes, the pads of her feet, ran slowly up his feet and calves. Her hand circled the small patch of hair on his lower belly, the slight paunch, the dip below his hips.

He reached his hands up into her, but she still didn't touch him. He arched his back, made low, quiet sounds. She kissed him only once and thought of leaving without ever letting him inside her. Thought of sliding out of his bed and back to that big, empty house. Instead, she held his ass, his belly again, waited, waited. Another mewling groan from him; his back and ass rose up. Finally, she cupped his balls, then touched him, slipped him inside her. Teenage, desperate, he came, and she did too.

"Freddy," he said.

She startled. She'd passed out, stayed longer than she meant to.

David had pulled on his shirt and shorts. "My mom's been trying to call you," he said.

She nodded, still not looking at him. Fred had loved David's mother since the moment she met her. She didn't trust how open and generous Barb was, but over the years, Barb had won Fred over. Fred was terrible at phone calls, and when she and David lived in New York, they'd only spoken to Barb once a month. But since they'd moved down, right up until the week that Fred left David, Barb and Fred had had coffee or dinner once a week at least. In all the years that Mom was jealous, angry at Fred for liking Barb more than her, she'd argued (at their wedding, over holidays, any time they were in town and Mom counted and compared the minutes, hours, Fred and David spent at her and Barb's houses and Mom felt like she'd lost) that when David left her, Barb would desert Fred too. But now, Fred was the one who wasn't answering Barb's calls.

"Please tell her that I'm sorry," Fred said.

She wanted him to tell Barb that she missed her.

"Monty sold the house," said David.

Fred got out of bed and grabbed her shirt. No one had told her that the house she was borrowing was on the market.

"They close September first."

Fred reached under the sheets for her pants and underwear and pulled them on.

"You can come here," David said. When she didn't answer, he said, "Fred. We have to talk about this."

"I'm sorry," Fred said.

David shook his head. "Me too."

Fred climbed back out the window, went back to her soon-to-be-sold-to-someone-else borrowed house. She felt something hard and heavy pressing on her neck and shoulders. The house she'd bought with David felt like giving up, all those concrete walls like a trap. She couldn't sleep so she swam again, then sat out on the porch and scrolled Zillow. She put in their old zip code, the zip code up by the university where she used to work, and she scrolled and clicked through tiny, one-walled kitchens, shared rooms, closets called bed-rooms, windows facing brick walls, windows looking down onto the alleys where the buildings kept the trash.

A month before, only two weeks before Mom died, Fred had flown up to New York. To see her friends, to get her footing, find a place, figure out whatever life she still had there. She'd known, of course, that she couldn't stay indefinitely at Monty's. She had said vaguely, when she told David she couldn't move in with him, that she'd only ever felt at home in New York. She had no idea how she'd pay for a new apartment, first and last, security. David had always been the one to do the banking, the bill paying. This now felt shameful to her.

Fred had told friends she was coming up, and they had all been happy: So excited! Cannot wait! Hooray! When she and David left the city, it had been so sudden and jarring: all their stuff in storage, the whole city locked up, quiet, empty-feeling. Fred had cried, said they'd be back soon; she'd made her friends promise, joking (but maybe also proof that Allie was right about her narcissism) that none of them should have any babies or any fun at all while she and David were gone. It was only meant to be a couple months, to save money, for Fred to sell a book. A little break and beach, and David would find another job, and they'd be back.

Our couch is always your couch, her friends had said.

Her friends with lots of money: *Our extra room is yours whenever you need.*

Call me anytime and I'll come extract you from that fascist state.

Thirty-two months after that conversation, one month ago, Fred had put a nonrefundable flight on her credit card. (Presumptive, she thought later, so obviously embarrassing.) She texted the friend she thought of as her closest. Like nearly every writer Fred knew who still lived in New York, the friend's husband did something in tech that no one understood (some of the other husbands worked in finance, were corporate lawyers, had trust funds; it had been a prickly point with David, especially in their conversations about staying in Florida, the way these wealthy spouses felt like an indictment). But her friend was on Fire Island for the week. The apartment was shut up, no one to let Fred in. Two other friends had very young kids. Another was dating someone who had roommates, so the boyfriend was working remotely on the couch where, otherwise, Fred might have slept.

(I was at home in New York with a spare room but was still not returning any of Fred's phone calls, texts, or emails. After that first year with Cass, we saw each other much less: we'd meet for dinner after I got off work; she'd come take Cass while Brian worked. *Your sister lives in the city?* a friend of mine said, when I mentioned Fred and I were getting dinner. Another pre-K parent asked me who that woman had been, the one without a kid, in the black jeans, at one of Cassie's birthday parties. *My sister*, I'd think, sometimes hours or days later. It felt different, out loud, on my tongue. *Sister*, I thought, sitting, talking to her, watching Cassie, after a phone call with George. After a long visit with Mom and Dad. She would know all the things they did that made me squirmy, angry, before I told her. I could tell Fred about arguments, grown-up tantrums, and she wouldn't wince and call it trauma, call it awful, ask if I'd ever considered *establishing a boundary*. *Sounds exactly right*, she'd say, pulling Cass up to her, careful, doting. *Of course they fucking did.*)

She finally called a friend with kids and offered to babysit in exchange for the foldout couch in their basement office.

"I'll watch the kids, and you and Greg can go out," she said.

"I'm so sorry, Freddie," Emily said. "Xander's been acting, out and I'm worried about warping his schedule right now."

Fred was quiet. So was Emily.

"I know how annoying it all sounds," said Emily at last.

Fred got a cheap Airbnb at the last minute, a small studio in a smoky elevator building in Murray Hill. She put that, too, on the credit card, a larger chunk of money than she'd laid down in months.

She didn't tell her friends a single thing about her life. Not that she'd left David, she'd quit writing, she'd not followed up on seeing any of the long list of apartments that she'd bookmarked before she'd come. Underneath the *Oh my god, it's so good to see you*, the *Promise me you're moving back*, the *I'm so sorry David couldn't come*, the hugs and late nights talking, drinking, eating, Fred was slowly and methodically detaching from whatever it was she thought her life was there.

In every interaction Fred had in New York, she was reminded of what she'd once had living in that city: a richness and a lightness, walking from work uptown to their apartment, running into a friend, stopping to see art and texting David to meet her for dinner, long conversations about nothing over coffee. She'd thought this was her life, that it would be forever. The person she'd loved most in New York she couldn't call, because Tess had died five years before.

Her last night in New York that week, Fred went out with a handful of the friends that she had left and got drunk. She hadn't been drinking back in Florida; Maeve didn't drink, so it seemed like the right thing when she was there. That finger or two of whiskey she used to have sometimes with David felt too sad when she was by herself. That night, though, she sat in the backyard of a bar off Atlantic Avenue in Brooklyn, rickety tables and wrought-iron chairs and Christmas lights strung over the white wood fence. She had one fancy gin drink with chartreuse, lime, and prosecco, then one more. The third was because the first two had gone down so easy, because she'd thought so many sad and desperate and sometimes unkind things about her friends while she was there. With the gin's help, she allowed herself to love them, to luxuriate in talking to them, telling stories, bringing up and talking about old friends.

The first twenty minutes of her walk back to the Airbnb, she'd felt like she was floating, AirPods in and peeking in the uncurtained windows along the streets of downtown Brooklyn, bare arms extended out, cars whooshing past. She walked over the Brooklyn Bridge and carefully avoided her old building, Tess's building. She worried her body might not let her walk past Tess's; it was, of course, no longer Tess's. She worried she might climb the fire escape, through the same window they used to climb through—a drink for Fred, a cigarette for Tess—after Tess's kids and husband were asleep; that she'd settle herself somewhere quiet in their too-small kitchen. Regardless of who lived there now, Fred thought, if she walked by, she might climb in and ask if she could stay.

Instead, she walked and walked. She felt how surely Tess was gone, saw how likely it was that she might never live in this place she'd loved for so much of her life again. It was only the last couple blocks up Third Avenue, the car exhaust much thicker, her legs and arms all achy and exhausted, that she thought maybe—and then waiting for the elevator, and the stale air inside once the doors closed, that she felt sure—everything was coming up.

She ran from the elevator to the apartment, canvas bag open in front of her in case she retched in the hall. Pulling her wallet out of her bag and shoving it in her back pocket, clutching at, then dropping, then picking up again, then finally getting the keys in the door. She stayed crouched half an hour over the toilet in the tiny bathroom, grime on the underside of the seat lid. She dry-heaved, but nothing came out. The whole trip had felt like this: wanting release, something certain, solid, but then nothing, just this almost-not-quite grasping, heaving, this awful thing inside her, refusing to get out.

When she came back, Maeve and Tallulah met her at the airport in her car. She'd lent the car to Maeve while she was gone. She felt herself tear up at the sight of both their heads; she'd prepared herself, her whole flight, for them not to be there. *Fred Fred Fred how was your flight how was your trip?* A hug over the seat from Maeve. Fred reached back to grab Tallulah's foot.

That morning, after sex with David, after the news that this house where she was staying would soon disappear, she pulled on her shorts and bra and shirt and socks; it was hot already, barely six thirty but already close to 90 degrees, the humidity so thick it made her think of how when we were kids, George would sometimes mimic swimming in the hot summer air, moving his kid arms and hands in frantic strokes.

Outside, warming up, Fred was quickly wet with sweat: between her breasts and shoulder blades, her forehead and upper lip, her lower back above the thick elastic of her waistband. Wild fist-size bunnies sprang out of the bushes as she jogged past, startling her even though they did this every morning, every time she jogged by. She did ten sprints, high knees, butt kicks, skipped in high leaps while pumping her fists. She jogged slowly toward the main road, where she did repeating one-mile sprints back and forth. After each mile, she jogged for ninety seconds. Her phone tracked her times: 6:01, 6:03, 5:57, 6:07, 5:54. At last, she jogged back to the house and peeled off her clothes and lay naked in the pool for a long time, legs and then arms churning.

Mind and body finally spent enough to feel emptied, Fred looked up to see a klatch of that same type of vulture she'd seen with Tallulah, a thick swarm of them, high above the pool. She thought of William Faulkner, tied with Virginia Woolf as her favorite-ever writer. (She'd tried to get me to read *Absalom, Absalom!* at least ten times.) Faulkner had said he wanted to come back in his next life as a vulture (he'd said "buzzard"), because, he said, *nothing hates him or envies him or wants him or needs him. He is never bothered or in danger, and he can eat anything*.

There were more than a hundred vultures, Fred thought. She could see the outlines of their bodies, a flash of tail, a curve of wing, the same sharp contours of heads and beak. As they circled closer, she could see that what she'd thought was sleek looked wan and hungry.

Starving, she said, still trying, failing, to float, arms and ankles circling. *Starving*, she said again, out loud.

She righted herself, the balls of her feet settling on the pool's prickled concrete, still looking at those vultures, swarming, desperate. She climbed out, dried off, pulled on her linen pants and button-up, and found her phone. After half an hour on Zillow—studio apartments in Crown Heights, Bed-Stuy, for $3,000—she expanded her search. A cabin in the Everglades for $1500, but no hot water and no air conditioner; a place upstate for $2000 that was half an hour from the nearest grocery store.

She wasn't looking, she thought, for an apartment. She was looking for a place that might tell her who or what she was. Where no one would bother or endanger her; somewhere where she also wouldn't starve.

Those years in New York, she'd liked what it meant when she said she *lived in New York*. I liked it too. The way people nodded, asked questions, as if it proved that she'd accomplished something, when really, most days, all *New York* was was coffee, breakfast, prep for class and teach it, lunch and dinner, on her phone, on her computer, a life like any other life. (And what of this, too, was Mom; Fred wanted to feel *special*, to prove somehow—the way we all wanted to—that she wasn't *just like everybody else*).

She did love, though, the subway, the noise, the lights no matter how late or early, unknown bodies, hours walking through the city, early mornings running along both rivers. Her friends, her work. *New York* had started as the place she'd gone (we'd gone) to prove that she was the sort of person who might live there, but then time had passed, and it had become the closest Fred had ever felt to feeling like a place was hers.

It isn't ours, though, David said, when he'd argued that they had to buy the house in Florida. *I can't live again reliant on some asshole landlord. I just want,* he said, *to breathe.*

And Fred knew, too, the pull of this: the ocean, air, all that quiet, open, empty space. New York had sucked us up into its rush, its clank and force, the constant, desperate, clawing need for more. She worried often (I did too)- that it had turned her into someone she didn't like or trust or want to be.

She put the address of the house they'd bought, where David lived, into her phone and took a tour: the arid rooms, the concrete front, the backyard where David said, in a year or two, they could put in a pool. It was *a clean slate, just a start. You have to have a little vision*, David said. He'd spent his whole life pouring himself into other people's houses. *Trust that I can make it something that you'll love.*

Fred closed the app, set down her phone. She looked up again to find the birds, but they weren't there. She picked up her phone again and typed "vultures." Scrolled and clicked and scrolled and read.

"Obligate scavenger birds," her search revealed. "If vultures are not present, carcasses tend to remain longer in the environment, decomposing and producing greenhouse gases." Fred did an image search and looked at pictures: beaks bloodied from the inside of a carcass, white feathers on necks and faces, red, exposed skin on heads. She took screenshots and saved them, then put down her phone, went into her room to grab the gun (still in its canvas bag), and drove out to the beach.

10

George spent a lot of time out by the pool because Dad didn't like it there. The wind off the water, the palm tree rustle: Dad got bothered when his work papers (and his hair) got mussed. George threw a ball for Libby, who ran back and forth out to the dock, ball clenched in her teeth. *Libby!* George said. *Ball back, Libby! Treat?* Libby yipped, running larger and larger circles around him, finally running down to the sand that Mom and Dad had had installed in front of the sea wall. She squatted there, ball in her mouth, one eye on George, who lunged toward her and wrenched the ball from her teeth while she shat.

Dad hated mess but had fallen gradually in love with Libby. (*Because she's bitchy like Mom,* Jenn said, when she called and told me this.) He would let her leap into his lap. The first few times, he didn't allow it; *Not on the couch, sweet girl,* George heard him say. He pushed her down. But she kept jumping up, her body curling into him. Eventually, he started calling for her when she wasn't right there waiting as soon as he sat down.

Dad had started asking questions about George's work, and this was also, for George, reason to stay outside. Dad loved talking about money. He knew about the balloon payment on George's house because they'd talked about it when George had done it, and Dad had advised against it. Dad only ever liked to borrow money when it made good financial sense. George had placated Dad with talk of various bonuses that he'd been promised. Except he was now, technically, no longer employed.

"Whatever happened to all those cryptocurrencies?" Dad said now, ambling his way out to the pool with his first rum drink of the evening. George had encouraged Dad to go in big a couple years before, but Dad had balked. "The Bitcoin market is . . ." Dad stopped. He lowered himself slowly into the Adirondack chair next to George. Self-awareness was rare for both George and Dad, but even Dad could tell, halfway through that sentence, that he should either get back up and walk away or find something else to talk about.

Libby jumped into Dad's lap.

"The Bitcoin market is not in great shape," George said, trying to coax Libby down.

"She's happy here," Dad said.

"She's my fucking dog," George said.

"George," Dad said, "is everything okay?"

"I just need a fucking break," George said. "I'm going out."

George at eight, nine, ten, asking for *a break*: he used to bang his head against the coffee table, stubby fingers clutching at the edges, whenever Mom and Dad asked him to do something he didn't want to do. Often it was something he *did* want to do, just not in that moment, not if it meant going upstairs, getting changed, pausing what he was already occupied with. *You better stop right now*, he'd say. *If you keep making me do these things I don't want to do, I might turn out like Fred.*

George at twenty-three: big new job just started, calling Fred to ask for help, wanting her advice about finding medication for what he thought might be long-ignored depression and anxiety. *George, you have health insurance*, Fred said—jealous, likely; she and David wouldn't have consistent health insurance until Fred was thirty-six. *You go on the website, call them, find a doctor.*

I don't want to, George said.

George. Fred worked to keep her voice careful. *You know I can't prescribe you anything*. Talking, talking, Fred trying to explain how she got help, got better, and then to David, after, *I'm the family mental health provider now, I guess?*

Two hours later, Mom and Dad calling Fred and putting her on speaker: *What did you say to our baby to make him think he's sick like you?*

George got into Mom's convertible, kept the top up. He drove half an hour aimlessly, past the house where Fred was staying, over the two bridges, along the thin strip of land with the river to its west and ocean to its east. George went west again, toward US 1, over the train tracks into a strip mall. When he pulled in, he still had not admitted to himself that he had come in search of Maeve. That he'd been thinking of her smiling, chin in hand, while he played with her kid in the pool that night at Fred's. He parked and walked immediately into the Bonefish Grill, passed the hostess, and sat down at the bar.

He'd chosen his least ill-fitting shirt—notably expensive, pale blue, buttoned up. A kid who looked young enough to be in high school took George's order: rum and Diet Coke, the bang bang shrimp, the breadcrumb-crusted baked tilapia. The intermittent fasting had transitioned to sporadic, inconsistent, all-day fasting, and then a lot of eating and too much drinking late at night.

The first slow sip of the rum and Diet Coke was not unlike the feeling that George used to get chewing on the toe of his favorite stuffed cat, named Cat—the fabric worn down, always a little wet.

Mom would yell, *Georgie, that's disgusting; stop*, but he'd keep gnaw-ing, tilt his head, angle his body behind mine or Fred's or Jenn's so Mom couldn't see.

After his second sip of rum, George opened Instagram. No new pictures had appeared on Allie's page, so he scrolled through all the old ones. She always selected the photos that made her look good, with little to no thought to him, his awkward slouch, weird grimace, double chin. She was a full foot shorter than him, those perfect lips. All the trips they took—his birthday, her birthday, Valentine's Day, summer, Tahoe, Paris, Vegas. *So fucking predictable*, he knew Fred said, but these places were predictable, George thought, be-cause they were *fun*.

He checked on Allie's boss's wife: no new posts, no reels. Was she mourning, he thought? He thought again of DMing her. He was so much richer than this guy who was seemingly loved by both George's wife and his own. This was infuriating. He thought maybe he would tell her about her husband and she'd leave him, that maybe she'd move in with George instead. He stared again at her pictures, her three kids, the lines around her eyes and chin. Her name was Clara. He thought maybe she'd be grateful, appreciate more, all George had to give.

"Didn't get enough of me last night?" Maeve said. She'd come up from behind him with his bang bang shrimp.

He started, and she laughed. "Guess not," George said.

Maeve had not ever had it easy. Her dad left. Her mom drank too much. Yet George knew that Fred was always jealous of her. Could see it when we were kids. Her mom drank too much, but she was fun and funny. They were close and easy, Maeve and her mom, more like friends. Fred envied the mess of their house and its tightness, smallness, closeness. Sometimes Maeve's mom stayed out late (*probably fucking some dumb asshole*, Maeve might say), and Maeve and Fred stayed home in front of the TV and got drunk or stoned all by themselves instead of going out and feeling lonely, anxious, at a party on the beach with too many other kids. Maeve's mom got them takeout, microwaved them Stouffer's mac and cheese, hot pockets, Costco mini tacos—shit Mom would never have bought us. Laughing, watching *The Real World*, *Behind the Music*, passing tubs of Betty Crocker icing back and forth. Those nights were Fred's favorite nights, I think.

"You girls drunk again?" Maeve's mom would call out once she got home.

"Of course not," Maeve would say, and they'd all laugh.

"I'm glad you girls stayed home," she would say. "When Freddy's here, I'm always less scared of what you'll get up to."

This was a time in Fred's life when she loved alcohol the most. But when she went to college, drinking hadn't felt as fun without Maeve there to watch, to guide her, huddle up with her in bathrooms, Applebee's booths, car backseats and whisper, gossip, laugh and laugh. What had felt fun began instead to feel sloppy, scary: skinned knees and elbows that she couldn't account for, the cottony, afraid feeling of waking up and not knowing how you'd gotten home. Her whole life, she'd worked to stop Dad from dying, and now she felt like maybe she was dying. The university called and told Mom and Dad she was *in crisis*. They weren't always great or glad about it—Mom on the phone, still not convinced by the idea of therapy: *Why the fuck am I paying all this money for someone to talk to you?*—but they got Fred help, and slowly, gradually, she got better.

In that same time—Fred's freshman year of college, my high school junior year—I went up with Mom to help Fred move out of her dorm. I was, at that time, consuming fewer than three hundred calories a day. Fine, downy hair had begun to pop up above my lips and on my cheeks. I rode horses both before and after school each day. (Mom and Dad hated spending too much money on the horses. *They stink*, Mom said. *Too many rich people*, said Dad—he was, of course, also rich, but his money was new; he was still cheap). I loved the horses, though not the shows, the other kids; our trainer used to tie our reins up in a knot and send us over a line of three-foot jumps, calling out to us to put our arms out straight, then touch our heads, then touch our toes, heels down, head up, back straight. Full speed, on a two-thousand-pound horse, shifting the placement of my hands, the positioning of my seat, squeezing my legs: in every other aspect of my life I was afraid, but up there, I wasn't. Sitting in my horse's stall was the closest I had ever come to loving something that didn't need or want things from me that I couldn't or didn't want to give.

Fred gawked but didn't say anything about my weight loss when she saw me. (*She's just jealous*, Mom said later, after Fred called and said that she was *concerned*.) She had gone from 90 to 140 pounds in that same year. I thought of taking her aside and telling her about the pleasure I felt, my body gnawing at itself from the inside; the clarity, the ease and cleanliness of shrinking, melting. How good it felt to look in the mirror and not recognize myself. All her problems, I wanted to tell her, were a direct result of all the space she seemed incapable of not taking up.

Mostly, though, Fred didn't look at Mom or me the whole time. She was in bed, silent (*a lump*, Mom said, and cried that night at the hotel) when we came to take her to breakfast at nine thirty; asleep in a big, comfy chair in the library, the sun setting, after she told us she was studying and Mom sent me to look for her. Mom worked all day cleaning, organizing, throwing out the carpet she'd bought when she'd moved Fred in that was now covered in stains, doing load after load of musty, months-old laundry, carrying Fred's furniture and books down all those dorm stairs by herself, letting Fred—swollen-faced, in the same sweatshirt and sweatpants she'd worn the whole time—support herself on Mom's small shoulder as they walked off campus and into the hotel restaurant. Only crying quietly in the bathroom after we'd dropped Fred back in her room.

In that same time, Maeve had found her way to her mom's, and then a lot of other mothers' and fathers', OxyContin, Xanax, Klonopin. The drug use had escalated, as had the lying, then the stealing, then the pain clinics, then, finally, the heroin.

It was easy, now, to lay out Maeve's past and let it look and feel like escalation, slippery slopes, etc. To see all of it—the drugs, the alcohol, the minor misdemeanors—as inevitable and predetermined: late-night drives out to the beach to find a party, older friends and guys Fred had never met, a bottle or three of sweet rum at the drive-through liquor store attached to the gas station that never carded, sold by the same guy every night playing the same Sublime record (*40 Oz. to Freedom*), lamenting that 40s were illegal in the state, looking long at girls' bare legs and arms as they counted out their cash. It was easy, now, to look back at all of it and say this here was why Maeve had had such a hard time in all the years since; except, back then, when we were young and she was cool and easy, when Fred and Jenn and George and I spent most of our time feeling small and lost and scared, nearly everything that Maeve did had looked and felt to Fred, to all of us, like fun.

Maeve had been clean since Tallulah but was still only sporadically talking to her mother. She had a belly, and her skin was pockmarked, but her legs were long and thin. She'd lived with her mom the first year with Tallulah, but she hated feeling beholden like that, and so for the past year she and Tallulah had lived in the motel close to the highway, week to week. No kitchen, but a hot plate and lots of left-overs from work; the bathroom sink worked just as well for dishes.

Maeve didn't live in the motel because she couldn't afford anything else. The Bonefish job was one of the best she'd ever had; health insurance after the first year and consistent-to-good money from November through the start of summer. From May to November, it still stuck pretty solidly at fine. But she had bad credit and a small but traceable misdemeanor record: three possession charges; two DUIs. There were almost no rentals in the school district she wanted for Tallulah, the one we'd all come up in; the rentals that did exist were run by people who thought their willingness to ignore her bad credit was sufficient reason to overcharge for some shitty place, to not respond to phone calls about broken pipes or busted air conditioners, to make vague threats to call the cops for nothing when Maeve tried to dock the costs of various repairs from her rent.

So instead, Maeve and Tallulah lived at the motel. The owner was nice enough, female, older, unobtrusive, grateful for the extra cash in summer. A shitty, algaeed pool in the front parking lot, a motel neighbor, Liz, whose four-year-old Maeve watched sometimes in exchange for Liz watching Tallulah. When Liz and Maeve both had the night off, they would sit outside and talk while their kids slept.

When she and Fred were in high school, George seven, eight, nine, ten, Fred and Maeve used to drive him and his friends to soccer, baseball, basketball in Fred's little black convertible with the top down, music on too loud. Alanis Morissette, those same Sublime songs, Nirvana, Counting Crows, Cake, Reel Big Fish, Blink-182. It was possible Fred and Maeve were drunk some of those times, but in the end, everyone still made it to their practices and games.

George had loved the way Maeve looked from the backseat of that car—cool and pretty, bare shouldered, eyes squinting in the sun and arms often in the air—he'd loved the way her fingers pulled at the hair stuck to her chin and lips but she kept talking, kept turning to him, laughing, singing, no matter how hard the wind whipped hair in her face.

"You know Mama Maeve?" the bartender said.

George looked at him, his long hair, tanned arms: the sort of guy Maeve would have fucked in high school. He was probably, right now, dating a girl like Maeve had been. George glanced over at Maeve, setting down food at a table of four women over sixty, smiling at them, answering their questions, folding an unfolded napkin, clearing an errant appetizer plate. Fred thought she wore too much makeup, but George thought it just enough, lipstick almost as red as Allie's. She still had that way of being in her body, easy, open. Her pants were tight and black, flattering. It was impossible for George to look at her and not also see the sixteen-year-old, hair in her face, singing, turning back to tell him stories, ask him questions, the girl he woke up thinking about when he was eight and nine and ten.

Fred had hostessed at a restaurant very similar to this in high school, the Italian chain Carrabba's, the sister restaurant to Bonefish. She had wanted an excuse to be outside the house after dark for which she could not be castigated or accused. (We all wanted to be out of the house in high school: Jenn worked retail; George played lots of tennis; I was always riding horses; *we aren't ever coming back*, Fred had said that day when I was eight and she was almost ten, except only Fred would think that such a thing was possible, allowed.) Fred often got stoned with coworkers in the parking lot before work. The sous-chef was a kid she had ridden the bus with, kindergarten through fifth grade; she snuck him Tupperware containers filled with Sprite and vodka that she pilfered from the bar. He—this friend—would die a few years later. South Florida in the late 1990s, early 2000s: of the three hundred kids with whom Fred started high school, eight would die of overdoses before the age of twenty-three.

———

"She's friends with my older sister," George said now, about Maeve, strangely angry at this kid. He looked back at Maeve and saw now all that makeup, years of sun exposure, the dark coarseness of the tops of her hands, the crease and pucker of the skin around her mouth and eyes. She looked like a mom.

"She does not fuck around," the kid said.

An hour later, George had eaten his shrimp and his tilapia, his garlic smashed potatoes, his crème brûlée. Maeve had brought all four. The kid had introduced himself as Travis. George had watched Maeve greet then serve then clean up after two rounds of her four tables, watched her laugh as she came out of the kitchen, turn her head and say something indecipherable as she walked through the swinging door, hot full plates in a row down both her arms. Up at the bar, talking to Travis while he filled her drink orders, dropping the fresh cocktails while clearing out the empties, quick and deft on the computer, dropping checks, clearing more plates, wiping and then resetting at least half her tables before the busser could help. Half the tables now sat empty. Travis stood scrolling through his phone.

"Georgie Kenner," Maeve said, sliding onto the stool one down from George's. "All grown up." She had a stack of cash and receipts that she laid out and began organizing, counting. Travis brought her a Diet Coke and half an order of bang bang shrimp.

"You have plans?" George said, emboldened by his third drink.

"Sleep," Maeve said. "Maybe a bath."

Tallulah slept at Fred's when Maeve worked late. Maeve used to come get her, lifting her up out of Fred's bed all careful, quiet whispers, strapping her into the car. But this was, Fred said to Maeve, *an unnecessary disruption to her sleep.* She tried hard not to make it sound like judgment. *It's no big deal for me,* Fred said.

Fred loved it, of course, Tallulah's tiny body flailing next to her, the steady sounds of her breathing, easy rhythms of her waking, stretching, padding out into the kitchen as Fred made breakfast for the both of them. She loved it also as a way to keep from going to David's every night.

"Could I . . ." George started. He didn't know, had not ever known, what he was doing. He was still married. He wanted the girl he used to watch singing Alanis Morisette, head back, laughing, hair stuck to her face, to take him to her house and prove to him that he wasn't a worthless baby piece of shit.

"I don't drink," she said.

"You want to go out to the beach and swim?" he said.

This was something Fred would say, and it was thinking of her that made him say it. George had never liked the ocean as much as Fred did. But he liked what suggesting this might say about him.

"I'm really beat," Maeve said.

But later, after Travis walked down to the other end of the bar to take an order, Maeve looked at George and broke her last piece of fried shrimp in half. "What the hell," she said.

George had to push back the passenger's seat in Maeve's car because there was trash on the car floor: water bottles, Coke cans, Gatorades, half-eaten bags of snacks. Maeve didn't apologize for the mess. It took three tries to start the car. Maeve had changed out of her chef's coat and black clogs into a tank top and flip-flops. She still wore the same black pants. She'd thrown her hair up into a bun, and he could see the places where her makeup had begun to cake and crack, mascara smudged.

"What's it like for you," Maeve said, "being back here?"

"Really fucking weird," George said.

Maeve laughed and turned the car out of the parking lot. "I bet."

She'd put her window down, so George did too, rested his arm over the window's ledge.

"What about for you?" George said.

"I'm not sure it counts as being back if I've mostly always been here," Maeve said.

"I thought you . . ." George was awash with that strange shame of knowing things about a person that they hadn't told you, information he had gleaned from other people's conversations, that he had either seen or sought out on the internet.

Maeve lifted her arm off the car's side and let it hover out the window. "I tried to leave a few times, but it never really took."

George felt chastened. He lifted his right arm out the window, just like Maeve's.

"I'm sorry about your mom," Maeve said. "She was . . ."

"A lot," George said. The tennis guys in high school used to pretend to be Mom: *Get that little shit, Georgie!* they'd screech, waving their hands the way Mom did. *Move faster, George! Eyes on the ball!*

Maeve laughed.

"Thanks, though," George said. "I wish . . . She did her best."

Mom about George, straight into his thirties: *Where's the baby? How's my baby? You girls let my baby be!*

Us to her: *Jesus, Mom, he's* [insert any age past ten and up to thirty-four]. *He's six foot three.*

Maeve's window was still down, and George watched as the wind snatched at her hair and threw wisps around her face.

"I don't think any of us are good at feelings," said George.

"Fred thinks she is," Maeve said.

It was the first time either of them had brought up Fred.

"She tell you that she quit?" Maeve asked.

"Feeling?" George said.

"Writing books."

"Bullshit," George said.

"She just runs and swims and listens to long, boring audiobooks."

They stopped at a stoplight, and Maeve looked briefly at him. "She watches football docuseries, parents my kid."

Neither Maeve nor George spoke again until they got to the beach. They'd not seen a single other car on their way there. George didn't want to talk about Fred. Maeve regretted bringing her up. She pulled into the same public beach access lot she went to with Fred, with Tallulah, the same place where Fred parked when she ran, gun on the floor. None of them, of us, ever parked at any of the larger, lifeguarded, snack bar–endowed public beaches because: tourists. It was summer, though, and the tourists were all gone.

George and Maeve left their flip-flops in the car and walked out onto the sand. George wondered how many of her clothes Maeve would take off. She pulled off her black pants, revealing worn blue cotton underpants, kept her tank top and bra on. George yanked at his own pants, stumbling as they caught on his ankles. He tried not to think of Allie. A breeze came off the water, and bumps rose up on his bare skin.

Late-July south Florida ocean is more like a bathtub than an ocean. No waves, so warm it borders hot. George hadn't been swimming, besides the half hour with Tallulah, since he got to town. All that time beside the pool at Dad's house, he'd never thought to dive in.

Maeve stood in the first trickle of water, burrowing her toes in the wet sand. George was grateful for her eyes not being on him as he pulled at his jeans one final time and almost fell over. He folded them beside Maeve's pants, took off his shirt, the moon three quarters full, and breathed in. Fred used to get drunk and swim out here when she was in high school. She used to, still drunk, come into my bed at night and sleep next to me, hair damp, skin sticky, smelling just like this. I'd thought at first it was an accident, that she'd come up the stairs and turned right instead of left on her way to her bed.

But then it happened again, and again: many weekend nights when she was fifteen, sixteen, and I was thirteen, fourteen. I loved every night like that, when my bed smelled like Fred.

George that night with Maeve: it felt like trying on a different way of being. He could not say how or why this was appealing. It felt thrilling, late at night, walking slowly to the ocean with Maeve in front of him, like if they started talking, they would rupture some of what was happening between them. George wanted to be nine, ten, sixteen, with Maeve also his same age. He wanted to be wifeless, uncuckolded, all filled up with possibility, everything before him. He wanted to swim.

Maeve, too, wanted to be another version of herself. The sort of girl who knew enough to seek out a boy like Georgie. She worried that parts of her had been destroyed: youth, her lemon-scented blond hair, a pheromone she'd given off when she was younger. Something in her that had once been bright and easy, an impulse toward pleasing, smiling, giving, had been worn down to a hard, dark nub; not big or strong enough for anyone to notice, not big or strong enough for her to get a hold of anymore.

This could be, too, Maeve thought, what was happening with Georgie. Of course she knew George wanted to fuck her, always had, at least abstractly. He wanted to fuck some vague idea of her that didn't actually exist, that used to exist but didn't now. But when he looked at her, she knew he saw those bright, light parts she could no longer feel.

Maybe they didn't have to fuck for him to see this, her to feel this. He was, after all, Fred's baby George. They could swim instead.

The water was perfect, lolling, easy. The smell was almost more than George could handle. All that rum sloshed in his stomach as he watched the lapping water. His wife had left him. Mom was dead. The water was so still, salty, bathlike. No clouds. The three-quarter fucking moon.

George and Maeve swam out without talking. Maeve never got scared when she was swimming, but George thought a couple times—a quick flash in his brain—of sharks. When we were little, sometimes, Fred or Jenn or I would yell to him, *George, I think I saw a fin,* and he'd go frantic, churning, kicking, running through the shallows back to shore. One of the articles that Fred sent George about the climate (Fred didn't think he read them, and he often didn't read them, just like he never read the books she bought him for Christmas, but this one he did) was about how sharks were hunting closer to the shore now, given the warmer water and a dwindling food supply. They didn't want to attack humans, the article said, but they might get to a point at which they had no choice.

The water dropped off and got deep a hundred feet out, and soon neither of them could touch the bottom. George watched Maeve's face change, become more open and approving, as their eyes met. They stayed ten, fifteen feet apart and treaded water, churned circles with their hands and feet. George swam farther out, eyes closed, legs kicking, arms working, strong and light and buoyed; he dove under, before, suddenly, he got scared and popped up again.

Time became slippery, elastic. An hour, half an hour, ten minutes. George's arms started to hurt; he thought more and more of what might be lurking underneath the dark surface. He breaststroked slowly back to shore, climbed up and out, dried himself off with his pants, tipped his head to one side then the other to knock the water from his ears, slipped his shirt back on. He sat on the shore and watched as Maeve swam back and climbed out, tank top and underwear soaked through, translucent, looking straight at him. He looked past her to the water. It felt more illicit, intimate, not talking, not touching all this time.

"I need to go to sleep," Maeve said.

"Me too," said George. She drove him back to his car. It was past midnight, and the roads were empty. George wondered the whole time he drove home what would happen if he got stopped. He was wearing a soaked shirt and his underwear, wet jeans on the seat next to him, likely technically still drunk. What would Fred or Allie, or Jenn or Dad or I, say if he got arrested, if he had to call Dad or Jenn or Fred to come bail him out? He drove thirty-four in a thirty-five, thirty-seven in a forty. When he got home, he went right to bed so he could be up early to walk Libby; he only believed what had happened because as he lay down, he smelled the sand and salt still on his skin.

11

When Maeve came to get Tallulah the next morning, Fred noticed how easy Maeve seemed, somehow more like she'd been those years before.

"Work good?" she said. Tallulah was diving for rings in the deep end, and Fred and Maeve sat close to one another, making circles with their bare feet in the pool.

"Usual," said Maeve.

This moment would come to matter later, Maeve not telling Fred about her night with George. She would argue that she hadn't had a night with George, they'd just gone swimming, though this felt like both more and less a breach than if they'd fucked. Fred hated secrets, being left out. She hated feeling as if anyone was talking about her when she wasn't there. Even though she herself kept secrets constantly, most of all from us (*you don't even know my friends' names*, she said to Mom one time, grown up and in New York, at my house for dinner; *she's never let me meet her friends*, Mom said after Fred left).

That year, those days I was alone with baby Cass and Fred showed up with breakfast, coffees, those first months she was with David, she hadn't told Mom and Dad about him, but I did. They were in one of their stretches of estrangement, and I talked to Mom and Dad every Sunday, after seeing Fred on Saturday, and I gave them bits of her. Always they were hungry, grateful for it. At Brian's and my wedding, Cass was eighteen months (Mom had advised, for the sake of the pictures, that I wait until I felt sure all the baby weight was gone), Fred found out that I'd told Mom and Dad about David, about grad school applications, her different jobs, her failed attempts to publish her short stories. *We hear there's a boyfriend*, Mom said, her third vodka soda in hand, face too close to Fred's. If not for Cass, I'm not sure Fred would have spoken to me after that.

"Lu was great as ever," Fred said. Though Talullah had had a tantrum after dinner because she missed her mom.

"You could stay here, you know?" Fred said. "There's so much room. No rent." Fred wasn't thinking when she said this; she'd felt the tug on Maeve from some outside force and wanted it to stop. The house would be gone in less than two months.

"We like the place where we are," Maeve said, watching Lulah, hoping that she hadn't heard Fred. This was true enough; Maeve liked the motel, and also, she wanted time and space, felt certain saying yes would turn into feeling beholden, out of her depth. She wasn't sure she trusted Fred enough.

Maeve wrapped Tallulah in a towel, got her dressed.

"Those birds creep me out," Maeve said, looking up as Tallulah changed into her shorts and T-shirt.

Fred looked up to see a swarm of vultures. "They're starving," she said. "They make me really sad."

Maeve nodded, looking up again, wincing, then hanging up Tallulah's towel. "We'll see you later, Freddy," Maeve said, and they left.

Fred felt embarrassed. Maeve felt sorry. Even though she hadn't given George her number, Maeve still checked her phone as soon as she had Tallulah settled in the car.

———

Fred put on her linen pants and button-up, a baseball cap, because she'd learned to hide as much as she could out in public in this town where we grew up. She needed groceries, and to be somewhere that was not that house and not running or swimming. Sometimes, when she couldn't stand the bigness of the house without Maeve and Tallulah, she'd sit an hour or two alone in the car, windows down, out by the water, reading about the climate or invasive species on her phone, or looking straight ahead and listening to her audiobook. When Maeve and Tallulah didn't come for dinner, she ate in the big bed, *Last Chance U* playing on her computer, the door closed, all the lights off.

The week after she left David, she'd lost all hold of time. She'd stay up all night, then run early in the morning, then sleep through the day, then be up again at night. She spent some nights out on the all-weather daybed on the screened-in back porch, the ceiling fan on high, unable to sleep, sweating, birds and raccoons rustling. She did video after video of twenty-minute yoga with a woman named Adriene who she thought of sometimes, in those first weeks, as her closest friend. She'd have potato chips or an uncooked tub of tofu for dinner, forget to eat or buy groceries and then gorge herself on late night gas station snacks. For so long, she'd relied on David's cooking, David's coming home from work with groceries, David's texting her to ask her to meet him at their favorite place once she got out of class. She had needed to leave, but leaving felt awful: like she was lighter, but also empty, scared.

That week, though, the first after she left David, she'd been running in the middle of the day when she heard someone call her name. She'd taken David's name when she got married. *Another fuck you,* Mom said; *even her so-called* feminism *couldn't overcome her need to feel separate from us.* But she heard the name that she'd had before she married David; this felt apt and ominous. *Fred Kenner,* she heard again. She hated stopping when she was running, but then a car, a dark-blue, grumbling old Mustang, pulled up next to her, the window down. *I would have known that stride anywhere,* the man said. Early sixties, maybe, sun damage so bad his skin was reddish-brown and worn. He wore a tank top like Fred had only ever seen in Florida, thin strapped, fluorescent green. *Fred Kenner,* the man said again, and Fred stood still and felt his eyes on her, felt the shortness of her shorts, the way the sweat had made her T-shirt stick to her. *I used to watch you,* he said. *God*—the O long and from somewhere deep in his throat. *I'm Garth,* he said. He didn't offer her his last name. *I used to watch you. In high school. God, I used to love to watch you run.* Fred still hadn't spoken. She looked past him, down at her bare legs. His car was still running. She'd rolled the sleeves of her shirt into her sports bra's straps in order to cool off her shoulders. Now she wrapped her arms around herself, ran her hands up and down her upper arms. *You look exactly the same,* he said. *I don't,* Fred said finally. *That was almost thirty years ago.* She willed this man to stay inside his car. *Well now,* Garth said, *that is a real mind fuck.*

Dad used to stay up late and study the splits of every girl in Florida: whose first mile was faster, whose kick was best, who Fred could catch in the last half mile. Fred was running twice a day by sophomore year and at the gym three days a week with a private coach. She was fast in high school, but she'd never had the talent that the top girls had. Even so, she'd loved it. What she saw in this guy, his face and posture, was what she saw in Dad those days he went out to the track with her on weekends, the thrill of watching something wild and embodied, pretending this need to somehow be part of it, to co-opt it, was support. By senior year, vomiting in the bushes before races, a little drunk, but oftentimes still winning, Fred had blown up all and any offers that she might have gotten to run the way she'd planned to run in college. She'd wanted then, much as she wanted now, to disappear herself for a while.

She didn't want to be looked at the way this guy was looking at her now. It reminded her of running back then but also it reminded her of writing. The power she felt—being good, getting better—was altered, destroyed, broken, by all the ways that being good meant other people looking, wanting, standing too close to her to try to make her theirs somehow.

The guy asked more questions about where Fred was living, what she did. Fred answered brusquely, quickly, lied about it all. *Fred Kenner*, he said again, her arms still wrapped around her torso, *what a trip*. She turned away. *Don't ever stop*, he said, as she took off.

At Publix, Fred wore her hat down low and shopped mostly for Tallulah: boxes of Annie's mac and cheese, eggs (organic, free range) and milk and butter, the challah she'd introduced Tallulah to and with which she made her French toast the mornings Maeve came late. She got the potato chips she mostly lived on when Tallulah and Maeve weren't there. Mangoes, clementines, fresh berries. Two bags of organic semisweet chocolate chips. She got raisin bran, granola, yogurt, peanut butter. Tofu, veggie burgers, lentils, black beans. The little packs of organic fruit gummies for Tallulah, and then three bags of the neon sour gummy worms that she kept hidden in the drawer next to her bed. She took a number for the meat counter without thinking. She hadn't eaten meat in over twenty years.

"What's your bloodiest cut?" she said to the guy when he called her number.

"My what?" he said.

"I want the cut of steak with the most blood," she said.

The guy looked at her. Tattooed flowers ran up his left arm and into his plain white T-shirt, the same vine curving up his neck.

"You know what carrion is?" Fred said.

The guy looked past her to the line of people waiting. "I just sell meat," he said.

"I want your bloodiest steak," Fred said.

"What weight?" the guy said.

Fred tucked her hair up tighter in her hat. "Two pounds?" she said.

The guy pulled and cut a long piece of parchment paper, slapped the meat on top and weighed it, wrapped it, stuck it with the price, and handed it to Fred.

Fred held her breath and focused on the flowers on his arms. She didn't look at the package as she took it from him. "Thanks," she said.

"Enjoy your blood."

When Fred got home, she put away the groceries and googled what large, meat-eating animals lived in this part of Florida. She googled carrion and how or whether it could be ordered. All that came up for this last search was a bunch of websites for a Nintendo Switch game.

She put down her phone and poured herself a glass of whiskey, opened the potato chips, and went outside with the wrapped-up steak. She held the paper up and sniffed it, but it had no smell. She sat down among the rocks and sticks. Mosquitoes landed on her foot, her neck, her hand; she slapped at them. She looked up to find the vultures, unwrapped the meat, looked around the yard—behind the big Bismarck palm, the dead citrus trees, the scrub grass—for other animals. A fourth mosquito burrowed into the space beneath her ear and bit before she could slap at it. A tiny bird flitted onto the branch of one of the citrus trees, twitched, flew away. Fred lay the meat down and unwrapped it. Not as bloody as she hoped it would be. She lay back a minute in the dirt and waited, slapping at more and more mosquitoes, eyes up to the sky.

12

Georgie, the next morning, still smelling salty, sandy, felt afire. He didn't even mind Libby's refusing to give the ball back. He drank three cups of black coffee and made it to his first 2:00 p.m. meal of the day without a single glimpse at Allie's Instagram. He made small talk with Dad before Dad's morning check-in with his secretary, followed by his string of Zooms with his old ladies. Libby continued to favor Dad, and this, too, felt less annoying to George.

"Where were you last night?" Dad said during his first break, holding Libby in the crook of his arm, rubbing her head.

"Just needed to get out," George said, reaching for the dog.

"Right," Dad said. Libby yipped and squirmed away from George. Dad quieted her, turning his body so George couldn't get hold of her. "Of course."

Dad and George worked best when there were sports to watch— plays and rankings, details and statistics to unpack. Fred, too, had long loved football, until she declared herself too disturbed by all the CTE, the blatant racism and misogyny, blah blah. Mom had been the biggest, most aggressive Florida Gators fan of all of us. It was July, though, and neither Dad nor George had been paying enough attention for a preseason conversation.

Dad took Libby back into his room for his afternoon Zooms with a bag of Lay's potato chips, a Diet Dr Pepper. George wrote email after email, reaching out to old investors, guys he used to work with who had moved to firms in New York. After college, before Allie, when George and I were still close, texting all the time, he'd come for three weeks to stay with Brian and me and Cassie, to try to find a job. But he'd gone to UNC, and most of the New York places wanted Ivy League. The three kids he knew who got New York jobs all had family friends to help. Mom and Dad had all that money but they knew no one, knew very little beyond the few square miles between their offices and home. George made three second rounds of interviews, but always came the point when he felt out of his depth, not in terms of job knowledge or ability but in terms of how and when to lean forward, make jokes, unbutton or not unbutton his blazer, sit or stand or shake hands. In Houston, George also wasn't always comfortable, but the guys who hired him were so much like the guys he used to watch in high school, he found it easier to know what and how to pretend.

By two o'clock, George figured that he'd earned a rum and Coke. He thought that he'd call Allie, ask if they could stay married, tell her he forgave her, imply that something intimate, barely clothed, had happened with Maeve. Maybe a little healthy competition was what Allie needed, would make him more attractive to her. He made it all the way to scrolling to her name and then got scared.

He made himself another drink and reopened his computer. He'd do more searching, seeking, call her once he had a couple jobs lined up, could threaten he was moving or threaten he was coming back. He scrolled through emails from his former bosses. His work email had been disabled, but he'd forwarded almost all his correspondence to his personal email before he left. He still couldn't quite make sense of how or why he'd gotten fired. No one had said explicitly he had to leave. But the office worked mostly on commissions, a yearly bonus based on money brought in, and he'd been taken off all three of the deals that he'd been working on.

He'd been offered some of his last year's profits, profits he thought that he was owed but was then told would come only with contingencies, as an advance on starting his own shop from which his bosses would have legal rights to a large cut. He had worked hard to convince himself this was a vote of confidence. He'd always meant to go out on his own. Old contacts, again, had to be contacted, deals found and organized, investors committed and signed up. He couldn't help but think his bosses simply hadn't liked him, thought him absurd, childish. Too often, he'd caught on too late when jokes were made.

Now, he talked to a bot on LinkedIn about other, similar companies, scrolled through old work emails as if somehow the answers would appear. He read first sentences, whole paragraphs he'd written, at first looking for people he might email to ask to partner with him on new deals, but then for proof, perhaps—none of what his bosses promised felt as if it might come to fruition—of what it was about him that made people want to cast him off.

Reading all those emails, George remembered and felt queasy: meetings, before and after presentations, on those trips they took—Tahoe, Vegas—in the chartered plane, the walks to restaurants, the ride up the gondola to some Park City mountaintop, before people got too fucked up or too focused on the deal that they were making. All the time they were together outside the context of their jobs, George had the sort of woolly and uneasy feeling that they were making fun of him behind his back.

He had felt a version of this his whole life—the little, lesser baby brother, the accident. *Our precious little gift*, Mom said, and we all cringed and laughed.

George continued to scroll and thought about the faces the guys made sometimes at dinners when he talked, the way some of them turned their bodies when they were standing in small groups at bars so that he felt pushed out. Brett, his boss, was not much older than him. He'd started the shop with a friend and money from their parents, two years out of Vanderbilt. The last year, George had done two deals alone with Brett. He opened Brett's Instagram. Brett, unlike the boss of Allie's who she was fucking, had a new house that Allie had been jealous of. The company Christmas party had been there last year, and Allie had not been able to stop talking about the vaulted ceilings, big, grand curving staircase, three outdoor fire pits, the pool and tennis court. (*Your health, though, George! You could get in at least an hour hitting every day.*) When they got home, George had looked up how much the house cost, shocked by how cheap it was, not much more than his and Allie's—shocked and then ashamed to have not gotten a deal like this for his own house. George googled it again now, wrote down the sale price and the date of purchase, the date Brett put in the offer.

The last big deal he'd done with Brett had been a pipeline from an oil field deeper in Texas to a Houston port. A more efficient route, construction promised to be quick. Brett had done a similar deal the year before and knew the regulatory landscape well; it was a near-certain high-margin payoff for investors. The biggest deal that George had ever done, a billion dollars over twenty different individuals and funds. Brett and George had come to New York three times to bring in two private investors and a small bank they'd not worked with in the past. (*It's all just storytelling*, Brett said, *making these guys feel like they want to be a part of this from the jump.* George thought of Fred, of course.) Brett had found the contractor for the job, the same one he'd used on the earlier deal, before George had been brought in, a friend of Brett's dad: old Texas, loud and brash. George read through more emails, all from Brett, acting as liaison for the contractor, arguing for their skill and efficiency in past deals, celebrating when he'd talked them from 1.1 billion down to one. How and what made George see it all more clearly now? Maybe talking to Dad, all that CNBC and talk of real estate.

Anyone who did what George did knew real estate was one of the safest avenues through which to launder large sums of money. He googled Brett again and found three apartment buildings in three different states, all purchased at insanely low prices by an LLC in his name.

"Motherfucker," George said, feeling smart. He wanted to call Allie but felt a quick twinge of remembering the thing she'd done. He thought of calling Maeve but didn't have her number. He thought of calling Jenn or Fred or me or Mom, but Mom was dead. He opened a Google Doc and recorded what he'd found, went through all the emails with the costs the contractor had laid out, the various investors and their pledged amounts. He looked up similar jobs, similar deals his firm had done. Recorded and collected and collected and recorded and by five he was worn out, his forehead and his temples damp with sweat.

He had been the point man in New York. *They're a little faggy up there, like you*, Brett said. The other guys had laughed. But George had done well courting them. A 7 to 10 percent return on investment, and Brett with his magic touch, promises that the thing would be done in three years. A billion sounded like a lot, but there was no end to the need for oil, gas. For the people who needed extra caressing: the pipeline would be *better made than the other routes, less likely to leak and therefore more environmentally sound, blah blah*. He'd blathered that to Fred on one of those visits to New York. He had once, answering a question Fred had asked about the nefarious effects of private equity, unironically used the word "bootstraps." But he saw now very clearly that Brett had lied and stolen, had some sort of kickback deal with the contractor, and had received nearly fifteen million dollars in real estate for what he'd done.

13

Fred lay a long time by the steak, but nothing came to eat it. She'd had to go inside to douse herself in bug spray and now she worried that the DEET had scared the vultures off. She thought of driving to David's, bringing the meat with her and asking him to cook it, offering to cook it for him—he'd given meat up, too, after they met—taking off her clothes and fucking him. But she worried if she saw him, after feeling Maeve was getting further from her, with an expiration date on her borrowed home, she might ask him if she could have a small space somewhere in that house she hated.

She kept looking for a New York apartment, for a cabin somewhere in the Everglades. She thought again of Tess's kitchen. She'd driven six hours south one morning before sunrise and tried to find Joy Williams's acre of land. She'd redownloaded the email app on her phone and started reading emails, a trickle still from agents, editors, publicists who hadn't noticed that she'd stopped blurbing and reviewing books. She scrolled through years of old correspondences with former employers, people who had hired her to edit their books. The tutoring company where she'd worked—she'd taken the LSAT once, the year after her first book came out and no one bought it, and she'd scored pretty well—had shifted all their work online; she emailed her old boss. She'd signed up for email updates from a doula school in upstate New York and now she checked the fees and looked vaguely into housing. Another year, when they'd been low on money, Fred had picked up serving shifts again.

David did fine enough, but not for New York; he never broke a hundred K a year. Fred's career, from the outside, looked good to great. She wasn't famous, wasn't wealthy, but at the right bookstore in Manhattan, a bookseller might recognize her name at checkout and give her his employee discount, and she'd feel a little thrill for half an hour. Some years she made okay money; some as little as ten grand. She'd worn a dress, received an award, but you couldn't flush the toilet or do the dishes in their apartment if someone was trying to take a shower with hot water. They had to walk six blocks to wash their clothes. Fred hated that she couldn't just appreciate the life they'd built together, hated the achy, desperate part of her that lingered too long outside the full-length windows of the brownstones on all the blocks on her walk home. She hated how ashamed she felt when certain of her friends came over, settled on their old ratty couch, perched on a stool in their flimsy-cabinet-covered, tiny corner kitchen; she felt like our parents then.

Six hundred square feet was charming at twenty-five and thirty, their own little square in this city that she loved, but then she was thirty-five, then forty. The windows looked onto an alleyway, and their bed was nestled in a corner that some days felt cozy and other days felt dingy, dark, and cramped. A vaguely metallic smell came up from the street when it rained. Fred had yearned plenty, all those years, for some big thing: a movie deal, a book that outperformed, a long-term full-time job that was not a lot of work and would allow her plenty of time to write. She yearned for David to stay himself but also to become the sort of person who would start his own firm. Neither of them was good with money. They weren't bad with money—they didn't go to fancy restaurants; Fred wore her clothes so long that David often had to throw them out in secret when she wasn't home. But every couple years, if she'd sold a book, they'd leave the country for two weeks. She bought too many books, fresh fruit, takeout, drinks, a blazer or two every other year. In all the years when things weren't dire, and even sometimes when they were, David was still the only person in his family to have gone to college, to have a good and steady source of income; they continued to send his parents five hundred dollars a month.

One month, the ends didn't meet, and Fred had called and asked if I would lend her money, *just to tide them over*, until her next book payment came. I'd been divorced a year. Mom and Dad had helped me get our place in Park Slope. *I heard you guys are struggling*, Mom said when she called Fred the next week. *What the fuck, Jude*, Fred said when she called me after she hung up with Mom. *Every fucking thing I tell you, somehow it gets back to them*. Mom feigned concern, Fred said, but really she was smug. *If she was concerned for real she'd ask to help*, Fred said. *It was concern, though*, I said. Concern couched in the metallic glint of also feeling smug, hardened and affirmed by all those years of being told that she'd been wrong, of reading all the unfair (Mom thought) depictions of moms in Fred's work. (*You should hear what my friends say*, said Mom to Fred. *Since when does she have friends?* Fred said to me.) Of course Mom cared about Fred. Loved her. She also took more than a little pleasure in the ways that—when Fred and David were broke, stayed another year in that shitty apartment—Mom felt like she had won. *I should have known better*, Fred said to me, *than to ask you. I gave you the money*, I said. *You always fucking take their side*, she said. *There are no sides, Fred*, I said. She laughed and hung up.

Another month, instead of calling me, she'd called her agent. *I need work*, she said. *Can you get me more work?* Her agent was good, knew what it meant when someone called and said, *I need money ASAP*. She'd gotten Fred on a listserv for ghostwriting, and Fred went to a bagged-lunch info session at a WeWork in midtown a few weeks later. Nothing ever came of it.

Now, though, sitting in Fred's long-lapsed email account, was an email asking for a ghostwriter for a full-length novel. *Writer sought for a commercial novel about a surrogate who absconds with the baby she's been paid to carry and the mother who will stop at nothing to get her baby back!* Without thinking, Fred sent a response with the requisite info: her CV, a writing sample, links to pieces she'd published online. Within hours, she had an email back asking if she might be available the next day for an interview. The compensation, the email told her, would be two months in the carriage house outside of Paris that belonged to the woman who was seeking the ghostwriter, as well as forty thousand dollars.

Fred wrapped the meat back up and put it in the fridge and went to the beach to go running. As she did now every time she left the house, she took the gun with her. She ran forty minutes out, barefoot, the callouses on her feet so hard that twice a shell stuck in her foot and she only barely felt it. She ran the forty minutes back, took off her shirt, and swam a long time past the break until every part of her felt spent.

When she got back to the house, it was finally starting to get dark. She took the meat out of the fridge again. She got the gun out of the car and placed it on the pack of meat and brought it all back outside, sprayed herself with bug spray by the pool. She unwrapped the meat and set it on the ground, sat cross-legged, the weight of the gun cold and heavy in her lap. She still had no idea why she'd taken it that night. In all the weeks before our mother died, in all the years she and Fred didn't talk, Fred had nevertheless thought about their finding a way to something better. She felt unmoored and stunned that the possibility was gone. The gun was the thing in that drawer that felt most like our mother: hard and sharp, small and dangerous, something you had to be very careful with. It could hurt you, destroy you. But also, if you could only find a way to keep it on your side, do everything exactly right, it would destroy the whole world, burn every bit of it right down, in order to take care of you.

Fred had not ever held a gun, and it was heavier than she'd thought it would be. She'd watched a video on YouTube about basic usage, had flipped open its fist-size cartridge, counted its four bullets. She'd learned to clasp and unclasp the safety, to wrap her right hand over her left. (She was left-handed like the rest of us.)

Mom had always hated vomit, looked physically revolted at even the suggestion that you might be sick. She was incapable of any complicated or nuanced feeling. *Everything is fine*, she'd say, *it's great, just stop, don't be pathetic*, when actually you felt like you might die. Once, at Macy's, she held up a pair of size six jeans from the sale rack (I was a size six then) and yelled, *The only clothes that are ever on sale here are fat people's clothes.* At Fred's and Jenn's track meets and mine and George's tennis matches, she shouted the loudest—*that's my baby; go, go baby; get her ass, Freddy!*—sometimes freaking out our teammates, the competition; whispering to Fred, after she'd finished her race and the slower kids were still out there running, *Someone should tell those kids to join the band.* She was up at five each morning to pack each of us a lunch we'd learn, soon enough, not to eat. A heaping sandwich, cookie, chips, an apple and a sweet syrupy drink: if you ate those things, you'd be fat and therefore gross and so you took the lunch and said thank you, always had to be grateful, but then had no choice but throw it away. All that food, bought and prepared, just like the love that we were told was there for us to grab and have—it would be embarrassing and gross, pathetic, if we ever actually wanted, needed, asked for whatever sustenance or comfort it (either the love or the food) might provide.

Fred clutched the handle of the gun with both her hands, fingers still a safe distance from the trigger, resting, testing the trigger's resistance. She wanted to talk about Mom, her lack, her absence. To call David or Dad, George or Jenn. Clutching tightly to that gun, thinking endlessly of everything that she'd done wrong, Fred wanted to call me.

14

Fred didn't know the story of the gun because, as I've said already, she didn't listen closely, didn't call and wade her way through all the palaver you had to wade your way through about whatever Mom and Dad had had for dinner, vacations they were planning, all Jenn's kids' various accomplishments. You waded through this because sometimes Mom or Dad would get in a rhythm, and then they'd talk about their lives or one another, cases, clients, and in so doing they'd become, just for a minute, the people Fred had never quite acknowledged that they were.

The story starts with the rumor in town, when we were kids, that Ellen Davis's mom lost it, left on a sailboat, moved to Turks and Caicos, the year before Ellen started kindergarten, a few weeks after Ellen's youngest brother was born. The rumor was that she got a job as crew on a tug and never wrote or called, never came back.

This was not the sort of thing that anybody talked about with or to Ellen. It was something we, and our parents, whispered about when we saw her at National Honor Society induction, a track meet, baseball game. When she was part of the group of kids Fred went to prom with junior year (Ellen, my age, was then a freshman, the date of one of Fred's male friends—this was before Fred started skipping school and drinking too much to do things like go to prom with good kids who let their parents take their pictures all in a group before they left).

Ellen was nice, sweet. *That girl*, some of the moms would say, watching her hug her dad after some school event or other, sit in the bleachers at one of her brothers' baseball games. Watching as she packed up both boys' bags, reminded them not to forget their cleats and snacks and water, grabbed hold of their arms as they walked through the parking lot to her car. Grown up before her time: So how inevitable was it, Ellen marrying someone almost twice her age?

Junior year of college—like every summer while she was in college, the honors program at UF—Ellen got a job doing administrative work for the optometrist where she'd taken both her brothers to get glasses in third and fifth grade. Again, her small hand on their small arms, guiding them into the windowless room where they joked about the way the lights made them nauseous, the way the paddle up against one eye felt cold and strange. Ellen at fifteen, sixteen, helping them pick out durable frames and glasses. She got a job at the front desk of the main location the month after she turned twenty; the pay was mediocre, but she got a discount for her brothers' glasses and eye checks.

Dr. Schultz was only five years younger than her father, having franchised his name, with large lens stores all over the state. Ellen hadn't even registered at first the way he stood close to her, the way he lingered, leaned over her desk asking questions, the moment she caught him looking at her when she got up to lead a client back for her exam. He'd divorced his wife, mother to his two young sons, six months before her first day. His wife was a pediatrician. *Abrasive, hard-ass*, he said to Ellen once she realized he was flirting with her, once they'd been on one date, then another, then a third. *Just wants all my money. Never fucking wants to let me see the kids.*

Of course, later, Ellen would track back and understand, see clearly, the blueprint for how he'd gotten exactly what he wanted from his ex-wife.

She finished college in one final, packed semester, came back to our town. She married Dr. Schultz and got pregnant quickly. A whole life, she thought, all ready-made for her. She helped out at the older kids' private school and tried not to run into their mother, their mother's friends. Most of Ellen's friends from growing up were still away at college, but Dr. Schultz liked to keep her close, so she went to dinner with people who felt less like friends and more like other people's parents, spent most of her time loving, caring for the kids.

After Brooke was born, Ellen was the opposite of postpartum depressed—high on what her body had shown itself capable of, a long, straightforward labor without medication, the thrill of the sensations of her daughter coming out into the world. She was, like some new mothers, enmeshed, obsessed, up all night, sleeping only with the baby on her chest, nursing and then watching her breathe, her lips purse, face scrunch, chest rise. Exhausted, worn out, but also happy and relieved. She'd hardly noticed Dr. Schultz until two days after her six-week check up at the obstetrician, when he took a sleeping Brooke off Ellen's chest and placed her slowly, carefully into her crib. *What*, said Ellen, bleary, shirt off, her chest and belly wet and sticky with milk. He reached for the drawstring of her cotton pants. She realized too late he meant to fuck her. *I*, she started to say, *Mike, I'm not—*. It felt impossible that he would want this, want her, think that this was something she was up for. She realized quickly that he didn't care.

The first time she stayed silent. She didn't want to wake the baby. She did not pretend to want it. His grasp on her wrists was harder, firmer, than it had ever been. The second time, Brooke cried the whole time from the room next to theirs, and Ellen did as well. The third time, she stayed still again. He seemed to like it more when she fought him, asked him not to; he'd come more quickly when she'd cried, when she'd asked softly, not sure even that he heard her, to stop.

Her skin began to feel cold, exposed, fear in her pores. She was at first afraid to go outside without wearing lots of layers and then afraid to go outside at all. Her husband seemed to love her more like this and he seemed to want her more now that she did not consent. He never hit her, never yelled. In her deepest, clearest fantasies of getting away from him, Ellen failed to find a word, a name, a way to talk about what her husband did.

One of her brothers, in the meantime, had flunked out of cop school. He'd flunked previously out of the University of North Florida. He smoked too much weed for cop school, and this had, in fact, been the reason he flunked out. But as part of cop school he'd acquired a handgun and, after a year of Ellen's husband coming into their bed to fuck her almost every night, Ellen drove over to her father's house while both her dad and Mike were at work. Teddy was in shorts, no shirt, playing *Grand Theft Auto* in his room with the blinds closed. *Go for a walk with us,* she said, Brooke in her arms. Outside she said: *I need a favor, bud. What's up?* Teddy said. Ellen peeked beneath the visor to make sure Brooke had fallen asleep. She asked Teddy for the gun, and he gave it to her without a single question. Ellen was as close to mother as Teddy'd ever had.

Ellen kept the gun in Brooke's room, in the cabinet high above the wipes drawer. Mike only ever went into Brooke's room to put her down when he wanted to fuck. For two months, Ellen checked on it every morning after he left for work. She was relieved and also frightened by the weight of it. She had no plan and mostly cried and fantasized about leaving this place and finding her mom in Turks and Caicos.

And then, during her weekly grocery outing, Deborah Kenner—our mom—had come up to Ellen at Publix, all big gestures, too loud. Ellen was wearing three long-sleeved layers though it was ninety degrees and sunny, thirteen-month-old Brooke strapped to her chest. *Ellen, honey!* Mom said. *I'm Fred and Jude's mom! Jude and Fred Kenner?! Oh my god, this baby, Ellen! How beautiful!*

Of course! How are you, Mrs. Kenner? Ellen said.

Honey, Mom said, *call me Deborah.* Ellen went home thinking vaguely of how much Deborah Kenner seemed to like her, seemed to want so much to please her. She thought hopefully of Mom's job—two parents of two friends of hers had used her; another one had had her used against her; all had talked about her within earshot, saying that she was very, very good at what she did.

15

Before the Zoom the next day, Fred ran, swam naked in the pool and then showered, put on moisturizer and mascara. She owned no makeup besides this. She stood in front of the mirror, pressing lightly on the skin beneath her eyes, around her lips. She was early to the Zoom and she spent that extra time staring at her face, shocked and confused by how old she looked. *It's just my face*, she whispered, trying to not to think of the ways it wasn't what she imagined when she was out in public, teaching, talking, when she didn't have to stare at it like this. Her eyes were too small, nose too big. Her scowl line made her look angrier than she was. She put three books beneath her computer to shift the angle, turned off the overhead lights so the desk lamp lit her from the front.

The woman, when she came on, was rich-person-in-her-forties glowy, clear-skinned. Her face hardly moved, but her hands and neck crinkled when she talked. Her hair was pulled back tightly from her face.

"I feel like I know you!" was the first thing she said.

Jesus fuck, Fred thought.

"I stayed up all night on your website," said the woman. "I read your whole blog."

Substack, Fred thought but didn't correct her.

"I just feel like you know, you *know*, what it is to be a woman."

Fred laughed and then quickly quieted her laughter. "I think most women know that," she said.

"Oh, but you know how to *talk* about it," said the woman. "You're so honest! So raw!"

The woman's name was Lucia. She and her husband had relocated their family from Los Angeles to Provence during the pandemic, the two of them as well as their twins (born by surrogate, as the twins would be in the novel that Fred wrote for her).

"And oh my god," Lucia added. "I'm so, so sorry about your friend."

Fred nodded, looked down. "Thanks," she said.

"I just love your work," Lucia said.

Fred sat back. There was no surer way to ensure Fred didn't trust a person than to have them compliment her. But she recalibrated. This was not a person who happened (obviously incorrectly) to like and admire her. This was a woman who could give her a job. "That really means a lot," Fred said.

Fred felt her body shift as they talked: her posture, the volume of her voice, her laughter, how often she leaned forward. All sense of Fred, of what she might want or think, drifted from her. She became only what she felt this woman wanted, needed. This was perhaps the greatest skill passed down to all of us from Mom: We could forget completely who we were or what we wanted. For most of our lives, we hadn't even thought to wonder what that was.

Listening to Lucia talk about her *deep desire for children*, about how she'd always known that she was meant to be a mother, about the betrayal that her body had enacted on her in the face of this, Fred felt not only sad for her but wholly convinced of the rightness of these feelings. They felt true to Fred and also true *for* Fred. She felt, listening to this woman, that she too needed, wanted to have children; less because she'd always needed, wanted children and more because her body understood that that was what Lucia wanted Fred to need and want.

By the end of the call, Lucia had cried twice, and Fred had teared up. Lucia had recounted her experience with fertility treatments, her miscarriages, their eventual search for a surrogate. "Obviously," she said, "the bad stuff would all be made up." They loved their surrogate, she told Fred, but it was such a complex, high-stakes relationship. She'd studied screenwriting briefly. "I just felt like there's a story here, you know?"

Fred nodded, smiling as she might have at Cassie trying out the monkey bars for the first time.

"You don't have children, though?" Lucia asked, looking at her screen and likely something else that Fred had written.

Fred shook her head. "Not yet." She felt Lucia scrutinize her face, undoubtedly wondering how close she was to menopause. Before Lucia could ask any kind of leading question, Fred added, "I think we could make something really amazing."

"I know," Lucia said. "I feel certain of it."

Once off the call, Fred closed her computer. She stood up, sat back down. She spent an hour on Instagram looking at pictures of Lucia's twins as they grew from infancy to toddlerdom into active, grinning, tanned, French-speaking six-year-olds.

Fred five years before: She had an appointment with her OB to get her IUD removed. She and David talked and talked. *You don't have to be afraid,* her husband said. *It's normal to be scared.* But the word *fear* wasn't enough. *Afraid* was a lost job, a dwindling bank account, an empty subway late at night. What Fred felt was fifteen and by herself, a tropical storm offshore, swim advisory, rip tide, knowing that if and when she got caught up, she could not fight, flail, claw

her way back. She'd built a life in which she could convince herself sometimes that she had power, had control, and she knew that
would be shown to be ridiculous, absurd, in the face of children, in
the face of love like that. She wanted David to promise absolutely
that she wouldn't do or be done harm, that she wouldn't fuck it up.
Of course, he couldn't. Fred couldn't figure out how to have children
without that.

She'd walked uptown and across town to her OB's office on Eighth
Avenue and Sixty-Seventh Street. She'd gotten the text reminder
and the calendar reminder, the email alert. She'd only had the IUD
for three years, which meant she had four more if she wanted them.
It was summer, hot and stale. The clang and shake of the Upper
West Side on a July weekday. Fred walked past the Film at Lincoln
Center sign on Sixty-Third, turned and looked briefly through the
dark glass doors. A man came out, the door swung open, and she
walked in where it was clean and cool and quiet. A little window by
the door sold coffee, pastries. Fred stood in line for both and then
stood in the lobby, eating, sipping her drink. Her phone pinged to
say the appointment would start soon.

Fred turned off her phone, drank her latte, ate her almond croissant in thin, flaky bits. On the movie poster behind her, Robert
Pattinson and Juliette Binoche; director, Claire Denis. It was a
Tuesday, and matinees were only ten dollars. She bought a ticket,
a box of Junior Mints. Fred and two older women who sat talking
through the credits had the whole theater to themselves. The film
was violent, jarring: a group of convicts sent into space to live but
also die. Lives as government experiment. Robert Pattinson was
the father of a baby, the result of forced sex; what was the word,
Fred kept thinking, was it still *rape*, for sex in which neither party
had agency?

She didn't think about the missed appointment. When she got

outside, she had an email and a voicemail from the OB's office and deleted both. She got another coffee, black and iced this time, from the window outside the theater and walked a long time by herself. It had rained while she was inside, and the heat had lifted, and she walked only on the shady side of every street. She was thirty-six that year, and her life was close enough to what she'd always wanted. She'd just published her third novel. It had been about her friend who died and had been her most successful book by far. She'd won a PEN/Faulkner; the book had gone into a fifth printing. It was still not a life-changing amount of money. The whole six months after publication, she'd cried often until she realized she was devastated because as hard as she'd worked on the book, Tess was still dead. All the time Fred had been writing, she'd felt close to Tess again, but then the book came out and it felt like whatever intimacy she'd found in the writing was gone, released into the world. Over and over this happened when Fred was in a novel: it felt precious, sacred, the closest she had ever been to loving absolutely, and then it would become a book and she'd realize how small and separate, insignificant, that love looked out in the world.

David loved her, she thought, too absolutely. He did not live in constant terror. She thought a million times of all the what ifs: *What if I'm awful, not right, what if I destroy you? What if my love, and then whatever love I might give to a baby, holds something rotten at its core?* She worried all the time that David would find something or someone to love that deserved it more. I knew all about this. When Brian and I had Cassie, I saw how his love was less specific than it felt when I met him. That it wasn't me he loved so much as he was good at loving the people he had chosen to sit inside the roles where love was meant to be felt.

What Fred thought, walking home from that strange movie, from that appointment that she missed, was that if she was going to get pregnant, she wanted it to be a challenge, to feel ordained. She knew a woman on the internet whom she'd never met in person, another writer, who'd gotten accidentally pregnant with her IUD still in. What Fred thought—and remember, here, it was her whole job to be a liar, her whole job to build worlds and choices that were really only stand-ins for the random, abstract things one silly person felt and thought on random days—was that if she got pregnant with the IUD in, it would feel inevitable and therefore like proof that she was up to it.

She finally told David a full ten months later. He didn't have to prod her, had not seemed in any way suspicious; he had been suggesting, the past couple months, that they finally get some tests done. She'd told him early in the morning, coffee brewing, sun just barely up: *I never got my IUD removed.* She watched the way her betrayal quaked through him, face and hands and legs and fingers, his chest and shoulders folding and then still. She realized that she had hoped for anger—that closed fist, those expletives—but instead his face went flat and sad and empty, voice almost a whisper. Fifteen years together, but this was a tone, a posture, she'd never seen on him.

She tried to touch him but he wouldn't let her. She tried to talk but he asked her to please stop. He got his coat, his keys, his wallet. She waited, still and quiet.

He came back long after nightfall and started sleeping on his old futon. They hardly spoke for weeks. Slowly, he started asking her again what she might want for dinner; she'd order in his favorite Thai food; he let her touch him, found his way back to their bed. He didn't leave her. *You fucking piece of shit*, she'd mutter to herself on her run each morning, looking at herself briefly in the mirror as she got out of the shower, wishing she could hear some of that fury from her husband. She stopped being afraid then that he would leave her and instead began to worry, nearly every second, that one day very soon she would destroy him—this lovely, sweet, kind person—piece by piece, unthinking, with the power of her selfishness.

Two hours later, an email from Lucia: *Congratulations! I truly cannot wait to work with you dear Fred!* A contract attached, suggested timeline, payment schedule, a request to sign and return within a week.

16

George showed up again the next night at Bonefish. He got a rum and Coke, the bang bang shrimp, the baked tilapia.

Dad called me from outside by the pool. The daily storm had come and gone, and the air had cooled, was still. He threw the ball for Libby, and she brought it back for him. I was alone in my apartment, had just that week been fired and (relatedly) been broken up with. He didn't ask (because he didn't know) about any of this.

"I thought he came to stay with me," Dad said.

"Where'd he go?" I said.

"Out for dinner," Dad said. "He said he needed some *time to himself*"—the last phrase drenched in petulance.

"Any word on Allie?"

Jenn and I had been monitoring her un-updated Instagram.

"I'm worried about his job," Dad said.

Dad was careful and responsible above all else, worried for us about the practical things. He paid close attention to the ebbs and flows of stocks and markets, could be thrown off, brought down, by the subtlest dips. He looked at every bank account he had every day.

"How are you, Dad?" I said. If Fred was the one he loved the most when we were younger and couldn't stomach now, I was the opposite. Too weird and *lacking drive* in middle and in high school, my main interest—riding horses—a drain on his bank account and, because I didn't want to show, without opportunities for trophies. But now I'd gone to law school, had a child, checked two of his favorite grown-up boxes. We were close, if close meant we talked often but never about much.

"This house is too big," he said.

They'd built it only three years prior. Dad loved building houses; he loved the plans and choices, would be on the phone all hours of the day with his contractor and architect.

"Why not sell it?" I said.

He talked five minutes about rising interest rates, inflation, the market cooling. I got my keys and wallet, started walking toward the river, a mile and a half from my apartment.

"Where would I go?" he finally said.

"Another house, Dad," I said, having stopped for an iced coffee, a chocolate croissant, unsure almost all the time what to do with my days. "Somewhere smaller that's less work."

He paused as if this was the first he'd thought of this. He and Mom had only ever lived in houses they'd built, Dad overseeing every detail. *He's addicted to it*, Mom said, each time he found another lot and once again started construction. *He thinks the contractors are his friends*, Jenn said. He'd go out there every afternoon to watch them work.

"Jenn and I could start to look," I said, knowing Jenn would love the project.

"Not right now, Jude," he said.

While we talked, Maeve, again, brought George his appetizer and his main course. Again, Tallulah was with Fred.

George skipped the third drink to keep his wits about him.

Just like the first night, Maeve sidled up to George after she got cut and did her cash-out, while she drank her Diet Coke, ate her half-order of bang bang shrimp. She drove them out to the beach. They left their flip-flops in the car. Instead of jeans, George had worn his looser, easier-to-remove khakis. The water was warm and calm and just as dark as it had been. George dove down and up and down again, his body loose and easy as he breaststroked past the second wave break, entering the section of the ocean where Dad used to float out on those rented boards with Fred.

He treaded water and he watched Maeve. Maeve dove down and down again.

"Georgie!" called Maeve. "I should get home." She'd gone back to shore, and he hadn't noticed. He'd swum out farther so as not to look too long at her. He crawled quickly back, climbed up the sand, and pulled on his shirt. Once again, her tank top stuck to her torso, the soft curve of her belly, her breasts cupped firmly in the light beige of her bra.

He pulled on his pants.

"I don't work tomorrow," she said as she drove him back to the Bonefish parking lot. He saw her face at sixteen, grinning, saying something to Fred that he wasn't meant to hear, that he couldn't, the music and the wind. "I'm with Tallulah the next two days by myself."

He thought of asking if this meant she would also be with Fred. He thought of asking Maeve if she knew how to get Fred to be nice to him again.

"I should work," he said, feeling silly even before he finished. Although he did have things to do with the new information about Brett.

She drove exactly the speed limit. They kept their windows down, elbows and forearms resting on each of their doors' ledge.

In the Bonefish parking lot, George hesitated, reaching for the handle but not opening the door. The engine ran. Smudged mascara made circles above Maeve's cheekbones; her hand with chipped turquoise nails held tight to the clutch.

"I have a meeting," she said. NA. She'd told him briefly she went three times a week. She looked at him and she suddenly looked too grown-up, worse than older: she looked every bit her age and also like she'd lived too much life for him to ever understand. "See you later."

George opened the door and exited the car. After he closed the door he turned back, looking at her through his still-open window. "See you soon," he said.

She laughed then, long and loud.

That same night, Fred couldn't have known where Maeve and George were, but she was antsy, anxious, walking the length of the house back and forth, Robert Caro in her ears while Tallulah slept. She wished she could go to David's, lose herself in the familiar hot of his skin. He and Barb were both texting about places she could stay once she lost the house. Barb had offered Fred her guest bedroom. Fred replied to neither of them and continued scrolling, searching, spending hours in the middle of the night looking at pictures of houses and apartments that she couldn't afford in New York. She'd read through the contract for the ghostwriting gig three times. She thought of absenting herself, committing to a book that was all craft, a puzzle with no angst, no Tess, no Maeve, no siphoning from any of us.

In high school, Fred had sometimes accompanied Maeve on dates. Of course, they weren't called dates; they were *meet-ups* with guys who wanted to fuck Maeve, who Maeve wanted to fuck. Fred was there as an escape in case they sucked, entertainment if they left. Later, in New York, with me and Brian, me and Cass, Fred used to say: *My ideal place is as third wheel—to be loved but not essential, to know I can't ever fuck it up too much.*

She made sure one more time that Tallulah was asleep, took out her AirPods, and sat out back, where she watched the moon reflected in the pool, listened to the crack and crick of bugs and squirrels moving through the backyard, wind mussing leaves and making heavy palm tree branches bend. She left the gun and meat stored safely in her underwear drawer and the fridge. She lay her head back and looked for all those starving vultures, closed her eyes and thought of Mom.

17

For a few weeks, Ellen Schultz felt better. Late at night after Mike fell asleep, in the middle of the day pushing the stroller back and forth, she thought that if she had to, if she wanted, she could call Deborah Kenner, and Deborah would make everything okay again. She still wore thin cardigans over her arms and shoulders no matter the weather, long linen pants, closed-toed shoes. She brought Brooke, fourteen months now, all squishy wobbly limbs and toddle, to a playground with swings that she could strap her into, up, down, up, down, grabbing hold of one or both her feet and kissing them. They'd sit on the grass and watch the birds hover high over the river, and on the walk home Ellen would get a large black coffee, hot year-round, and a muffin for Brooke, the size of her head.

Mike never yelled. Not once. He never hit her but if he didn't like the food she'd cooked, a gift she'd bought, he'd stand—slowly, carefully—and throw it in the trash. Some nights, when his boys came over, eight and ten now, tall and solid, she'd listen to Mike itemize the failures of their mother, *toxic, selfish, weak, pathetic, parasitic,* and she'd understand that he was also talking about her. He was still kind sometimes, careful, doting. He did all the after-dinner cleanup so that Ellen could put Brooke to bed. Ellen still nursed Brooke to sleep each night, hot, squirmy skin against the hard angles of her hips and ribs. Mike was careful with Brooke, playing in the pool on weekends, taking his boys to basketball and soccer, cheering for them, tearing up once when the younger scored a goal and ran up to hug Mike to celebrate.

Ellen had run into Mom in May, and in August, just like always, she and Brooke went to the coffee shop. She was making her way up to the counter when she heard, *Ellen Davis!* She was no longer Ellen Davis, she had become Ellen Schultz. She saw people who looked vaguely familiar all the time, parents of kids she knew but who seemed unable to place her. She thought this was because she'd had a baby, because she wore the cardigans, because she'd lost too much weight and her face had settled into hardened lines and angles, empty blankness.

Parker Monaghan had been three years ahead of her in high school, quiet, smart. She remembered hearing that he drove a Toyota Camry so old and rusted that it was missing sections of its floor. Because people broadly liked him, this had been presented to her as charming and eccentric, cool. They'd both been on the swim team, and he'd congratulated her when she was a freshman for getting third place at regionals in the 200 free. *Ellen Davis!* he said again, and Ellen saw a flash of his adolescent body in his school-issued Speedo, tall and awkward, tanned and sinewed, a light, wet patch of dark-brown hair on his chest and abdomen. She grabbed her coffee and muffin. *Hi!* she said, not sure she should acknowledge that she remembered him.

Parker Monaghan looked solid, grown-up. Ellen could feel her body cant in his direction. He touched her once and briefly and then knelt to meet Brooke. Brooke clutched tightly to her muffin. *I promise not to take your muffin*, Ellen heard him whisper. She watched Brooke settle, nodding. Parker Monaghan stood up, face flushed, open. *A baby, huh?* he said. Ellen nodded. *Best thing in my life*, she said. *She's beautiful*, he said. She felt a rush of what his skin might feel like touching hers again, the way his body had looked padding to and from the pool each morning before school. She worried there was something broken in her, how quickly and intensely she imagined fucking him. Brooke in the stroller, hot coffee in Ellen's hand, and she thought of pulling Parker Monaghan into the bathroom, letting Brooke sit quiet with her muffin until both she and Parker Monaghan were spent.

Her face got hot, and she clutched harder to the stroller's handle, looked past Parker to the door. Parker was back in town, he explained, before starting his residency in pediatric orthopedics at Miami Children's in the fall. *This fucking place*, he said, then reddened, nodding toward Brooke, apologetic. *It's fine*, Ellen said. *I can't believe how much I missed it*, he said. They talked another couple minutes, no exchange of information.

He had touched her one more time: an older guy in shorts and a neon-green tank top bumped her elbow, and hot coffee spilled on her wrist, and Parker got a napkin and began to clean it without asking. She'd blanched, stepped back. *Sorry*, he said. *Sorry*, she said. He'd handed her the napkin, offered to hold her coffee. *Ellen Davis*, he said one more time—she didn't correct him and say *Schultz*—*so good to see you.*

On the walk home, Ellen stopped twice to touch the place he'd brushed her hand. When she got home, Brooke was asleep, and she left her in the hallway in the stroller and lay on the couch and masturbated with the same hand Parker had touched and came for the first time since Brooke was born.

That night, when Mike got home, she had already bathed Brooke and fed her dinner. Together, she and Mike ate—steaks, asparagus, cubed purple potatoes roasted with thyme and salt and pepper— while Brooke played on the floor close to them, toddling after the large yoga ball Mike had bought for Ellen as a gift, and then Ellen put Brooke down while Mike cleaned up. When Brooke was settled, Ellen came back into the kitchen and approached Mike from behind, her arms first around his waist and then, slowly, angling her hips toward him, reaching her hand, the same one Parker Monaghan had touched, the same one she'd reached up into herself, into her husband's pants.

Mike grabbed her wrists with his hot, wet, soapy hands. *Stop it*, he said. So much worse than angry: grossed out, rimmed with condescension, as if Ellen was a small, sad girl. *What's wrong with you?* He said. That night, he didn't fuck her, didn't touch her. He kept his body from hers as he finished wiping down the kitchen, the skin around his chin rippling, tightening, each time she got close. Once the kitchen was clean, he made himself a third drink and went upstairs.

Ellen got the gun out of the cabinet above the wipes and sat outside a long time looking at the river. She wondered what it would look like, what she would look like, after, what Mike would have to see if he found her.

18

Two nights in a row, Fred sat crossed-legged on the ground, the meat a few feet in front of her, gun on her lap. She'd talked briefly on the phone with Lucia in France. Lucia sent her pictures of the carriage house: big windows, a wrought-iron bed, a small garden; she sent the train schedule in and out of Paris. *I'm almost jealous*, she wrote, *you'll be so free!* Fred looked at those pictures. *Free*, she said out loud, then set her phone down; *free*, like not trapped underneath the roiling ocean; *free*, like forty-two and by herself in someone else's house. She thought again of Faulkner, his dream about the vultures, no hate, envy, need, or wanting; how that also felt like death.

Fred had tried half an hour outside with the meat and without bug spray, wearing long sleeves and linen pants, but the mosquitoes had torn up her ankles, the tops of her feet, and her neck. The meat started to stink from the heat. The third night, four raccoons came—eight wet, black, beady eyes, those swishing, bushy tails. Fred sprang up; the gun fell off her lap; she almost fell into the pool. The raccoons watched, keeping one eye on the meat and one on Fred.

"Scat!" Fred said, but the raccoons stayed still. Fred picked up the gun and swung it at them. "Scat! Scat!" she said again. She thought briefly that she should shoot; she could make real live homemade carrion. She had become strangely mournful about the fact the vultures hadn't come.

She could see light from the house next door, hear cars whooshing past. The gun would be too loud. Someone would come.

"Get away!" Fred said.

The largest of the raccoons came two steps closer.

Fred stepped back. "Go!" she said, desperation drawing out the O.

She lunged quickly for the meat and picked it up. She felt the raccoons inch closer, and her skin pricked; she turned, irrationally, and ran. Her bare foot caught on a root, and she fell face-first into the rancid meat: the ball of her foot bruised; elbows, knees, and wrists scraped; dirt already crusted in the cuts. She felt bile rise up in her throat but picked herself back up. "Scat! Scat! Scat!" she said again, though mostly to herself. She collected the meat and the gun and ran into the house.

Inside, she put the gun back in her drawer and threw the meat away, into a garbage bag and then the big can in the garage. She took a scalding shower, cleaned her legs and elbows, got dressed. She thought of going to David's but didn't want to answer any questions about her cuts.

The morning after, George showed up. He thought maybe Maeve would be there, but he also hoped she wouldn't be. He wanted to talk to Fred. We all liked, at odd moments, we all wanted, sometimes, to talk to Fred. She pretended to be so open, *vulnerable*, as if she wouldn't hold whatever you disclosed against you. Except later, she'd snatch at it, if and when it might serve her; she would put it in her *work*. George knew he couldn't talk to her about Maeve, about Allie, maybe not even about Brett and all that money. He couldn't talk to her about Dad.

Still, none of us—even Jenn and I, who were still checking in almost daily—were talking about Mom.

George found Fred swimming, mercifully wearing running shorts, a sports bra. George tried not to gawk at her taut stomach, the clearly defined ripple of her arms.

"Hey," he said, hoping that in this greeting he could convey that he was caring, thoughtful, raised by his three sisters. An oil and gas trader, sure, but he'd minored in philosophy.

"Hi, bud," Fred said.

"You already go for your run?"

"I did." Her arms rippled as she stroked toward him.

What is it you do all day? George thought but didn't say. "Where's David?" he said, even though he knew the answer.

"You know where," she said.

"What happened, though?" said George. "He was—he *is* . . ."

"Nice," Fred said. "I know he is. How's Allie?"

George didn't mean to say this, but: "She left."

"Well, fuck," said Fred. "Did she . . ." She left the question unfinished.

George sat on the pool's edge. "I'm pretty sure she's fucking someone else."

Fred swam toward him, put her hand on his knee. "Mom would have really loved this."

They both laughed.

"What now?" Fred said.

"You tell me," George said. "How'd we fuck all this up?"

"She wasn't that great," Fred said.

George let both feet fall into the water. "So then what now?" he finally said.

"I think I need to not give a shit about what now for a while."

"What does that mean?" said George.

"*Striving*," she said. "Grasping. Fighting. I want to figure out what I am when I'm not that."

George stayed quiet, looked down again into the water.

"It's all so fucking desperate," Fred said. "Prostrating myself on the internet to sell books that just don't matter. Or books that only matter because they hurt people I love. I have to figure out what's so wrong with me that I can't stop."

George drew a circle in the pool with his finger, flicked the drops of water at Fred's face. "I thought the dead-friend book was good."

He felt more than saw Fred blanch.

I read the Tess book the same day it came out. Fred never got us early copies, always made us wait through all the prepublication press, trying to guess which parts of us she'd laid bare this time. I listened to the audio, which Fred read herself. Straight past sundown, I walked around Manhattan, my sister talking in my ears about the pain, confusion, isolation. I sobbed and thought of calling, took my phone out of my pocket, but then realized that the book was fiction; anyone could buy it, read it, listen to her: I felt tricked. I didn't for a second doubt that everything Fred said inside those pages was true. I was angry that she only ever offered versions of herself this true inside her work.

Twenty-six the year she started grad school, Fred felt older than all the kids who'd come straight out of undergrad, older even than her older, wealthier colleagues who'd not ever had jobs. Fred and David had met two years before and already gotten married. She'd waited tables, taught high school, become an expensive SAT tutor. She was maybe a year or two older than most of her classmates, but she often felt too enmeshed already in a life outside of the world of classrooms, talk of art and process, practice; Fred felt too practical to feel close to most of the people that she met.

(Add to this, too, our family: Fred had grown up watching Lifetime movies, reading Mom and Dad's pulpy paperbacks; once, on a high school trip to Europe, Dad convinced her to skip their designated two hours at the Louvre to find a second lunch. Her colleagues' parents were professors, *intellectuals*; they used the word "film" unironically, spoke Mandarin, Italian, French.)

Fred's favorite class was taught by her youngest, least well-known professor. In a program largely peopled by bold-lettered names, almost no one had heard of Tess. None of the students, including Fred, had read Tess's two books. She taught a class called "The Anti-Social Novel" (a term Tess claimed to have coined): characters cast out of society, their communities or families, *clinging to the edge of the map of their lives*. Iris Murdoch, Desző Kosztolányi, Shirley Jackson, Violette Leduc—the only writer they studied that Fred had read, or even heard of, was Joan Didion.

Tess talked with both hands and did not ever stop talking. She wore multicolored knee socks and big floral skirts, small, fitted T-shirts, blousy floor-length dresses; her hair was long and very straight, and she had an assortment of differently rimmed glasses that most of her students believed were not visually necessary.

At Fred's first one-on-one visit to office hours, Tess leaned over the desk, her face close to Fred's. She complimented her thinking and her reading and her writing, pointed out a sentence on Fred's earliest submission, circled it and wrote, *yes, good*. Just understated and rare enough that Fred believed it, and, Fred, who later wouldn't even have copies of the newspapers or magazines in which either she published work or her work was covered, still had that note from Tess.

All to say: Fred loved Tess from the start.

Once, early in that first semester, Tess mentioned offhand in class that she hated the student-faculty cocktail parties—they had all just gotten an invitation to their first of these—in part because all they served was shitty wine. Playfully provocative, hindsightedly predictable, Tess said, *You'd think these guys could swing for some good beer.*

Classic, basic cool-girl performance, but Fred was in love, bought it, drank it in.

So then, Fred and two friends, both girls, went, the next week, hours before the party, in search of beer for Tess. In the back fridge of one of the overpriced grocery stores on Broadway, they found a smattering of five-dollar-apiece craft beers and carefully, unknowingly, selected a half dozen; none of them drank beer. Fred clutched the cardboard container handle all the way back to the party, her other hand cupped underneath, canvas bag swung over her shoulder. They climbed the stairs together laughing, the party in an emptied-out seminar classroom. Fred cast about in search of Tess and finally saw her across the room, talking, laughing, close to a large window, in a cinched-waisted blue-and-purple dress. Fred bounded toward her and held up the beers. "We got these for you!" she said.

The guy who was talking to Tess looked long at the beer, not smiling. He was short and thin, dark hair, face scruff, a much more well-known novelist. "How very sweet," he said.

Fred looked at the guy, then at Tess, then down, then at the beers. She was seconds away from self-immolating. And then Tess, as she would a thousand times in the almost ten years that followed, swooped in to save Fred: "Replacing the bad wine! How very sweet," she said, parroting the guy but without his mocking and condescension. She took a beer and offered one to Fred, the guy, Fred's friends.

Fred drank half her beer and bolted. She wouldn't, couldn't talk to Tess again that night. She walked the hundred-plus blocks to her and David's apartment still ashamed. *Silly, stupid, desperate*, she thought the whole walk home. Someone like Tess, outside of class, outside of her professional, paid obligations, would always be too brilliant, charming—all those multicolored heels and knee socks—to have any extra time for someone like Fred.

Slowly, though, they made small shifts toward friendship. Long office hours turned into meeting Tess for coffee after or before class, turned into dinner, turned into Tess asking Fred to come watch her kids while Tess and her husband, Ben, went out. Her second year, Fred would get a teaching fellowship, but that first year, it felt like all Fred did was look for work.

Tess and Ben and Oona and Hal all lived in a small one-bedroom close to the river, blocks from Fred's apartment in the East Village, rent stabilized so impossible to leave, chock full of toys and that tiny, messy, always too-hot kitchen. Tess and Ben's bed was lofted in their living room. There was a fire escape off the front room where Tess and Fred would sit some nights with a glass of wine or whiskey (both) and a cigarette (Tess) after the kids were in bed.

Fred loved kids but hadn't babysat since high school. She'd said yes when Tess asked only because she loved Tess; tutoring paid better. The kids were seven and nine and wanted to impress her; they'd already be fed and showered by the time Fred got there, so babysitting consisted of an hour talking about the books and movies they liked, manga and video games that Fred had never heard of, then getting them to brush their teeth and letting Hal read to her, his long, thin body settled easily next to hers and his head on her shoulder, Oona going into her top bunk with a small reading light and her own book.

The first time Fred sat for them, Tess and Ben came home after Fred had spent half an hour trying to find the book from Tess's shelf that might evoke the most exciting conversation when Fred was found reading it, that might prove to Tess how smart, how effortlessly curious and engaged Fred was. As it turned out, neither Tess nor Ben noticed the book (Annie Ernaux's *A Woman's Story*) when they came in. Ben went quickly into the children's room to check on them, and Tess led Fred into the kitchen, smelling of gin and her single post-dinner cigarette, whatever herbal scent she wore. She poured herself and Fred a glass of water and leaned forward, elbows on the counter, skin chapped from the cold.

"They were good?" she said.

Fred recognized this as a type of performance: Tess a little drunk but wanting to seem not to be, an at-home mother-and-wife self but wanting, in front of Fred, also to be something more.

"Great!" Fred said, taking one long sip of water and then gathering her coat and bag, putting the book back. "Oh, keep it!" Tess said. "I still haven't read that! You read it for me and report back."

More walks, more time, more babysitting, more coffee. Fred got the fellowship and was on campus more; she tutored less and finished grad school. Tess sold her next book. Fred was constantly afraid of scaring Tess away, her want, her need, too much. She'd think of her three times a day but only let herself text or call Tess weekly. She'd canceled coffee, a lunch, once or twice, to prove she could. She quickly became the kids' favorite babysitter. More and more, Tess or Ben would convince her to stay and have a drink, those nights out on the fire escape, watching Ben watch Tess. Going home to David, spurred and churned by all that watching; those years some of the best sex she and David had. Just home from Tess's, the warmth and closed-in tightness, Fred would think she wouldn't mind so much if her birth control failed—it would be years, still, before those painful conversations about babies—as long as her kids were like Oona and Hal.

The first Thanksgiving Fred was out of grad school, Tess helped her find an agent, and Fred's first novel sold; Tess helped her navigate initial interest that eventually fell off to a disappointing offer that still managed to feel thrilling, in part because Tess was with her the whole time. (Fred did not tell Mom and Dad the number because she was embarrassed; *You're back to tutoring?* Mom said). Fred and David, for the first time, did not fly home for Thanksgiving; instead, they joined fifteen other people stuffed into Ben and Tess's eight-hundred-square-foot apartment, everybody bringing something. It was cold outside but all the windows were open, oven on, the cold air rushing in but everything inside still warm, not least because of a big glass vat of whiskey punch, muddled and mixed, by the front door. Oona and Hal were now eight and ten, telling every-body stories, drawing portraits, grabbing grown-up hands to give tours of their room. So much food and all of it rich and delicious. The children sneaking some of the pumpkin cookies Fred had made with David, sneaking crumble off one of the pie's tops and hand-ing it to Fred. David and Fred walked home a little tipsy, clutching one another, thinking that evening—the room, the people, the food, those gorgeous, earnest kids—was the exact shape and texture of the grown-up lives they'd not even fully known they'd wanted. David, like Fred, just some kid from Florida, wanting to make this life, this city, theirs.

Here, it feels worth noting how unfathomable a life like this would have seemed to any of us. Like if you've ever been somewhere and heard a song and, without thinking, started singing because you heard it so much when you were little, because it's embedded so completely in your brain, only to look up and realize someone, maybe everyone, is smirking at you, realize that song, but also ev-erything that you came up with, every bit of you that has been built up since you were small—the food you ate, the books you read, the movies, but also the whole way of thinking and being, let's call it *values*—that it was crass and brash, worse than vapid because you'd never known to see what else life might be.

How unfathomable to watch Tess and Ben, their friends—and here, now, one more detail from that evening: Tess's mom, Christina, who'd flown in from San Francisco, a Berkeley linguistics professor. The way she sat and laughed and talked to everybody, leaning forward, touching elbows, shoulders, asking questions, her voice low and quiet and conspiring; the way she fit right in, listened while the children talked. More than once, Fred saw her grab hold of Tess's hand. All of this drew Fred to Tess, made her feel as if something magic might be happening, as if maybe, over time, with Tess's help, Fred could become someone else.

Fred's first book came out, but no one really noticed. Mom and Dad came up, and we all went to the book launch. Brian and I were still together, and we got a sitter. Mom and Dad felt hurt because Fred didn't come up to them before the reading or right after. She made no effort to introduce them to her friends. She invited us to the after-reading dinner, but Mom and Dad were angry—also, likely, they felt out of their depth—and instead they went back to their hotel to eat alone. For months afterward, they talked about how rude Fred was.

Tess helped Fred get an adjunct gig at the same place Fred had graduated from and where Tess now taught. Tess brought Fred misshapen scones that she'd made with the kids, and they'd share them in their borrowed adjunct office before class. Sometimes they shared work—a paragraph, a first few pages. Fred did her best to hold her want in check, not to send Tess every word she'd ever written, not to call or email or text Tess with every thought, fear, snippet of something that she'd read.

Tess's third book came out the year after Fred's and also didn't get much notice, a Briefly Noted in *The New Yorker*, the longlist for a prize but not the shortlist. Ben was a bartender and worked nights and watched the kids while Tess taught and wrote. They didn't have health insurance for the grown-ups. The kids were on CHIP.

And then: Tess was turning forty-four and Fred a couple months from thirty-four, and Tess called her.

"Walk?" Tess said.

"Of course," Fred said.

"Busy now?"

"I can be to you in ten."

What did Fred think walking over? How many hundred thousand times had she walked to Tess's over the years; how many other times had she just walked past? Not to mention those times she let herself in through the almost-never-locked front door of their building and left a treat—a box of cookies, candy, a book, a note—with Tess, Oona, Hal, and/or Ben's name on it. A text from Tess a couple hours later: a picture of one of the kids reading, Tess and both kids biting into the same big cookie at once. (*You should see the way she is with strangers,* Dad used to say after visits to New York, *how nice she is to them! They're not strangers to her, Dad,* I'd say. *They're not her family,* he'd say back.)

There are so few moments in a life that feel explicitly like they might cleave time up into before and after. *Start a story with a rupture,* both Fred and Tess would say to students, but maybe neither had ever felt one quite as monumental as this.

Fred buzzed, and Tess came down; they hugged. It was fall, and the whole city felt opened up for them; New York is never as much its perfect, cinematic self as how it tastes and smells and looks in fall. Classes had just started, and Fred wanted to tell Tess what stories she was teaching. She did this often, prepping for her, still hoping to impress, to prove her worth.

"I need you to promise not to make a face," Tess said. She'd always been thin, *gamine* was the word that Fred thought often. Did Fred smell it on her, sense it on her, that day?

"I promise," Fred said.

"Acute myeloid leukemia," Tess said. "Blood cancer, but it's spread to my liver and my lymph nodes and my bones."

A feeling that Fred would equate to her whole body melting, disintegrating: muscles, skin, bones, nothing felt solid.

"Riddled. Addled," Tess said, trying the words out.

Fred stayed silent.

"You said you wouldn't make a face," Tess said.

But my face is melting, Fred thought. "You're too young," she said.

Tess shrugged. "They say that might work in my favor for a while."

The prognosis was an almost unfathomable not knowing. Blank, open spaces in which experimental treatments and immune suppressants lived. New drugs all the time, etc.

"Modern life is shit," Tess said, "but the doctors say there has never been as good a time to have cancer as right now."

"I think fuck them," Fred said.

"I'm not sure that will make them more likely to help me."

The land of sick was new and different. Ben started looking for a job with health insurance. Tess kept both her classes the next two semesters. Fred filled in when necessary, did all the reading, course prep.

Fred started a GoFundMe, though Tess didn't want her to. *I don't think I can stomach all the pity*, Tess said. *I'll be your block*, said Fred.

She started going to the appointments, because Ben had still not found a different job but had picked up day shifts so he could be with Tess at night, when her body seemed to be revolting, angry, over whatever it was inside her.

The prognosis was, historically, three to six months, but there were pills that had been keeping people alive longer, though those people had only been taking the pills for nine months. One woman in Cincinnati had just made it past a year.

"Like a frozen bullet right at my head," Tess said. "That might, at any point, unfreeze."

Fred looked straight at her and smiled.

The kids were big enough to know most of what was happening. Oona had started watching TikToks made by kids of cancer patients and often refused to go to school. Hal got very quiet and did exactly what was asked of him, and Tess would grab his face and hold it too long, and he'd look at her, face and body still. Tess said to Fred that his not reacting scared her most of all.

Fred went uptown to teach her class and then Tess's. She still got up every morning and ran and worked on her next book. She was not around them 100 percent of the time: Christina took the whole family to Europe for a week, and Fred got a couple of pictures from a boat along the Seine; outside the Musée d'Orsay; a group of paintings by Tess's favorite, Chaïm Soutine, from the Musée de l'Orangerie. Only puked three times today, Tess texted, with a melting-smiley-face emoji.

What an awful, terrible thing, is what people say, showing for the thousandth millionth time the endless inadequacies of language, of any human response to death and dying when it looks and feels like this. All that empty time Fred used to not know how to fill, all that love she'd stored up, not knowing fully how to offer it. She loved David, who was good and kind and steady, funny, impossibly good-looking, weirdly and consistently charmed by Fred. Love like that made Fred suspicious—love that she didn't have to work to earn, that came so surely every day. What loving Tess those months offered was like the early years of Cass for me: the constancy, the tasks, the doing, the opportunity to prove over and over that she could be there for her, that, given the opportunity to earn love—which was the only way we'd ever been taught love could exist—she would earn it. Though she would never have said this out loud or even thought it, Fred carried with her a half belief that maybe if she could work hard enough, love well enough, that somehow Tess would live.

And here, too, briefly: Fred on my couch, having walked to my place straight from Tess's, crying, desperate. Cassie at her dad's and David out of town. I ordered Indian, the tofu tikka masala I knew she liked but was embarrassed to order. She ate and cried and talked, and I sat very still and listened. *Freddy, you're allowed.* After half a bottle of wine, she lay her head on my lap, and I turned on a movie. She talked more and cried more until she finally fell asleep.

Tess didn't live. The bullet unfroze and she died.

Fred wasn't there that day. Ben had taken Tess back to the hospital because she was shitting blood and couldn't eat or even drink a glass of water. The kids had begged and pleaded to come, and so Ben had taken them too. *It was the only lucky thing*, Ben said, the fact that they were there. *An IV hit*, Tess said in the cab uptown. *Just to hydrate me. We'll be back home for dinner, a Housewives episode on the couch.* She weighed nothing by then, was still mostly herself.

She was dying, sure, but also, she'd mostly kept on living.

———

Fred had to teach a class on Denis Johnson that day. *So fucking weird*, she said to me later. A story about a hospital, called "Emergency." The last line: *I save lives*.

She kept waiting for some part of her to break down, break off. Instead, she taught her class, and no one knew a thing about what happened. A whole person vanished—Oona and Hal's mother, Ben's wife—and these kids raising their hands, asking questions, and Fred writing on the board, asking, *What do you guys think?* Waiting for her body to know how to register that Tess was gone.

"My friend died," she said one day on the subway, when a woman asked her if she was okay and she realized she'd been crying. The woman's face right next to hers, mint and coffee on her breath.

"Oh honey," said the woman.

"It's fine," Fred said. "I'm fine."

"You don't have to be, you know," the woman said.

Fred nodded. She stopped crying. Her coat brushed the woman's, Fred's bag open between her legs, the mess of papers and books, tissues, too overt and visible.

The doors opened.

"My stop," Fred said, although it wasn't. She got off, climbed aboveground: midtown, a part of town she never went to. She walked its blocks, looking at restaurants, shop windows, so grateful that it held almost none of Tess.

Junior year of high school, Fred got second in the state in the one-mile. It was her fastest-ever time, her highest-ever place. The only time she ever broke five minutes. Around the corner of her last 400 meters, her quadricep tore. She kept going, around three more turns, she passed two people on the last stretch. Briefly, from up in the stands, I thought I saw her wince. The girl who won pushed past her at the finish. Fred leaned her whole body forward, waist bent, arms loose, toes first. And then she collapsed.

That's what that book felt like for Fred. She didn't stop or think or feel, she just kept pushing. Whatever broke or tore inside her, she didn't register in all those months. It was the best she'd ever felt inside a novel, head down, stretching. And then she finished. And then she collapsed.

For a year after the Tess book came out, Fred hardly touched her computer. She ran and cried, she taught and read. She'd sent an early copy of the book to Ben and Oona and Hal, and though they'd all signed off on it, none of them was as responsive to her texts or phone calls after that. She got more and better teaching gigs and said yes to everyone. Every other week or so, she'd get an email from a person who had lost someone; she spent hours reading and responding to each one. But then, sometimes, she'd meet people who had read the book and thought they knew everything there was to know about her. They stood too close and presumed their way into her most private, intimate thoughts. She was confused, surprised, emboldened briefly and then hurt by the response. The book garnered lots of attention, but the talk was all about her anguish—*raw and honest*—and Tess's suffering. *What did I do?* she said to David late at night. *I don't ever want to write a raw and honest book again.* The next year, she wrote another book with much less angst in it. Multiple points of view, an awful family somewhere far off in the distance, of course; a person who struggled with substances, but mostly, otherwise, made up. *My imagination's shit, apparently*, she said to David, when no one seemed to care about it. This felt related to, all tied up with, everything she'd tried or failed to write since.

"How's Dad?" Fred said to George. She didn't want to talk about Tess, what she'd written since, who she'd betrayed (me).

"He's sad," George said. "Looks lost a lot."

"Do you guys talk?"

"He asks me about work."

"About Mom?"

"What's he supposed to say?"

Fred was still in the pool, on her back now, twirling her legs and arms to keep herself from sinking. A smaller patch of vultures had flown by while they talked. Fred let her legs fall down, leaned forward, stood up straight. She grinned at him, our little brother, thought of telling him about the job in France, about the vultures.

George stood up and took off his shirt, walked over to the deep end. "Maybe I'll stop striving too," he said, and dove in.

19

"The famous writer!" said Ellen Monaghan as Fred walked through her big glass door with great blue herons etched in the center, the day after Fred saw George. She'd ended up at David's that night but had stayed only half an hour. He'd found the cuts, had touched each of them; his face shifted toward a question. She shook her head and grabbed his hands, eased him inside of her, then flipped him onto his back so she was on her knees, putting pressure on her cuts as they fucked. She'd come home and sat outside a long time, without the meat, head tilted back, looking for the vultures, scratching all her bug bites. This morning, she'd overslept and had time for only four quick miles before coming here.

She had four more days to decide whether or not to go spend three months in France.

Fred remembered she'd known Ellen in high school. Ellen looked so much like a mom now, the way she moved briskly, the crisp, soft blue of her sleeveless shirt. Her skin shone, taut. Fred reached up to her own bare face, the stretches of her chin where the skin thinned, the bloodied bumps on her neck from the bugs. She eyed the two holes at the bottom edges of her linen pants.

"I saw your face in *People* magazine a couple years ago and almost peed myself!" said Ellen (Fred's third book had been in *People*, a "Book to Watch Out For" but not "Book of the Week"; Mom and

Dad both stocked the magazine at their respective offices, and this had excited Mom's paralegal and both Mom's and Dad's secretaries). "And now look—you're here!" Ellen grinned at her.

Fred had also googled Ellen. She knew her husband was a pediatric orthopedic surgeon. Ellen had a website that called her an interior designer, but now, walking into her house, Fred noticed all the pictures from the website were of Ellen's own home. Ellen had three kids, Fred had learned on Facebook. Fred had been hired to help the oldest, Brooke.

"I told Brooke," Ellen said, "how lucky she should feel!" She whisked Fred through the high-ceilinged kitchen, shimmery stainless steel and spotless granite, the windows looking out onto the wide water, the long, large pool. It reminded Fred of our parents' house: the same plastic wood, high windows, empty walls, the same hardly-lived-in feel.

"I thought we'd put you two in the dining room," said Ellen.

Fred looked down at her flip-flops, specks of sand still at her ankles, scratchy bumps and welts. She reached her hand up to her face again and tried to remember if she'd put on moisturizer after her shower.

"You look wonderful, by the way!" said Ellen.

"You too!" Fred said.

In the dining room sat Brooke, phone in hand, scrolling, typing, all wrists and elbows. She wore cutoff jean shorts and a camisole, purple bra straps visible. "Brooke! Brooke!" said Ellen, reaching for the bra straps and shifting them beneath the camisole straps, then grabbing her daughter's phone. "You are just about the luckiest kid!"

"Since when?" said Brooke, pulling away from her mother, grabbing her phone back.

Fred watched Ellen's back and shoulders clench.

"I'll put it away," said Brooke, stuffing the phone in the back pocket of her shorts.

Ellen stepped away from Brooke, turned toward Fred. "Make sure she doesn't take it out again?"

"Of course," Fred said. She had a quick flash of an image: Ellen upside down in her bikini, two guys from another school holding her ankles, the nozzle of the keg in her teeth; the kids around her cheering, beer bubbling from her mouth, the red and purple striped triangle of her top slipping, a shock of bright white skin contrasting with the darker hue of the rest of her torso.

Fred sat down in the high-backed dark-wood chair next to Brooke. They both waited as Ellen walked out.

"Why are you here?" asked Brooke, once the smell of Ellen's floral perfume had faded.

"To help with your essay," Fred said.

"I mean, why in the hell would you come back to Florida?"

Fred smiled at her. It was possible that Ellen had had a nose job. Brooke's nose was large, a little crooked; it looked familiar to her in a way that Ellen's straight and pert nose did not.

"I love the ocean," Fred said.

"Good thing, I guess," said Brooke. "Since this whole place will be underwater soon."

The house was all open. The dining room sat in between the kitchen and a living room with large leather couches, a fireplace and massive flatscreen, a baby grand piano. Big, wide windows everywhere, all that light, the view.

"Sometimes," said Brooke, "I think about a big wave crashing through that window, just fucking flattening all of this."

Fred looked at her, a totally normal-looking kid, acne on her nose and in the space between her eyebrows, a smattering of scars on both sides of her chin from picking at her skin. She wore her hair held back, messy, but messy in a way Fred figured she had thought about. Fred liked teenagers, always had. She had taught or tutored high school students for most of her twenties before grad school, done a year teaching high school in the city the year after her first book came out.

Brooke got out her computer—brand new, Fred noted, but with food crumbs among the keys. She opened Word and then an already typed up document, handed it to Fred, went back to her phone.

"Not how this works," Fred said, nodding toward the phone. Brooke looked at her, then back out the window, put the phone back in the pocket of her shorts.

"Okay," Fred said. "You read it out loud to me, and we'll talk about each sentence."

"You're serious?" Brooke said.

Fred laughed. "I am."

The essay, "Our Dying River," was about the algae that had spread into the river, the spores that sometimes made whole sections of water uninhabitable for the fish and manatees and plant life; how Brooke's asthma acted up when she walked along the water; the dogs that had died after lapping at the river's edge. The letters Brooke had written, the club she'd started after school, the strange dissonance of feeling like none of the grown-ups in her life—the people tasked with helping, taking care, etc.—gave a shit about this thing that all of them could clearly see was dying off. The spores came from Lake Okeechobee, which had been built to make the land around it more conducive to farming. When Okeechobee got overfull in summer, its dams were opened up, releasing too much freshwater into the river's balanced brackish, the whole ecosystem thrown off kilter, the algae spores so toxic and pervasive that sometimes even the beaches were shut down.

"It's really good, Brooke," Fred said, after an hour sharpening sentences, teasing out points, asking questions and clarifying syntax, sentence order, transition paragraphs.

"It's also terrible," said Brooke.

Fred nodded, looking past her to the water. A heron was gliding just above its surface; a large motorboat with a big, long wake sped through the channel, looking briefly like it might hit the marker. Fred flinched, and the boat zipped past.

"It really is," said Fred.

Ellen gave Fred a check (*or I could Zelle you? Venmo?*; *Check is fine*, Fred said), and Fred drove for a long time, windows down, music on. Driving like this, on these roads where she had driven when she was a teenager, she felt forty-two and sober, sixteen and very drunk, twenty-five and pissed, having fought again with our parents about some slight that Mom had offered about her job or work, but really about every word that Mom either had or hadn't said in every second, minute, hour, and day before that. She thought of the algae accruing in Lake Okeechobee, years of pesticide spill from farms that existed only because the natural floods had been stymied by the lake. All that intervention that had looked like progress, now fraught with destruction, now impossible to turn back.

20

Fred began feeling worse just as George had begun to feel better. He had written out a script to talk to Brett. He was going to get his money back.

He threw the ball for Libby, followed her frantic running around the yard and out onto the dock. Dad was on one of his Zoom calls. George had broken his intermittent fasting because he was too nervous, had driven to the bagel place a quarter mile from Mom and Dad's and gotten a bacon egg and cheese on a plain bagel, an orange juice and a large latte, two packs of Sweet'N Low. He'd used a tiny piece of the bacon from his sandwich to entice Libby from Dad's room. Now he looked over his script and scrolled through Allie's Instagram. He went back into the house and took a single shot of rum that he immediately regretted. He went into his room and put on swim trunks and dove into the pool and swam three laps, then got out and lay on one of the larger loungers to dry off.

"You're really taking to the tropics," Jenn said. George startled. Jenn stood next to the row of sliding glass doors that led out to the pool, holding her toddler, Devon.

George sat up, pulled on his shirt.

"I had a mediation cancel," Jenn said. "So I thought I'd stock the fridge."

———

Jenn was the meanest and also sweetest of us. All those kids, doting, careful: *sweetie, honey, my precious baby angel.* The sharp, hard barbs she hurled at Allie: *It must be hard to find places to shop in Houston; I guess flavor's easy to come by when you use that much cheese.* The greatest damage that both Jenn and Mom did was not ever actually with the things they said but what they didn't—the way they wouldn't look at you, the way that when they did sometimes they looked like they might spit. Language is not just words but the silences between them; the way lips purse, contract; the angle of chins and shoulders. It was thrilling when Jenn whispered in our ear some mean thing she thought secretly but would also share with us, some silly, funny story about her kids; it felt so good to be singled out, taken aside by the big sister—a confidence in the walk-in pantry, in her room when everyone else was downstairs, with a couple of her kids in the backyard; alternatively, a snide remark under her breath to someone else, but also meant for us to hear. The language of a family often lives outside of what is spoken. Here are details, facts, instances accumulated and then offered, but what's missing is the feeling in your belly when your big sister says something nice to you, that feeling in the creases of your face, the balls of your feet, when she looks you up and down as only she can look you up and down and you know absolutely that whatever it is she sees makes her want to puke.

"You know I can shop for groceries, right?" George said to Jenn.

"Can you, though?" Jenn said. "Who shops at your house?"

It was true that Allie did it, that, standing in the middle of a random aisle with a list that Allie had texted, George felt confused and lost.

"I like it," Jenn said. "I like tasks." She'd doted on him when he was little, calling him her baby, carting him around. But she was gone before his eighth birthday, off to college and then law school, married early, always busy.

"Good thing," George said, nodding toward Devon.

"Oh, they're almost too easy," Jenn said. "They all take care of each other; I guess that's why I keep having more."

George thought of telling her about Brett, asking her to call for him.

The baby squirmed, and Jenn put her down to play with Libby. She walked over to Georgie, sat beside him on the chair.

"Most everything in life that's any good," Jenn said, "most anything that's brought me sustained bouts of joy: it all felt hard at first."

George nodded as Devon fell down, as Jenn put her hand briefly on George's shoulder, then stood and scooped up the baby. The biggest split was between her first four and her last two. In the year before she got pregnant for the fifth time, she'd cried inexplicably near every day.

"Let me do the shopping next week," George said.

"If I hear you two ate something besides takeout this week, then we'll talk."

He watched her walk back into the house, Libby still running circles around the backyard. He picked up his phone: *In Danger of Overheating*, said a warning on the screen. He clutched it in his hands, still cold from the swimming, until the warning screen turned off. Back and forth on the grass, barefoot, George kept an eye out for errant dog shit as he walked. Jenn sent Devon out to hug him, kiss him, *tell Uncle George you love him*. Dad stood at the door and called Libby in. The afternoon storm was coming, and George watched the block of clouds move in over the river, the sheets of rain far off in the distance, until the first smattering of drops hit.

Finally, twenty minutes later, the rain still falling but less heavily, George called Brett.

"Georgie!" Brett's voice was so confident that it felt thrilling.

"Hey Brett," George said.

"Was sorry to hear about your mom."

"Yeah, thanks."

Brett was quiet. George held the silence for a beat, then: "Listen," he said.

"What's up?" said Brett.

George went quickly through what he had discovered. He wasn't tricky or articulate or cunning. He was careful and deliberate, listed what he now felt pretty sure Brett had done.

Brett didn't speak for a long time. George thought maybe he'd hung up, but then he heard a clanging in the background, what might have been the clink of ice on glass.

"Well, fuck," Brett said.

Brett admitted to nothing, but George understood that he had heard him and that George had gotten it exactly right.

An hour later, Heather from HR called to say she needed to know the account info for the transfer of George's severance. George had not been told before that he would receive any severance. He gave Heather all the info that she asked for and ordered himself butter-milk fried chicken for dinner, with mashed potatoes, a side of fries, and a brownie sundae with the ice cream on the side.

21

"Are you . . ." The boy was just a boy, Fred kept telling herself. He lived three houses down from Ellen Monaghan, who had told this boy's mom to contact Fred. Fred kept telling herself he was a boy, though he was well over six feet: broad, strong shoulders, tight-fitting shirt, loose shorts, Miami Dolphins cap a little crooked over his tousled white-blond hair. He had looked her up and down when she walked in. Fred scratched the bumps on her neck, her clavicles and shoulders.

"Are you . . . feminist?" he said.

Fred hesitated and then resented that she'd hesitated. She picked the blood from underneath her fingernails and wiped it on the underside of her shirt. "I am," she said.

"You're from New York?"

"I grew up here."

"I googled you." He smelled of sweat but with a layer of Axe body spray. He leaned forward in his chair, bread and peanut butter on his breath, and Fred felt her body tighten. She leaned back, reached up to itch her neck again. "You hate cops?" he said.

Fred looked past him, toward the kitchen into which his mother had disappeared.

"I want to be a cop," he said. "Does that freak you out?"

"You want to get your essay out?" Fred said.

"You like it here?" he said. "Relieved to be out of the cesspool of New York?"

"It's beautiful here," Fred said.

He sat up straighter than seemed normal for a teenager, lifted his arms above his head to stretch. Fred looked down as his shirt rose up.

"You should get your essay out," Fred said. She fought the urge to wrap her arms around herself. She fought the urge to stand up, yell. She scratched her mosquito bites and then picked more blood out of her nails.

"I just think we should get to know each other. Since we're going to be working together, you know, *closely*."

"I don't think we should," said Fred. She nodded toward the laptop that sat between them on the table. "May I?"

The kid nodded, smirking. "You may," he said.

There was no passcode, just tabs and tabs of YouTube, email, Twitter, TikTok, Reddit. The window that was open was an interview that Fred had given. She stared at the picture of herself and tried to pretend she didn't notice. Instead, she nudged the laptop toward him. "Can you open the essay?" she said.

"I didn't start it," the kid said.

Fred looked around again for a parent, looked down at her phone, out the window toward the water. A massive power boat sped past.

"Just kidding," the kid said, reaching out like he might touch her. Fred drew back, and the kid laughed.

"What's wrong?" he said.

"Do you have an essay?" Fred said.

He reached for the computer, brushing her hand with his forearm as he did. "What's most important to me in writing is that we complicate the questions that have already been asked, that we *elasticize* our relationship to words and terms that have started to feel fixed," he said.

Fred stayed still a minute, her mind whirring. He was quoting her back to herself.

He clicked and moved his cursor, passed the computer back to her. "I tried to give them what they want," he said.

Reflect on something that someone has done for you that has made you happy or thankful in a surprising way. How has this gratitude affected or motivated you? was the Common App question he'd chosen. He'd written about his grandpa, how he'd taken him fishing early in the morning every weekend since he was a toddler and how essential those weekend mornings had been to his becoming who he was. It wasn't awful. Fred felt anxious, angry; she'd wanted the essay, she realized, to be bad. When our own grandpa, Mom's dad, had died, Fred hadn't been talking to Mom. She'd called her, told her she was sorry, but had failed to show up at the funeral.

"He also takes me hunting," the kid said. "But I know those college people don't want to read about that shit."

Fred stayed quiet, pulled the laptop closer to her. She would usually, as she had with Brooke, make him read the essay with her, move her chair so they could read together, walk him through the smoothing out of awkward syntax, show him places to explain, expand. Instead, she quickly shifted some of the less clear language, passing him the computer across the table each time and explaining what she'd done and why she'd done it. She highlighted four sentences she thought he could expand. The whole time, he leaned too close to her, the stink of his breath creeping up her nose. Twice more, his forearm brushed her elbow, once, her hand. *He's just a kid*, she told herself as she tried not to push her chair out, stand up, walk out. *He's just a kid.*

Fred drove back to the house too fast, sweating, windows down, arm stretched out into the hot, humid air. When she got back, she googled river algae, Lake Okeechobee, organizations that might help. One of Fred's most persistent shames was that, because she'd been so single-minded about *becoming a writer*, she'd failed to do anything useful with her life. From late 2016 through the first third of 2017, she'd attended eight and a half biweekly meetings in an attempt to *resist*; the purpose of the meetings had been to select committees to help choose committees to help pick the times when the subcommittees would meet to vote on how and when they would decide to focus their energy and their attention, and she'd given up. (I knew she'd left that eighth meeting early because they all took place at a temple in Park Slope, and she'd brought Cass and me Vietnamese sandwiches instead of staying the last hour.)

She signed up now for more listservs, agreed to receive text message alerts about "actions" and beach cleanups. She clicked on a link and read about reducing microplastic degradation by picking up plastic before it got swept offshore. She emailed a Hotmail account attached to a website that ran a video loop of the algae blooms next to a count of the dogs killed. Would it be possible, Fred wrote, for her to come in and talk about different ways that she might help? The guy responded quickly: *there's not an office or anything like that but I could meet for coffee tomorrow if you want.* His signature read, *sent from a tiny computer in my pocket likely destroying my brain.*

Sure, Fred wrote. *I'd love that.*

He sent a time and place, a coffee shop downtown in the late afternoon the next day.

22

Fred tried on three different outfits before landing on one she liked. Her linen pants had holes in them. Her button-ups were all too big and saggy. She finally chose the same black Target dress she'd worn to Mom's funeral, the only non-running and non-holey, wrinkled piece of clothing she had left.

She shoved the gun in her canvas bag at the last minute, less thought than reflex. She slid on flip-flops, drove the ten minutes to the downtown coffee shop, grabbed her bag from the passenger's-side floor. She was used to carrying at least three books, a notebook, often her computer. The gun's weight was negligible.

She had to stand in line to get her coffee, stood on tiptoes looking around for the guy. He hadn't responded to the email she'd sent with her own description. She got a muffin, a large coffee, realized, of course, she might see people she knew, regretted not wearing her hat.

"Winnifred?" The guy was somewhere between twenty and thirty, curly hair springing out from his head and down to his shoulders, round-faced, scruffy. He stood too close to her. He wore purple-and-black board shorts and an old, thin Bad Religion shirt.

"Fred," she said.

He didn't offer to pay for her coffee.

"Let me, can I," she said.

"Sure," he said. He got a seventeen-dollar sandwich, a cappuccino. Asked for an extra mayo packet.

Fred gave the girl her card again.

"Thanks," he said.

They found an outside table. It was humid, stifling, Fred already sweating. Only three other people had chosen to sit in the heat.

"The coolest summer of the rest of our lives," the guy said, grinning at her. "Where you from?" He spread the extra mayonnaise on the top half of his sandwich, topped it with ketchup.

"I grew up here," Fred said.

"Well, welcome home," he said.

"You're from here?" she said.

"Born and raised," he said. "Went to New College. Before it got fucked up by Crazy Ron."

Fred nodded, smiling. She broke off a piece of her muffin and chewed slowly.

The guy took a large bite of his sandwich, gulped his latte. He had a dollop of ketchup mixed with mayonnaise on his chin.

"So," he said, "you want to *help*, huh?"

"Yeah," Fred said.

The guy took another large bite. "You're a writer?" he said.

"I am," Fred said. She thought maybe she should say that she was sorry.

"We're focused on the river. You know our local congressperson, Mast? He's fucking useless."

Fred nodded, pretending she knew more about the local politics than she did. She thought that most days she was an aware person, she read the news, engaged—like picking at a scab—with all the various horrors of the world: floods and fires, fascists. When people asked her how she was, she shook her head and looked down, apologetic, *in spite of all of it*, etc., she muttered, *I'm okay*. And then she interacted with people like this, and she felt like our parents.

"It's hard to get anybody around here to give a shit," the guy said.

Fred knew Barb and her friends organized beach cleanups and wrote letters. She wondered if this kid made up the whole of what the website called a *coalition*, thought of Brooke again. She wanted a clear task, a goal, to prove her efficacy somehow.

"I thought I could, you know . . . narrative can sometimes engender action." She felt her body curdle even at the sound of this last phrase. Did she actually believe this? She watched the guy's face to see if he did.

"We want more people to pay attention. Last month, we delivered Tupperware tubs of algae-filled river water to every local legislator, every local news station. The dams can be disrupted." He looked at the table closest to them, where an older couple had just sat down. "I can get more granular, if you're up for it, on Signal."

Fred nodded.

He appraised her. "Just no *hope, change* shit, or whatever," he said. "There is no hope. Humanity is a failed experiment."

"Do you really believe that?" Fred asked.

The guy laughed.

Fred clutched the gun inside her bag. She wouldn't, she thought, pull it out, but it was a comfort to touch it. For all the ways this guy was likely able to see through her, he couldn't possibly imagine that she also had that gun.

"Look around," the guy said. "Show me the hope."

In college, Fred wrote her senior thesis on Virginia Woolf and Nietzsche. Specifically, she wrote about their approaches to death. Hope, said Nietzsche (I was the only one of us who read the thesis), is the worst of all the evils, because it *prolongs the torments of man*.

"Why do this, then?" Fred said.

"I want to act," the guy said. "Not hope."

Fred nodded, clutching again at the weight of the gun in her bag. She had at first been a philosophy major, added English the same year she'd started more rigorous therapy. People without hope, said Flannery O'Connor, don't write novels. Fred wondered if this was also why she'd stopped.

Fred left the guy, her coffee half-drunk, the bottom of her muffin a pile of crumbles on the plate. *Let's be in touch soon*, she'd said, without giving him her number.

She drove west and then kept driving. So many of the places she remembered as wild swampland were now razed. She thought of Tess, of David, the endlessness of the destruction, the heat and smell of that kid, with his not-bad essay about his grandpa, sitting close to her and quoting her own words back to her. She thought of Faulkner and those vultures. She thought of Woolf, who put rocks in her coat two months after her fifty-ninth birthday, two years after Hitler invaded Poland, and drowned herself. Over that last bridge, Fred thought, *what would it feel like*—turning the wheel a hard right, fast into the concrete barrier, down into the water; no want, no need, no envy.

Of course, I think, she wouldn't do it. She thought about it the way sometimes people do: a quick burst, the thrill, the rush and shock of imagining an end. What she yearned for was someone who would see her want to do it, who would beg her to come to them; she wanted a mom to tell her everything would be okay.

Mom was dead, of course, but let's say Mom called her. Let's say Fred heard Mom's voice, that somehow Fred conjured Mom next to her in that car. Woolf said (and this was also in Fred's thesis) the dead *slip like a knife through everything*. Maybe, that car, that day, Mom did. Her own mother, our grandmother, had only let Mom have a peach for dinner on the days she had a big lunch, always made Mom feel less pretty than her younger sister, made Mom feel, her whole life, like she was not quite good or right enough. But she also fought for our mom to attend the nearby all-girls private school they couldn't afford, where Mom got made fun of for her homemade polyester clothes and graduated early to escape. In the time that she was there, let's say Mom was assigned *King Lear* (she was). Let's pretend that Mom slipped into that car, Fred thinking of her, and Mom—because she was made up, remember, so she could do this—offered Fred that quote from *King Lear*'s Edgar that Fred had tacked to the wall in their New York apartment: "The worst is not/ so long as we can say 'this is the worst.'"

In real life, even though Mom wanted nothing more than to give us exactly what we needed, she often didn't quite know how. But let's say, in that car, that day, Mom did.

Fred did not turn the car, hit the concrete, drown. She drove straight instead, past the streets I used to drive to get to the barn where I rode horses. Past the first expanse of swamp close to the house she'd tried to convince David to buy. She stopped and looked out for more vultures, an alligator, a heron, any sign of wildness, picked up her phone, found the email address for Lucia, the surrogacy book woman. She read through the contract, photos, timeline, payments.

I'm so sorry, she wrote to Lucia.

Free, she whispered to herself once more, just to make sure. She thought of lying, saying something came up, but then thought better of it.

I can't, she wrote. She signed her name and pressed send.

She put her windows down and drove toward the ocean, hot, wet air on her bare face. Jewel's "Pieces of You" wailed from the stereo. Fred said, "This is the worst," and then, maybe, she laughed.

AUGUST

1

Jenn called me on the way to the hospital, but I'd gone for a walk, silenced my phone and didn't answer. She called three more times, and on the fourth call, I picked up.

"Dad's in the hospital," she said. One of her toddlers was screaming in the background. I heard one of the teenagers tell the toddler to *please shut up*.

I took the subway home and showered, packed, called Cass and Brian. Found a flight, ordered a car, grabbed the weed gummies that my now ex-girlfriend, Molly, had left in an upper cabinet in the kitchen. Flew home.

Jenn sent Anelise to come get me.

"Hey, Aunt Jude," my niece said, idling by the curb at the Palm Beach airport: hair up, cutoff shorts and a pale-blue sleeveless shirt. Back straight, so grown-up. Of course I thought of Cass.

"You hanging in there, kid?" I said.

She nodded, solemn, both hands on the wheel, careful as she merged onto the interstate. "Mom is freaking out," she said. "But, like, she loves to freak out."

I watched this drive I'd done a thousand times, the clumps of palm tree farms, a manmade lake, sun-bleached stretches of thinly bladed grass. I could see the wind pick up on the trees' branches as clouds blew in, the sky got dark.

"You want me to drive?" I said to Anelise as the drops began to pound. Her windshield wipers began to whish quickly back and forth.

"No offense, Aunt Jude," she said. "But my dad says you and Mom and Uncle George are all terrible drivers."

I liked Adam well enough. He seemed defined, most of all, by his ability and willingness to fall in line with whatever Jenn decreed. Brian had the same complaint about our driving. We weren't great. It wasn't about gender; Dad and George were also terrible.

"How's Cass?" Anelise asked.

"You might know better," I said. I'd asked Cass if she wanted to come with me when I called her. "I have soccer," she said. She was at Brian's another week but was working out each morning with a trainer Posey had found and paid for. She had to be up at campus two weeks early for preseason training. I knew she felt behind because of me. I'd held off for years on sports. I'd held off because I'd hated what sports were when we were kids.

My dad's in the hospital, I didn't say. "Of course," I said. "Good luck with it."

"Mom?" she said, with what might have been the barest hint of sorry; hard-fought, long-held ambivalence briefly shifting. "Call me, okay?"

"Okay," I'd said, and got in two more *I love you*s before we'd hung up.

Anelise looked at me, appraising, careful. "She seems good," she said about Cass.

"How are you?" I said.

"Oh, you know," she said.

"I don't know!"

"Bullshit junior-year stuff already starting."

"You still swimming?" All Jenn's kids, past the age of six, played at least one sport very seriously.

"We trained all summer."

"Sounds fun," I said.

She shrugged.

We'd left the storm behind us. The rain had spat and slapped, and then we'd gotten off the highway. The clouds shifted, revealing a patch of blue; the wipers scraped against the now dry windshield. We passed the old trails where Fred and Jenn used to run cross country, the tennis courts, the Wendy's, then the new developments, our old high school. I could feel my body shifting and reacting, the strange fact of all of this here as it had always been, same and same and wholly different.

"Welcome home, Aunt Jude!" Anelise said.

"Home," I said, smiling at her, trying out the feel of it.

2

"A car accident," Fred said when we got to the hospital. She didn't try to touch me. I had not returned her phone calls in over eight months.

Jenn had three of her kids and two cell phones and was yelling at the nurses. Dad had broken his collarbone and elbow, fractured a tibia. He had a black eye from the airbag but was better than any of us had feared.

George showed up with Maeve. They'd been at the beach. He smelled like rum and salt, and both he and Maeve had wet hair.

Fred looked silently at them and shook her head.

Dad appeared to be on some particularly strong painkillers, which meant his jokes had gotten worse, and every person in and out of his room seemed either amused or annoyed by him.

That he was neither alcoholic nor suicidal while also technically inhabiting the attributes of both was something no one said.

"Dad's alive!" Jenn said. "It's all fine! That car is too big."

We all looked at one another. No one mentioned that this made no sense.

Jenn handed me the toddler she'd been holding and went to get a coffee.

"Who's going to take care of him?" Fred said.

We looked at George, whose hair was still wet, his shirt clinging to his damp torso. I realized Maeve had slipped away without saying goodbye to any of us.

No one knew that I was currently unemployed. "I can stay through the week," I said.

"I can too," Fred said. "I'm not doing anything."

Jenn took me aside later, Anelise down the hall flirting with a resident. "We obviously can't trust either of them," Jenn said, meaning George and Fred. She'd stepped out to organize a car rental.

"Agreed," I said.

Jenn helped Dad with all the discharge papers. He hadn't yet switched his emergency contact or his power of attorney; no one had been able to get in touch with Jenn until after he had woken up and given a nurse the passcode to his phone and told them to call her. The hospital wanted to keep him another couple nights, but he and Jenn had both refused. He had to sign more papers to say he understood that he was leaving against medical advice.

"You're sure, Dad?" I said, as Jenn explained to the doctor that he was fine, that we would watch him, that he couldn't *just sit there* another couple nights.

"Jude, don't," Jenn said.

We took him home.

3

Libby lost her mind when we got to the house. Dad, scooting around on the wheelie padded knee support they'd given him to take pressure off his tibia, tried to lean down to settle her and almost fell face-first onto the plastic wood.

"Dad!" George and I said.

"She wants to be picked up!" Dad said.

George tried to scoop Libby into his arms, but she yapped at him, tried again to leap toward Dad. George finally picked her up, and she nipped at him. "Stop it!" he said, too loud, angry.

"She's upset!" Dad said.

"Since when do you care?" George said.

I glared at him.

"He hates dogs!" George said.

"I hate mess," Dad said. "Libby doesn't make a mess."

Dad wheeled himself toward his room. I found clothes for him. If Mom were there, she would have made him *shower off that awful hospital* before getting in their bed, but Dad was less horrified by the idea of germs than Mom. Also, the painkillers seemed still not to have worn off. I found him a soft button-up to pull over his taped collarbone, helped him pull loose, light pants over the cast that ran halfway up his calf. He smelled like hospital but also something rank and desperate. I wrapped my arm around his waist as he settled into bed.

"Judith, I am not your baby," he said. He pushed at my hand and I stood back.

George made both of us a drink, and we sat out by the pool, bare feet in up past our calves. Fred had offered to come back with us, but we'd refused her. I was annoyed, sitting now alone with Georgie, that she hadn't forced herself on us.

The moon was visible above the river, almost full, and there was a sound of rustling in the few clumps of mangroves that Dad hadn't had illegally removed. The drink that George had made was too sweet, gin and tonic instead of the gin and soda with a lime that I preferred. It was August, and the air was thick and warm. George swirled his feet, and I swirled mine, and the water spread out in concentric circles. Portions of us—our elbows as we lifted our drinks, our faces as one or the other of us leaned forward—spread in flashes across the surface of the pool.

"Maeve, huh?" I said finally.

He took a last sip of his drink and dipped his hand into the water. "We went swimming a few times," he said.

"Is that some euphemism I should know?" I said.

"We went to the beach a couple times."

"Did you fuck her?"

"Jesus, Judith."

I took my feet out of the water and pulled my knees up to my chest.

"We just swam," he said.

I looked at him, my brother. When Fred and Jenn had gone to college, the pressure, the attention, had shifted to us. All those dinners:

how was track tennis debate class your math test paper class rank. George sneaking into my room at night—ten, eleven, twelve—scared of the cavernousness of the house: the big windows, the big balcony. I would leave him only two years after Fred left us. Who can say what happened to him when he was left inside all that empty, open space all by himself.

George looked toward the water and said again that he and Maeve had only swum.

"And Allie?" I said.

"Fucking her boss," George said.

"Oh," I said.

"Yeah."

He took off his shirt and eased his way into the pool. I laughed at him but then decided to take off my pants and dive in too. I swam one long lap in my shirt and bra and underwear, the water colder than I'd thought it would be. George tried to lie back, arms out, and I swam up next to him.

"How's Cass," he said, "Poop Mom?"

When she was younger, Cass'd had chronic bouts of constipation. Straight to nine or ten, she would cry and grunt and sit stuck on the toilet, sometimes for hours. Big red blotches on her soft baby skin when she got off. I would sit next to her, on the floor or on the bathroom counter, hold her hand and remind her to breathe and to relax. In almost every other situation, she preferred Brian, but she held tight to me then. Sometimes, if too much time had passed and she got desperate enough, she'd let me reach up into her rectum and pull out the poop. *Judith*, George had said, when I first explained this to him, *that is really fucking gross.* But she was my kid.

Days after, I'd be doing something—gesturing while talking to a client, opening a door, washing my hands—and I'd glimpse my fingers and remember that they'd cupped a hard hunk of shit. When Brian and I split and Cass was at his house half the time, if and when the poop thing happened, even late at night or early in the morning, Cass would make Brian call me, and I'd come.

"No more Poop Mom," I said, feeling my voice break. I looked past George toward the dock. "My kid's all grown up." All those last times you never know are last times. All those late nights sitting next to her, so worried, feeling my whole body pushing, as if I could somehow help her get it out. The doctors all said it was nerves, nothing mechanical; I found her a therapist. It stopped within a year of Brian's new marriage. I hadn't sat with her like that in years.

George and I climbed out of the pool and sat at the edge again, feet back in the water. My face reflected wavily back at me as I leaned forward, crossed my arms, sipped the last of my sweet drink.

"I follow her on Instagram," George said.

"Of course you do," I said, flicking water at him.

"Hey!" he said, flicking water back.

"You understand you're in your thirties?"

"I think Jenn's kids think I'm embarrassing."

"All grown-ups are embarrassing to kids."

"How are you, though?" he said. "Jude. Really."

"You know," I said. I was infinitely better at keeping secrets than he was. "I miss my kid. I go to work."

"Don't worry, Jude," George said. "You'll always be Poop Mom to me."

4

The next morning, Maeve showed up at Fred's. She had an opening shift at Bonefish, and she needed Fred to watch Tallulah. Maeve didn't want to have to go there, didn't want to talk about George. But Liz and her mom were both working, and she couldn't call in sick.

Fred had run a quick eight miles before sunrise. She'd texted with Fanny about finding her more work, had texted George and me (I didn't answer) to ask us about Dad. She didn't want Maeve to come over, knew she had no right to be angry. She was both annoyed and confused. Maeve didn't belong to her. They were grown-ups, in their forties. But she couldn't help but hate that they hadn't told her. She didn't want Maeve to love George more.

I knew plenty about this part of Freddy. *Why do you always take their side?* she'd said.

"Lu, Lu, Lu," Fred said, when Maeve came around back and Tallulah came to hug her.

"Fred, Fred, Fred," Tallulah said.

"How's your dad?" Maeve said.

"Fine, I think," Fred said. "Jude and George took him home."

"You okay?" Maeve said.

Fred shrugged. She watched Tallulah change into her swimsuit right next to the place where the raccoons had stood and watched Fred fall face-first into that rancid meat a few nights before.

"You're hurt?" Maeve said.

Fred looked down at her scraped legs, but Maeve's gaze didn't follow. She meant George.

"You know, I read your books," Maeve said. She hadn't meant to say this. "A couple years ago. After the last one came out and I'd been clean a while." She'd found them at the library when she was there for one of those baby singalong classes with Tallulah where the women passed around noisemakers and all the older people who'd come to the library for the quiet shushed them loudly.

Fred felt her face get hot. "You never said."

"I didn't want to talk about it, I don't think."

Every time Fred put out a new book, every time she sent an early draft to her agent or her editor, a friend, she would wait for someone to point out that always somewhere in there was the same storyline of one friend, a family member, loved one, who was an addict (person with substance use disorder). (The review of her fourth book had called this character "a druggy," and Fred had been so furious she hadn't even noticed the review was good). It was *narratively useful*, all that recklessness embodied, when Fred's own life experience had often hewed too closely to hard lines drawn almost at random but with an eye toward always staying in control.

"I wasn't upset. It was so clear it wasn't about me," Maeve said. "Not even when I recognized it was me. You got all of it so wrong."

Fred thought of T. S. Eliot: *That is not it at all.*

"I was some metaphor for how dangerous you felt life was, or whatever," Maeve said. "It was all about you, whatever shit you were trying to work out. Which is fine, really. I don't really care about that. I do want you to know, though: I'm grateful for the ways you've helped us, and I like you, Freddy, but you don't know anything about me. You don't know anything about what my life has been."

Fred fixed her eyes on Tallulah's body moving underwater, head popping up from underneath the surface, diving down again.

"I used to be jealous of you," Maeve said. "Your fucking fancy college. Your fucking fancy stupid car, your house. People pay you money to write novels. You married David fucking Doyle. But you're so busy being sad about whatever you're so sad about. You go swimming all day. You have more time than I do to hang out with my kid."

Three stories about Maeve that Fred had never told: once a week, from twenty-eight to thirty-two, she fucked a guy we knew from high school who had since become an aide to our (former) local congressperson and was, both then and now, married with three kids. For an hour, in the ocean apartment he owned and kept as a rental property, he did whatever he wanted with his body to hers. In exchange, he gave her money that she used as her weekly budget for pills. He'd been mean to her in high school and he wasn't nice to her those days they met and fucked. She'd been his bartender at the hotel bar out by the beach, and he'd given her his number, tipped her well. She'd never before fucked a guy for money, but he'd thought he'd seen it in her, and she'd decided he was right. Maeve hated everything about this guy she fucked in this apartment filled with Florida kitsch, air conditioner on too high and always smelling slightly moldy, old shitty boogie boards out on the tiny balcony. But knowing what he wanted, and then giving it, every time: there was an ease and clarity, a comfort to it, that, even now, she missed.

For three and a half months, the last year she lived in Arizona, Maeve went to school to become a dental hygienist. She'd been clean the whole six months before that, had broken up with the boyfriend with whom she'd moved out there, spent thirty days inpatient, then found an apartment with the rehab's help. Alone for the first time in her life, she had a little whiteboard on her fridge where she made lists of groceries, work shifts, school assignments, tests, her monthly budget. Her mom had paid for her to get three root canals and three crowns the year before, and the hygienist, Ashley, had held her hand through all of it. Maeve had filled out the forms, turned her application in, while tending bar six nights a week. She'd sent her mom the acceptance email, even though it was a for-profit college and everyone got in. She took out a bunch of high-interest loans and cut her hours back to three nights, stayed up studying head and neck anatomy, did practice cleanings, ashamed and sorry the day she'd had canned tuna for lunch right before the only friend she'd made in school had to spend an hour inside her mouth with a mirror and a water flosser. She recited words like *stylopharyngeus* and *cricophyrangeus* to herself as she did the dishes, cleaned the bathroom, poured happy-hour beers. But then she got one B and three Cs, and the teacher she liked the most called her into her office and told her she had to *really buckle down* if this was what she wanted. She was already buckling, already exhausted, already owed too much on the loans and was about to have to apply for another round. Instead of buckling down, she dropped out.

The last story was that Maeve had not stopped using until after giving birth. She had wanted to be better. (Fred hadn't ever told this story because she'd wanted Maeve to be better too; because it felt too hard and sad and she didn't trust herself to understand it well enough to render it well.) Maeve'd felt sure, the first three months, she would stop using. But the father was some younger guy she'd waited tables with an hour north, and after she told him, he asked her not to ever contact him again. *I can't have a baby with some old addict*, he said. *You sure, you know, it's possible for you?* Maeve was forty but looked older. She'd terminated three pregnancies in the last two decades, had never meant for all that time to pass. She went out that night and shot up. Tallulah wasn't yet Tallulah. She was a weird feeling in Maeve's belly, a bunch of fear, frustration, anger. Maeve got high a few more times and then stopped going to the doctor. Tallulah came out via C-section, and a scowly nurse came in and told Maeve that they were legally bound not to let Maeve leave with her own kid. So then Maeve's mom came, crying and then yelling, swearing up and down that she would not ever let Maeve have Tallulah if she didn't get her shit together, if she didn't promise, swear on hands and knees. Maeve vomited and shook as her mother made her look at baby Tallulah, sallow, wan and too thin, one day old and in withdrawal: *This is what you did*, she said.

"I'm not mad, Fred," Maeve said now, shaking her head. "It's just, all the books are so fucking *angsty*. And the way you mope around here. I just need you to know how good your actual, real life has been."

5

For a week, we ministered to Dad. Jenn and Fred came over every day. It felt weird and also not weird at all. There was something elemental, calm and easy, about all of us being together. The way Jenn swept in, often with at least three of her kids, brought groceries, bossed all of us around. Fred laughing at her, but also playing with and entertaining whichever of the kids were in tow. *No one is going in that pool while we're here*, Jenn said. *Why not?* Fred said, a little whiny. *Do not test my patience, Winnifred*, Jenn said.

The days and nights that Fred came, she and I talked only when we absolutely had to. She tried, sometimes, to press further, but I'd shut down, turn away: *Do you know where this goes? Can you pass the olive oil? You have eyes on the baby?*

I watched her much more closely when I thought she couldn't see. It was hard to ignore her, to treat her coldly. I wanted to take her aside and whisper to her about Dad, about George, about Jenn, to take the kids out back with her and play and swim.

George offered to help but mostly sat and scrolled his phone, watched whatever was on TV: sports, finance shows. He snacked on the chips and salsa Jenn brought, took Libby to play outside with the kids. *We got it, Georgie*, Jenn said, if and when he offered to do more. *Maybe you could see if Dad needs anything? Maybe you could sit and talk to him?*

———

No one talked about what had happened to us in the past several weeks. Not about Dad's accident, or Mom. Jenn tut-tutted; Dad complained. *Stop talking to me about fresh air, Jenny; if you're over here to help, I don't understand why there's always so much mess.* On the phone with his secretary, searching again for his reading glasses, finding and wearing Mom's instead. He kept pushing back appointments because Jenn told him he had to. He looked at Fred only from a safe and certain distance, warily.

Jenn cleaned at least one room every time she got there: the kitchen, the living room, Dad's bathroom. I folded all the laundry that George and Dad had left in piles on the dryer. Mom's perfume still stunk up the master bathroom, and even though there were five other bathrooms, we all seemed to find ourselves in there. Remnants of Mom were all over the house: the Carr's crackers and Nutri-Grain granola bars that we all liked in high school in the pantry; extra tubes of her favorite lipstick in the first mudroom drawer, another in the kitchen—I'd take it out sometimes and take off the top, smear a little on my finger, rub the waxy sheen along the outside of my hand. Clothes and shoes still in her closet; three books, all thrillers, on the table by her bed. Twice, I took her car out late at night, her smell in the seat's creases. I drove along the water with the top down, music on too loud, that heavy, breezy ocean air.

In the week I was home, Fred twice more drove out west of town with the gun. She'd park the car and walk a long time, gun in her pocket, in search of woods or swamp. Sometimes. she parked at that old house she'd tried to convince David they should buy. Twice, she got her shoes stuck in the mud; once, she almost lost a flip-flop. She sweated through her shirt and pants, the temperature a good five to seven degrees warmer this far from the ocean air. It was different from the running: slower, quiet, much less pounding, harder to drown out the sounds of her own thoughts. She'd stop to take pictures of the way the light looked between the trees, glinting off the shallow stretches of swampy water. Once, walking along a path next to a large expanse of swamp, she saw the slap of alligator tail and then its big body slither, its jaw open, watched it pull a great blue heron down into the water: a desperate squawk and screech from the bird, the snap of teeth, and then a settling, the swamp still.

She went twice more to Busch Wildlife. After their last conversation, Maeve had caved and asked her mom to watch Tallulah. Fred stood alone and watched the same kid feed the eagles, watched the vultures swoop in. She thought of asking if she could have some of the carrion to take home, if she could work for them. What she really wanted was to have the thing that someone was starved for, give it to them, clean and easy. She watched the girl feed Alligator Fred and stood a long time in the shade watching the big limbs of the panthers and the bears, watching their bellies rise and fall.

On the fourth day, every shared room had gotten a deep clean. Jenn and I had both made separate trips to the grocery store: Jenn for food she thought Dad would eat, me for food that all of us might actually enjoy. At the store, I'd run into one of Jenn's old high school math teachers; she'd thought at first that I was Jenn and then apologized, *Fred! Of course! The writer! Nope*, I said, laughing, *the other one.* She stood quiet a long time, her face reddening. *Judith*, I said. *Of course!* she said, pushing her cart away fast.

———

Jenn wanted all of us to sit down and talk about Dad's birthday. She wanted a party. He'd be seventy-four two weeks from the day he'd crashed his car into a pole and almost exactly a month after Mom died.

"I think maybe we skip the birthday party this year," Fred said.

"Of course you do," Jenn said. "Of course you don't care."

Fred hated parties because Mom loved them. Jenn loved them, just like Mom.

"He just got out of the hospital," Fred said.

"A party is exactly what he needs," said Jenn.

"He's barely mobile," George said. I was impressed to see him talking back to Jenn.

"We'll keep it just us," Jenn said, looking only at me now. "A few presents, a cake."

"I could make a dinner," Fred said.

Jenn's mouth fell open.

"I cook now," Fred said.

"She's good," George said, eyeing me.

"I'm sure," Jenn said.

"Just the five of us is easy," Fred said. "I can do a cake, too, if you want?"

"Oh no!" Jenn said. "I'll do that!"

"Let's do it at your house, then," I said, turning to Fred. I didn't mean for it to come out as accusation. I didn't mean to look at her as long as I did.

"It's not her house," Jenn said.

"I'm happy to have it at the house I'm borrowing," said Fred.

"Anelise wants to have friends over that night anyway," Jenn said. "Fred as hostess! What a treat!" Neither the shape of her face nor the sound of her voice said she believed that it would be.

6

That night, after Jenn and Fred left, George and I sat and drank outside in the Adirondack chairs. The storm that day had been the best since I got there, long and loud and violent. Leaves and branches floated in the pool.

"What is it people do here?" I said.

"Swim?" he said. "Surf?"

"You been doing a lot of either of those things?" I said.

"I have the code for the tennis courts," he said.

George and I were the tennis players in our family. Jenn and Fred were faster, but neither could make contact with a ball with either a racket or a foot.

"Why not?" I said, getting up to find some shorts, my shoes, a bra.

We found old rackets in the garage, the handle tape half-stripped. George found a can of balls in the closet in the laundry room. I was a little dizzy from the drink that George had made me, from making awkward conversation with Dad while we ate the chicken Parmesan that he'd requested, that had not tasted anything at all like Mom's.

George and I walked the quarter mile to the tennis courts owned by the neighborhood association. "Are we going to get arrested?" I whispered.

"Likely not?" George said and smiled. He looked behind us, pressed the keypad four times, and the gate opened. "I know a guy," he said, smiling again.

George served to me, and we hit back and forth without talking. I missed near everything he passed to my backhand. I got him closer to the net with a drop shot twice, and both times he hit the ball out of bounds.

"Game?" he said, holding the ball up again to serve it.

"Your funeral," I said.

He laughed.

His serve was sharper than his earlier attempts. He grunted as his racket made whacking contact with the ball, and I leapt too late and the ball whooshed past me.

"Fifteen-love," George said.

I muttered *fuck* and felt my body tighten and hunch over. He served, I hit it back, he hit back, I backhanded tight and close up at the net, and he lobbed the ball out of bounds.

"Asshole," he said, throwing down his racket. Then he picked it up and walked back to the baseline. "Fifteen all."

Another ace, and then another point by me because he hit my return too hard. A point for him, and then deuce and then advantage me and then I won.

"Fuck you, Jude!" he said.

"Try harder," I said.

It was dark but still warm and humid. Sweat trickled down my back, on the sides of my face, between my breasts.

He hit my serve back hard and got the first point. I served softer, and he misread it and hit the ball out and it was fifteen-love. I won again, and we went to 2-0, and his face looked bright red even in the moonlight. He leaned over briefly, hands on his knees. I stood up straight, hands on my hips.

"You okay?" I said.

"Fucking awesome," said George, standing up and pulling at his shirt.

He had three aces, and we went to 2-1. I felt the prickle on my skin, wanting to win. My drink rose up in my throat, the taste of mozzarella, red sauce.

"Fucking chicken Parm," I said, bouncing the ball before I served the fourth game.

"Just serve, Jude," George said.

I did.

We went to 3-1 and then 3-2, and I could feel my heartbeat in my toes and arms and ankles. I could feel it in my head, white-hot, covered in sweat. I hadn't run this much in who knew how long. George was panting, wiping his face with his shirt, wiping his hands on his shorts.

"We could call it, Georgie," I said.

"Fuck that," he said.

"Fine," I said.

I won the next game and made some dumb joke about his needing to do more conditioning in Houston. He threw his racket again.

"I think I'm done now," I said.

"You have to let me come back," he said. "Two more sets."

"Georgie," I said. He was still panting. My head ached.

"Fine," he said. "You forfeit; I win."

"You're kidding, right, George?" I said.

"You don't finish the match, then you forfeit."

"This isn't a match, George. It's just . . ." I stopped.

He'd leaned over again, hands on his knees. His racket was still on the court, maybe twisted from the second time he'd thrown it.

"All right," I said. "I forfeit. Let's go back."

I went and got his racket, picked up all the balls. George sat down on the court and leaned against the chain-link fence. I set down the rackets and sat down next to him.

"Good game," I said, my hand on his back.

"Ha," he said.

"You okay?" I said.

He shook his head, wiped his face again with his shirt.

"Don't die," I said.

He looked at me, laughed, leaned back. "I'll do my best."

We were quiet a long time while our breathing slowed. At last, I got up and offered him my hand.

"I'm disgusting," he said.

"Georgie," I said.

"I am," he said.

I shook my head.

We walked back to the house in silence. I led him around to the back, and we stripped off our shirts, went for a swim.

"I'm glad I'm mostly able to forget how much I miss this," I said.

"You could come back here," he said.

"Georgie," I said. "You're fucking nuts."

"Everything's remote now. Cass has left the nest."

"I have a life in New York."

"Please, Jude—what life? Waiting anxiously for a text or call from Cass?"

I swam from him without talking, did four laps, fast, as he lay his head back. I hauled myself out of the pool and walked back to the outside shower. Water scalding, I let the burn of it hit hard on my face and back. I wrapped a towel back around me and found George still by the pool, his shirt back on.

"I think I'll go in and check on Dad," I said.

I stood a long time in the doorway, Libby lifting her head from her perch at Dad's feet, Mom's glasses perched on Dad's side of the bed.

"I'm okay, Jude," Dad said, unmoving. "Go sleep now."

7

The next night, Fred came for dinner. Dad was wheeling around more and more easily on his scooter; Libby had figured out how to walk close to him without getting her tail caught under its wheels. Jenn had brought over a big lasagna and salad from the Olive Garden but had left to bring the other two lasagnas she'd picked up to her kids. We sat inside because Dad didn't feel up to outside. It was close to 90 degrees, and the sun had not set yet, and Dad hated the wind.

I got plates, and Fred served, and George brought everybody waters, made himself and me and Dad drinks. I got napkins and forks and watched Dad watch how much more chaos we were than Mom.

"You kids," he said. He had been saying it a lot. We'd waited, the first couple times, for him to finish the sentence, but the statement always stopped there. "You kids . . ." as if whatever complicated things he thought about us, that long gape of silence, the slight tinge of accusation, held it best.

"I've got this app on my phone," Fred said. She was talking about running. Dad loved talking about running.

"The New York time was really something," Dad said, about Fred's last marathon (2:54).

I wondered, watching him watch her, his face lit up, what it might feel like to press slowly and steadily on his still-fractured collarbone. I shook it off.

"George said you don't write anymore," I said, instead, to Fred.

"I'm trying to figure out what else I am," Fred said.

I flipped open my lasagna, picking through the ricotta in search of meat chunks.

"You will, Freddy," Dad said, so sweet and earnest that some of the pasta and mozzarella, a little bit of chewed-up breadstick, rose up in my throat.

"We're all so very proud of you, Fred," I said, the condescension so thick even I felt sorry.

"You kids . . ." Dad said. And Georgie and I, Fred too—we laughed.

Fred left Mom and Dad's house without any of us hugging, without any of us touching. Mom had been the only one of us to hug consistently, though her hugs were so tight they felt likely to crack a rib.

Fred drove straight from Mom and Dad's to David's. She climbed through his window, took her clothes off, pressed his shoulders down onto the bed with both her hands.

She had not talked to Maeve since that conversation about her books.

Fred went for longer and longer runs even though her app told her to go shorter, told her to take rest days, to cross train; she'd gotten up to ten to fifteen miles a day, six days a week, often barefoot in the sand. Her knees and back, her shins and quadriceps all hurt. She woke up hungry in the middle of the night, boiled a handful of eggs each morning to have on hand for snacks throughout the day.

She'd gotten two more tutoring clients, had gone to help Brooke three more times. Ellen had twice asked her to "catch up," and though Fred had declined, when Ellen asked her a third time, it was after Brooke had written a draft so good that Fred felt obligated to tell Ellen about it. Fred felt hungry, tired, desperate. Ellen was so eager, grabbing at Fred's elbow as she walked her down the driveway, kissing Brooke on the forehead and Fred turning so as not to have to see Brooke flinch. Fred said yes because the idea of making Ellen happy, saying to her how impressed she was by her kid: Fred knew it would feel good.

8

I was sorry to hear about your mom," said Ellen. She wore a thin cardigan, had served them both tart, cold glasses of iced tea mixed with lemonade.

Oh no, thought Fred. *Not this.*

"You know," said Ellen. "My first marriage . . ."

The internet had not told Fred that Ellen had been married once before.

"Brooke has a different dad," Ellen said. "Your mom . . ."

Fred looked past her to the water, watched a heron glide by, tried to see if there was any algae, thought of asking Ellen if she was as worried about the river as her kid was.

"Your mom was my lawyer," Ellen said. "He didn't even want Brooke. Mike." The name fell out into the air as Ellen stiffened, her face suddenly a different level of alert, on guard. "He wanted to hurt me at any cost."

Ellen then, back to that night: gun on her lap, thinking maybe the best thing was to use it on herself instead of on her husband, maybe, her finger on the cold spring of the trigger, the only thing to do was to set all of them free. Except most of her life, she'd lived without a mother. *Brooke, Brooke, Brooke,* she thought. She put the gun back in the drawer, stood and watched her daughter sleep.

The next day, when Mike left for work, Ellen took Brooke to Mom's office. Twenty-three years old and a wife and mother, terrified. The receptionist was brusque, a clutch of silver bangles on both wrists that clanked when she set the phone down. *You need an appointment,* she said. *I don't,* Ellen began. Brooke knocked over a stack of *People* magazines on one of the coffee tables. *Uh-oh,* she said, grinning, looking at her mother.

I know Fred, said Ellen. *Her daughter.* Ellen and Fred had spoken twice in high school. They'd taken debate together but never once spoken in class; Fred sat in front and talked and gestured, Ellen sat in back and whispered with a friend. The two times they'd spoken had been: once, in line for a pep rally, when Ellen had lost the friend she'd come with and asked Fred if she'd seen her friend; once, both drunk at a party junior year, when Ellen did a keg stand and Fred vomited an hour later in a planter next to the pool and Ellen had asked her quickly, briefly, hand on her back, if she was okay.

What Ellen could not have known but the secretary did (her name was Joanne; she worked there thirty years, retired six months before Mom died) was that Fred wasn't speaking to Mom that day Ellen came to Mom's office. It was their first stretch of estrangement, had lasted close to a year. Joanne looked at Ellen and then at Brooke. *Let me see something,* said Joanne. She got up. *Stay here.*

Fifteen minutes, she said, when she came back. *She has a window. Fifteen minutes, and then she's due in court.*

Ellen, honey! Mom said, competent, put together, her blazer, her skirt, click-clack heels. *Come with me, sweetheart.*

"I was so scared," Ellen said now to Fred.

———

It was three full years of battles, failed mediations, threats, restraining orders, training his two older kids to testify against her, fifty-fifty custody for almost a year. Ellen had no job at first, no money. Mom instructed her to transfer as much money as she could out of their shared account before she left, but the daily limit for withdrawals was five thousand dollars, and Mike checked their accounts regularly, monitored Ellen's credit cards and scolded her the months he thought she spent too much.

She packed up the same day she took out the money. Her father had cried quietly, happily, he told her, when she'd called and asked if she and Brooke could move in with him. She left Brooke with him that day, and he called twice, when she fell down in his driveway and scraped her knee, when she refused to nap and ran circles around the bed he'd put her in instead. Ellen packed two bags and put the gun at the bottom of the second. She packed Brooke's clothes, diapers, wipes, her favorite stuffy, special blanket, the plastic truck Brooke's half brothers had picked out for her and that she loved. She packed her cardigans but left the dresses Mike had bought for going out.

She got a job at the café where she used to get Brooke's muffin, her hot coffee. If she thought at all about seeing Parker Monaghan again, she didn't let herself look for him too much at first. Mike found her and he came and sat and watched her. She'd told no one what he'd done. She had to walk around, serve people coffee, muffins, omelets with his eyes on her back, sometimes for hours. At their next appointment, she told Mom about these visits. *That motherfucker*, Mom said. She called his lawyer, right then, Ellen leaning forward, hands on Mom's desk. *You tell that motherfucker I will get so many restraining orders slapped on him he'll have to stay inside his house.*

The gun lived on the top shelf of her childhood closet for the next two years. Mike kept finding new ways to be threatening, teaching Brooke mean things to say to Ellen, idling his car outside her dad's house. Each time, Ellen would tell Mom, and she'd file an order or add another layer of protections or, if those weren't possible, get on the phone and yell at someone. Mediations turned almost immediately to court dates that went terribly, Ellen sobbing afterward in Mom's office. She hadn't seen Mike's boys since the day she left them, and now they were calling her incompetent in court. She hadn't done the things they'd said she'd done, but also, she had left, she had hurt them, nonetheless.

Mom was good at her job, and they appealed the initial ruling for split custody. Mike's first wife had also been appealing her split. He'd drunk too much one night and yelled and thrown and broken three water glasses and a plate, and one of the boys had told.

And then Ellen came out of work one day feeling okay, on her way to okay, wearing a tank top, her hair pulled back. Brooke safe at home with Ellen's dad, who had come to love the time he got to spend with her, who drove her, each day Ellen worked, to and from the day care she went to daily from nine to noon. *You fucking slut*, she heard, and her bones and muscles froze. From behind the truck next to her, she saw him bounding toward her—Ellen frozen—and then Mike's face up close, next to hers. *One night when you're sleeping*, he said, *or maybe in the middle of the day, when you're at work, I'll come take her, and you won't ever find her. I won't ever give her back.* She thought he'd spit on her, hit her. He leaned even closer so that their noses almost touched. He smiled. *You won't ever get her back*, he said again.

Ellen didn't cry and didn't answer her dad's questions when she got home. She picked up Brooke because she wouldn't ever leave Brooke, would quit her job if it meant she had to leave Brooke. She got the gun out of her closet, put it in her purse, and drove to Mom's office. By then, all of her was shaking. Brooke was looking at her warily, wanting to know why they had to go see Mrs. Kenner, why she couldn't stay behind with Grandpa.

Ellen, honey, said Joanne, *she's booked all day.* She looked at Ellen one more time. *Stay here,* she said. Half an hour later: *Ellen, honey, come on back.* By that point, Brooke was tearing out the pages of the *People* magazines, and Ellen's hands were shaking. She was still clutching tightly to her bag. A torrent, then, of what had happened, everything she hadn't told her. Halfway through, Mom stopped her. *Kristen, come here,* she said, summoning her paralegal. *Can you take Brooke and show her where we keep the secret candy stash?* Mom nodded at Ellen to stay seated. *She's okay,* Mom said. *Kristen has three of her own.*

Okay then, Mom said, once Brooke was out. *Start over.* Ellen told her more than she had ever told her, more than she had told anyone, about those nights Mike fucked her, the way her body felt, her skin, the fear, his hands on her, each day inside that house. At some point, she took out the gun, hands still shaking. *I can't,* she said. *I'm scared of what I'll do.*

Honey, Mom said. She took the gun and unlocked her bottom drawer, slipped it in, then closed the drawer again and locked it. *We will get that fucker,* Mom said. *You let me do it, though, okay?*

"I loved her," Ellen said.

Our whole lives, we knew Mom was ruthless. We had—Fred had, I had—not ever wholly registered this part of her as *good,* and it came at Fred now with such force. We'd been on both sides of it. If she was on your team, she could make the perfect case for all the ways that you were gorgeous, brilliant; if she wasn't, she could make just as strong a case for all the ways you were the opposite. You knew, as convincing as one case seemed, the other might come out again at any moment. Looking at this woman, Ellen, trying to ignore the flash of her exposed skin at that high school party, Fred saw what it might have been like to only ever know Mom as someone who was always on your side.

Both of them were quiet a long time, looking at the water.

"She saved my life," Ellen said one more time.

"I was so sad to miss the funeral," said Ellen.

Of course, Jenn and I had written all the thank-you cards, so Fred had failed to notice that one of the largest bouquets at the funeral had been signed, *the Monaghans.*

9

That same night Fred left Ellen's, Maeve called George because her car broke down. George usually kept his phone close by, but as no one ever tried to get in touch with him it was mostly silent, inert on the table until George flipped it to face him so he could scroll, scroll, swipe, scroll. (Brett had, in this time, had five million dollars transferred to George's personal account as "severance," and George didn't know how to feel about that.)

The phone's ring startled both of us; I was sitting there beside George.

"Hey," George said, his voice eager. "You okay?"

I thought of Allie, then looked at the softness of his body, open and unguarded. Not Allie.

"I'll come get you," he said. "Can you drop me a pin?"

He hung up, stood quickly, knocked into the table. His drink spilled, and he muttered *fuck*, and I laughed, stood up, and helped him wipe it clean.

"What's up?" I said.

"Maeve," he said.

I'd never liked Maeve. I didn't know her, had hardly ever spoken to her, so maybe my not liking her seems unfair. But just like Fred, I had gotten good at watching, learning. Just like Fred, I understood the power of secrets kept and shared. Maeve had always felt too reckless. I'd never understood how Fred hadn't seen or known to be afraid.

George, that night: "Maeve's car broke down," he said.

"Where is she?" I said.

He looked at his phone. "Close to the beach."

"She didn't call Fred?" Even as I said it, I realized this was likely not the right thing to say.

"I guess not," George said.

I thought maybe she had called Fred, but Fred hadn't answered. I kept this to myself.

George had had three drinks but had driven plenty after three drinks in his thirty-four years. Dad's accident had made him more cautious than he'd been the week before. He drove a tick or two below the speed limit, got to Maeve ten minutes after she'd called. He hadn't expected that Tallulah'd also be there, but of course she was. He wanted to ask, but didn't, what they'd been doing out by the beach this late at night.

Tallulah and Maeve were playing some clapping, snapping game as he pulled up. The car was visibly smoking, and he thought of whisking them both farther from it quickly. He had a quick flash of the whole car, Tallulah and Maeve too, blowing up.

"I don't know anything about cars," he said as he walked up, nodding toward the smoking hood. "But that looks bad."

Maeve laughed and grabbed hold of Tallulah's hands just as they reached out to slap hers. "Not great," she said.

"Want me to call a tow?" he said, wondering if she had AAA, thinking that she probably didn't, that a tow would cost too much.

"I let the fucking triple A lapse a couple years ago," she said.

"I could cover it," he said.

Maeve pulled Tallulah's car seat from the smoking car and strapped it into the backseat of Mom's convertible. "A lot easier with the top down," she said, lifting Tallulah and strapping her in. "I couldn't pay you back. If you call a tow. I could lie and say I will, but I won't, and I'd be grateful if you would." She double-checked the car seat straps and went back over to the smoking car to get her bag, a stuffed animal, and a book that she handed to Tallulah.

"This car is broken," said Tallulah, hands reaching up to where the ceiling would be.

"Less broken than ours," Maeve said, smiling at George.

George sat up very straight and put on his seat belt. He felt powerful and grown-up. "I can cover the tow," he said.

10

Maeve *had* called Fred first, but Fred hadn't picked up. She'd called George second. She could have called her mother but she'd appreciated, these past few months with Fred, not having to call her mother, or her sister, the same tiny clutch of people she had always called over the years for help. Or maybe it was the opposite: she liked to call her sister, who had three kids and a nice, boring husband; to call her mom, who tried well enough. She liked calling them just to talk, not to ask for a favor.

"I'm coooooool," Tallulah yelled as George drove them back to Dad's house. They needed to be close by for the tow. It was 85 degrees and humid, but windy in the back with the top down. Tallulah wore a short-sleeved shirt and cotton shorts.

"Could we put the top up?" Maeve said. But when George tried at the next light, the car just beeped; the button he was pressing blinked. And then the light turned green, and George's face turned red. He swore under his breath as Tallulah yelled from the backseat, "Mommy, I'm so coooooool."

It was late for a kid, nine o'clock, by the time they got to Dad's. I was outside by the pool. I'd thought George would wait with them by the car for AAA then watch as they drove home themselves.

"Jude!" he called to me in a half yell, half whisper, trying not to wake Dad.

"I want to swim!" Tallulah said.

"Oh, fuck it," Maeve said. "Sure."

Tallulah laughed, peeled off her shirt. We all watched as she dove in. She was small and compact, a short torso, spindly long legs. I thought of Cass, of course; it never stops. I thought of time, how fast and slippery. A friend of mine the one time I cried that I would only ever have her: *You don't want another kid*, she said, *you want Cass infinitely*.

Maeve stood close behind me.

"She's really something," I said.

"It's good to see you, Judith," Maeve said.

I thought: *Really?* But instead, I said, "You too, Maeve."

Tallulah swam down to the bottom of the pool and up again. There were no rings for her to swim for, but she kept swimming down, body stretched and reaching, then back up, then down again.

"You have a daughter," Maeve said. Of course she knew this. We had Fred in common all these years, the internet.

"She's sixteen," I said.

"So big," Maeve said, still looking at Tallulah.

"Impossibly," I said.

"Tow is ordered," George said, coming back toward us. "Guy said forty minutes."

"Thanks," Maeve said.

I watched Maeve look at George, and I looked back toward Tallulah. "I'll go find her a towel," I said, and went into the house.

On the table in the kitchen, my phone was buzzing. *Brian*, it said. *Fuck*, I thought, but also: *Finally, someone from my actual life.*

Brian now, Brian then: I found the barn he worked at my second year of law school. Mom and Dad had said I needed to take out at least half the law-school loans in my own name. I didn't get into any of the big names and went to the University of Florida and mostly hated it. I sat at the front of every class and paid careful, close attention because I wanted to get back to New York—I'd done my undergrad at Barnard. Brian offered me work exercising other people's horses in exchange for more lessons, in exchange for paid time riding. I hadn't ridden all through college. I missed it then, all that power underneath me. I still miss it now. I went out once a week, then three times, then every day.

I stayed late one night after Brian had run a dressage clinic, warmed up and cooled down all the horses while he taught. I was sweaty, worn out, hair in a halfway undone braid. He smelled like Murphy oil soap, that sturdy, solid body. In the tack room, on a bed of saddle pads, we fucked. He very carefully placed my right leg over his shoulder and cupped my ass with his left hand and pressed just so on my clitoris with his right as he moved slowly, carefully inside of me. Retrospectively, the sex was only ever good, but at the time it felt revelatory to not hate every aspect of my body, to see and feel the obvious pleasure he got from me.

I could hardly fathom how or why he wanted to be with me. I'd never felt as good as when Brian shifted my ass in the saddle with the palm of his hand, reminded me to sit up straight. We ran out of condoms. I got pregnant, was about to graduate. No one should make life choices when they're twenty-three, but he, and she, were probably the best I ever made.

My New York internship my second summer had turned into a job offer. Brian found work in Westchester, watched Cass during the week. People said how hard it must be—I went back to work when she was six weeks old, still larval, squirmy—and I nodded and made all the faces I knew they wanted me to make, but I loved putting on clothes every morning, kissing her and kissing Brian goodbye. I was good at what I did.

Sometimes, those years, I'd come home, and Brian would have left dinner out for me, underneath aluminum foil on the counter. Is there dinner? I'd text, hours before I was able to get home. Every night, he'd say. I'd slip off my shoes by the door and eat standing up, pull my hair out of its bun, pull my bra out from underneath my shirt. Some of those nights, I'd walk right past Brian's and my room and curl in with Cass, stretch my body out right next to her in her toddler bed, still wearing my button-up and skirt.

She turned two, then three, then four, then five.

The joke between them was that I worked too much. *Let's put Mommy's computer away*, Brian would say, making a show of handing it to Cass. He still taught lessons on the weekends, but now, often, Cass went with him. He made five hundred dollars a week. We paid four thousand dollars a month in rent. *I never see her*, I said. *What about me?* he said. *You're a grown-up*, I said. We were mostly not having sex. I was tired all the time and failed to listen closely enough to Cass at dinner—about dinosaurs and space when she was seven, about manga and Pokémon when she was eight. *Mom, Mom, Mom, were you listening? Of course, Cass. What did I just say?* I saw her look at Brian. *I'm just tired, Cassie. You're always tired.*

I never thought to stop. I made good money, except it never felt like good money because in every family we knew, both parents had jobs like that. *I work*, said Brian. *But*, I said. There was no finishing that sentence that didn't end with him annoyed and hurt. *Of course*, he said. I started to resent him. Coming home from work and taking off my shoes as I listened to them together in the kitchen, laughing, it felt like his fault that my kid didn't like me very much.

That's so cool, moms sometimes said at weekend birthday parties. *A horse trainer? That's fucking hot*, said one. She was on her third Bloody Mary in the kitchen while the kids all played on the indoor gym. *Sort of*, I said. And then I felt bad and made myself a Bloody Mary, walked out to the living room to find Cass.

I was thirty and had an eight-year-old and a great career and my husband loved me, was utterly devoted to our kid. I still felt, somehow, like my real life hadn't started yet. Even though, as Brian would remind me in so many of the months that followed, this life was mostly of my own making. *You don't make me happy* is a thing I said out loud to him, as if that were ever his job. It felt galling to deem my own unhappiness reason enough to blow up my family.

The divorce was quick and amicable. I was so smug. I loved the idea of being a single mom to Cassie, all that time with her all to myself. I'd bust ass, take names, all that, but I'd also be more present at home with her. She wouldn't constantly be looking to Brian. Of course, none of it worked out like I imagined. Cass only got closer to her father. She only resented all the ways she couldn't have him when she was with me, except when she was constipated and needed Poop Mom. But even that ended. Time kept passing. And then, again, I wasn't what she hoped.

A random dinner with Cass, at ten:

"How was school, baby?"

"I'm not your baby."

"*Cassandra*, how was school?"

"Fine."

"Can you tell me something that you did?"

"Sat at my desk."

"Something you learned?"

"Not much."

"Something you talked about with a friend?"

"That's between us."

"How's the baby?"

"You forget his name again?"

"How's Mason?"

"Really good."

"Your dad?"

"Pretending you care just makes it worse."

"I care, Cass."

"Sure."

"Jesus fuck."

"I'm not hungry anymore."

Her first year of sixth grade, we let her commute to school with friends on the subway. I didn't want to let it happen. *My days*, I said, *I can have Anna come get you.* Anna was the babysitter we'd had the last three years. *I'm too old for a babysitter*, Cass said. And then, one day, she didn't come home. A whole huge city. I had fought and fought not to let her have a phone. *She has an attention disorder*, I said to Brian. (She'd been diagnosed with ADHD when she was five.) *You're not supposed to talk about it like that*, he said. *It's not a good idea*, I said. We got her an Apple Watch until she lost three of them. A flip phone, until she lost that too. And then she wasn't home, and there was a whole city where she might have been.

I called all her friends' parents. *Maybe . . .* , said one of the moms. *Have you talked to Brian?* She was a stay-at-home, divorced too. Her kid had gone to the same elementary school as Cass, and she'd always stood very close to Brian at open houses, graduations, holiday productions, no matter that I was there, no matter that we were still married then. *I haven't*, I said. An hour later, I called him. *I can't find Cassie*, I said. I'd run from the subway to the school. It was winter. I was sweating under my coat. *Jude*, said Brian, *she's here.*

What the fuck, Cass, I said when I got there. She had a friend with her. Brian's house had a Nintendo Switch and mine did not. *Chill out*, Cass said. *Jude*, said Brian. He led me by the arm into the kitchen. *She said you knew.*

He had moved in with Posey after only six months, to the four-story brownstone that her parents bought her her last year at NYU. She also had a place in Westchester. They'd met when she'd hired Brian to exercise her horse while she was in Berlin making a (self-funded) film. *You know*, said Posey. I didn't like her standing close to me, conspiratorial. *They're like horses*, she said, nodding toward Cass and her friend. *Tweens.* She made a face. *They smell your fear.*

At fourteen, Cass got Brian to agree to boarding school, and Posey paid for it. I wrote her letters, emails, sent care packages each Friday with creams and lotions and all her favorite treats, until she sent me a terse email saying she didn't have room for all that stuff I sent.

Sometimes I went for walks with Brian and the second baby. We talked about Cass, of course, though I knew he kept things from me. I knew she told him things and then said to him, either before or after these disclosures, *don't tell Mom, okay?*

"You know, you're still young too," he said to me one day, walking over the Third Street Bridge in Gowanus. I thought about the life we might have had, tried to locate in my brain what it was I thought I was escaping when I asked for a divorce. Brian was not much taller than me, five eight to my five five, but he had those broad shoulders, large and heavy limbs. I had always loved the idea of loving him. It wasn't his fault, I thought that day, my leaving. I wanted to say that to him, but it felt unfair and too long overdue.

"I don't feel young," I said, staring down at the pudgy, bare ankles of his three-month-old. I was thirty-six that year.

"No," he said. "I'm not sure you ever did."

———

"You okay?" he said now, more than a decade later. Not my husband anymore but still checking in on me. "Cass is worried."

I'd started crying and I didn't want him to know that I was crying. He didn't know a lot of what my life was then. He didn't know that I'd started sleeping with my direct report and gotten fired.

"It's a lot right now," I said.

"Your dad okay?"

"Likely fine."

"That's great."

I walked out to the deck to hand Maeve Tallulah's towel.

"You talk to Cass?" he said.

"Very briefly," I said, turning back into the house.

"You know that's just kids," he said. I didn't argue this.

"How're you guys?" I said, not quite up for naming Posey.

"You know," he said. "Busy."

I stayed quiet.

"Jude . . ." he said. He'd always been so good at showing up and loving.

"Thanks for calling, Bri." I meant it. I was finally able to be grateful, for Cass but also for what Brian and I had been able to become.

Maeve and George came back in and asked if I could watch Tallulah while they went to meet the tow truck. "Of course," I said, smiling at Tallulah, who had wrapped the towel over her head so I could only make out her eyes. "You like ice cream?" I asked.

Tallulah looked at Maeve, who nodded, and Tallulah smiled at me. "You're just like Fred," she said.

"We'll be super quick," Maeve said.

I scooped Tallulah three scoops of vanilla, found an almost-expired bottle of Hershey's syrup. I left her in the kitchen and went into the room where Mom kept the kid stuff, where she'd set up two sets of bunk beds for Jenn's kids to stay, complete with stuffed animals, bean bags, stacks of toys. The closet contained Legos and more toys in clear plastic containers, all neatly stacked and labeled, kids' clothes in every size. I got Tallulah leggings and a T-shirt, found a children's book on the bookshelf. I washed her bowl and helped her change into the leggings, T-shirt. She was obviously exhausted; her hands kept going to her face. I picked her up and brought her back into the grandkid room.

"Maybe you could lie in this big cozy bed, and I could read to you a bit?"

She nodded, still not talking. I let her climb onto the bed and pulled the comforter over her chest, then settled into the bean bag chair close by.

The book I'd chosen was Cassie's favorite childhood book, *Amos and Boris*. Amos, a mouse, builds a ship to go to sea. He works and works and then launches the boat at high tide, and for a while he is blissful, floating, easy. I was tired, sun-spent. I sat and read that book I'd read a thousand times and thought about my kid, about how quickly she'd become too big for me to read to her like this: "One night, in a phosphorescent sea, he marveled at the sight of whales spouting luminous water . . . He rolled over and over and right off the deck of his boat and into the sea! A thousand miles from the nearest shore, with no one else in sight as far as the eye could see and not even so much as a stick of driftwood to hold onto. 'Should I try to swim home?' Amos wondered. 'Or should I just try to stay afloat?' He might swim a mile, but never a thousand. He decided he would try to just keep afloat, treading water and hoping that something would turn up to save him. But what if the thing that turned up was a shark or some big fish, a horse mackerel? What was he supposed to do to protect himself? He didn't know."

Tallulah had passed out after the second or third page, but I kept reading. *What was he supposed to do to protect himself?* Amos, the mouse, is rescued by Boris the whale, who happens to be heading to a conference (a whale conference!) close to where the mouse is headed. The mouse promises the whale he'll return the favor one day, and, eventually, he does. I was quietly crying by the second to last page. At seven, Cass had stopped admitting the book was her favorite, but still, on nights she stayed up late reading a dragon book about wars and murder, I would later find *Amos and Boris* next to her in bed too. Every rhythm of it felt like the weight of her head on my chest, those years when Brian and I were still together. She knew every tool that Amos packed on his boat, she worried for him every time Boris forgot Amos was on his back and sounded, she was relieved every time Boris quickly picked him up, apologized.

Sometimes, after the divorce, when I came to get her and she'd ask me what our plans were—her voice not absent accusation, her body ready to tighten and recoil if I got too close—I would say to her, *We're going to a whale conference!* and she'd smile at me, more willing to let me put my hand on her back as we walked toward the subway.

George and Maeve came back to get Tallulah.

"She's asleep," I whispered to them.

"I can get her," George said.

"I've got it," Maeve said.

Watching Maeve pick up her kid, I was reminded that she was also someone's mom. *It's Mama,* she said, scooping her arms slowly, carefully, beneath Tallulah's back and legs. George backed out of the room, and I walked behind them out to the front door, then stood there with the warm breeze coming in as George helped Maeve settle Tallulah into Mom's backseat and pressed the button to put up the top. (It turned out that the car had to be in park for the top button to work.) I stood there barefoot, looking at the palm trees, Dad's perfect yard. And then I closed the door and walked around to the backyard, sat and stared at the river's wide, blank, moonlit slate.

"You okay, Ma?" Cass said. I'd called and said, *Hey, kid.* She'd said, *Hi, Ma,* and maybe, likely, she heard my voice break.

"I'm fine, Cass," I said. Her asking, though, had tipped something big and heavy, also wobbly, a mismatched Richard Serra sculpture, under my ribcage. "You know me," I said.

I asked her to tell me about soccer, her coach, her half siblings, packing for school. I kept thinking of more questions so I could keep listening to her, I held the phone close to my face.

After we hung up, I sat a long time, contemplating calling Molly. I'd told her very little of my family. I miss you, I finally texted. But no bubble appeared back.

Molly, then: Not only was she my hire but my supervisor, a man, had fought to hire someone else. I'd pushed back hard, out of character. By then, I'd quit the corporate job and was lower on the totem pole than I should have been at Brooklyn Defenders. We sought to get parents their kids back, keep them out of foster care. It was mostly deeply painful, and I was grateful to have found my way to it.

On paper, Molly and my boss's favorite candidate were hardly different—both impressively educated, both top of their class. Our office was prestigious, though poorly compensated. I pushed for us to hire Molly because I thought she was the best candidate, because she held herself more confidently, but also: because I wanted to continue being in the same room as her for as long as I could. Her hands and forearms were disproportionately large compared to her frame, and I couldn't stop looking when she unbuttoned and rolled up the sleeves of her shirt. Maybe I thought I'd mentor her, take her to lunch. We'd be friends. Within a few weeks, I understood she had a girlfriend, and this knowledge shifted something further in me.

Is it possible to say I didn't know, I didn't realize at first? She was more than a decade younger than me. I knew that sometimes, masturbating, imagining her face or the way her ass looked in her A-line skirts would help me come, alone in my bed, after a glass or three of wine.

I did not pursue her, at first. After one too many unsatisfying dates with men in which I fantasized almost the whole time about the bodega ice cream I would purchase once I could free myself, after one specific outfit Molly tended to rotate in at least once a week that involved a particularly well-fitting skirt, I switched the options on my Tinder to not just men but both. I expanded the age range down another ten years, looping in Molly's generation.

I did not think, then, that I was trying to find Molly there. Molly had a girlfriend. I thought briefly, amusing myself, how absurd I was. How narrow my view of the world had always been. I thought, how strange: the internet.

And then, somehow, I was back at my apartment with a thirty-two-year-old with a razor fringe around her face, short, strong legs, average-size breasts. She had reached her hand and then her tongue inside of me. I was searching desperately to find her clit. She was laughing, pulling me up to her. *Want me to help?* she said. Then I was laughing. I thought, embarrassingly, of Brian, wanted to call him. *Look at me*, I would have told him, *finally less old, less walled in*.

I had six months of this and thought sometimes of calling Cassie, thought sometimes of calling Mom or Fred. I did, actually, call Fred a few times, walking home in work clothes from the night before just like the twenty-something that I'd never been, disheveled and hungover. I called Fred but didn't tell her what was happening, how it felt—a girl's hands on me, mine on them. I let Fred talk as I walked back to my apartment, and I waited for her to hear it in me, the shift, the way the aftermath of pleasure sounded, tasted. If Fred heard it, she never acknowledged it, but the sweet girl behind the counter at the bagel place who knew my whole-wheat-everything-with-egg-cheese-salt-and-pepper-order without my having to say it smiled at me knowingly. I'd turned to look to see if there was someone younger, closer to her age, standing behind me. The wall was mirrored, and I saw only my worn-out face, pulled-back hair, the smudge of makeup on the edges of my cheeks.

Once, all those years ago, I broke my wrist riding. Three hundred calories a day, fine, downy hair on my chin and cheeks, I pulled up quick on the reins at the end of a long string of jumps, and my bones were so weak from no food that the hard flick of my wrist made the bone crack. The doctor said, eventually, if I kept going like this, my bones would *turn to dust*. After: getting better, still counting calories but forcing myself to eat more, thrilled each time a piece of food passed through my lips without a thought. That's what it felt like, those months, something close to that. Indulgent, secret pleasure, like I hadn't known I could.

I had power over Molly, not just in terms of hiring and firing, not just in terms of her understanding that I had been the one to fight for her to get the job. But also: I could ask her to stay after so we could *just get this motion filed before morning*; I would order dinner.

Could she tag along with me to this discovery meeting uptown? Would she like to share a car back to Brooklyn, on the firm?

That this eventually led to fucking, to my feeling, acting, being, wholly out of control: it feels, in retrospect, predictable, embarrassing. If I could do and feel anything else with the constancy and intensity with which I feel shame, I might actually be a functional human being.

Three weeks after she mentioned in passing that she and her girlfriend had broken up: *Why don't we just meet at my apartment, since we're both in Brooklyn? I already hate asking you to work a weekend. At least we can do it on my roof?* Some drinks and the hot Brooklyn summer, and Cass with Brian and Posey and the babies in Europe for the month.

MOLLY: This place is so grown-up.

ME: I'm very old.

MOLLY (WAS SHE LOOKING AT ME TOO LONG?): Not at all.

ME: I don't have an air conditioner out here.

MOLLY: Your bedroom is bigger than my apartment.

ME: You want the loveseat or the comfy chair?

Seven and a half months of the best sex of my life and also total irresponsibility. Had we still been talking, I might have called Fred. She would have come right over, asked so many questions, thrilled that I was finally acting, feeling, both of which had been mostly her purview until then. I missed deadlines, phone calls. Molly and I fucked more than once in my office after business hours. *Jude, Jude, Jude*, Fred would have said. I would have laughed. She would have too. A few uncomfortable dinners with Molly's friends, Brian calling, Cass texting, both of them asking if I was sure I was okay. I thought I was. By the time I was in Florida, I had been let go from my job with a solid-enough severance, and Molly had broken up with me: *If I had wanted to be with someone working through this much shit, I could have just dated someone my own age.*

In Florida, that night, George gone with Maeve and Tallulah, me all squirmy, anxious, from the ways that book had jarred me back into that other, far-off time, I walked out barefoot to the dock and watched the river water slosh and knock against the pilings. I lay out flat on the damp wood, eyes closed, just like the mouse, Amos, on his boat before the storm.

11

At the motel, George offered to help carry Tallulah up.

"We're fine," Maeve said; then, as she was unstrapping Tallulah and trying to lift her past the downturned driver's seat, "You know what? Sure."

George picked up Tallulah and carried her up the stairs and into the room. He tried to ignore the brightness of the parking-lot lights, the way the concrete of the stairs went squish and crunch beneath his flip-flops. He tried to ignore what felt like grime on the carpet as he brought Tallulah to the bed. He tried not to think the thing that we'd been taught to think our whole lives, which was: if a life wasn't built with all the money love could buy (all the love that money was?), it wasn't safe, it wasn't right, it wasn't love that you could hold tight to or keep.

He tried to not feel sad for Maeve for living in this place that made him feel uncomfortable. To not think the word *ick*. Maeve and Tallulah deserved more, he thought. He thought of the money that Brett had put into his bank account.

"I like the pictures," he said, nodding toward a string of yarn with drawings taped to it. In among the drawings was a photo of Tallulah and Maeve, Maeve's mom: Tallulah tiny, Maeve awash in joy. George realized for all the time he'd spent with Maeve, he'd spent very little time thinking of her as a mother, as a grown-up. Suddenly he wanted to get out.

Maeve smiled at him. "Our décor," she said. "Thanks for the help, Georgie." And she walked him to the door.

On the drive home, George called Allie. He had all that money now. He thought that was how he'd get her back. He didn't care, it turned out, that she'd slept with her boss.

"I didn't think you'd pick up," he said when she did.

"Me neither," she said back.

When she'd kicked him out, he'd cut off her access to their savings, though he'd not canceled the credit cards. He thought of telling her the whole story about Brett and his discovery. He didn't have nearly enough money, obviously, for the lives they wanted long term, but now there was a cushion, something to get him started on his own, more still to put away for future kids. He thought again of her boss's wife and wondered if he shouldn't have called her instead.

"I miss you, Al," he said. He'd kept the top up but put the window down, warm air on his bare arms.

"I know," she said. "But I'm not coming back."

Why are you like this? he wanted to ask her. *Why can't you just love me like you said you would?* He wanted her to offer something, make all of it better. He wanted her to beg him to come back.

"What the fuck, Al," he said instead. "I gave you everything."

"Right," she said.

"You greedy bitch."

"Oh Georgie," she said. "You hate yourself. It's not your fault. But it is your fault you can't seem to break free of it. I can't live like that."

"Like what?" He'd brewed the coffee for her every morning, agreed to the backsplash color that he hadn't wanted, gotten her the Louis Vuitton bag that she'd picked out even after Jenn said it was tacky.

"You can't take your shirt off in front of me. We don't have sex. Libby is your only friend."

I took it off! he wanted to tell her. *I took my shirt off in front of Maeve and it was fine!* But then he'd have to tell her about Maeve. It seemed like her point might be bigger than just this.

"I've been working too much," he said. "That can stop."

"That's not what this is."

He stopped at a red light and kept his eyes forward so as not to accidentally see someone from high school, someone that Mom and Dad knew, one of Fred's or Jenn's or my old friends.

"I want to enjoy my life, George, and I don't think you're capable of that," Allie said.

Cabo! he wanted to yell at her. *Tahoe!* His favorite vacation spot was Vegas, for fuck's sake. *But you're not actually in any of those places,* she would have said back. *You're doing that strange. desperate thing of trying to prove you're having fun, but it's not true. You're miserable almost all the time. You're faking it.* It's possible Allie wouldn't have known to say exactly that, but she would have felt some version of it. George knew, I think, inside that gape of silence, what she meant.

"I'm sorry, George," she said.

He had planned a whole engagement, hired a photographer, rented out the backyard of a restaurant that she liked close to their house. He'd ordered roses, gotten a big ring with Allie's sisters' help. She had cried, and he had picked her up, and she had whispered good, kind things with her hot breath, those perfect lips, into the skin of his neck. He thought maybe he'd remind her of that—how happy she was, how good that day was, how nice those words had felt. He thought he could tell her, how good she felt, he felt, holding her like that.

"Al," he said.

But she'd hung up.

12

The morning after George went to get Maeve and Tallulah from their smoking car, George and I sat in the kitchen drinking coffee, and he watched me eat.

"You know intermittent fasting is disordered eating," I said to him, both his eyes angled toward my omelet.

"You're the expert," he said.

I looked past him toward the water.

"Sorry, Jude," he said.

I walked back to my room and checked in with Cassie. *Hi, Ma, all good, love you too, have you talked to Aunt Fred yet?*

Dad hadn't come down yet, so I went to check his bed, but it was empty.

George checked the upstairs bedrooms. Dad wasn't in the house. The temporary rental SUV Jenn had secured was still in the driveway, Mom's convertible still in the garage where George had parked it the night before. My body began to thrum the way it used to thrum when Cass was little, the way it still thrummed when she didn't respond to a call or text for hours or days.

"Dad!" I called. I went through every room a second, then a third time, every bathroom, closet, upstairs, downstairs, George behind me, changing course, then back outside again. Libby was also missing. I went out front, walked down the street, calling for him.

"You lose something?" a woman said, as she walked briskly past me.

"My dad," I said.

She stopped walking, quiet. "Good luck," she said, and started to walk again.

I went back inside—one more sweep of his room, the kitchen—yelling for him.

"Jude!" George said. He was outside by the pool. "He's out here!"

I went through the sliding glass. George was wearing basketball shorts, flip-flops, another too-small shirt. I'd yet to put my contacts in, and my glasses were somewhere upstairs, and I squinted as I walked out to the dock, where George was motioning to me.

I saw the walker before I saw Dad. He'd made it over the sliding glass door track, down the stairs to the concrete deck around the pool, over the grass to each stone step out to the dock, over the bumps of every slab of wood to the dock's end. Dad was behind the walker, prostrate on his belly, his casted leg stretched out behind him. For a second, minute, some stretch of time that felt impossible and cataclysmic, I thought he was dead.

"Judith!" Dad said, not dead. More emphatic than he'd been in days. "Come here!" Libby was licking at his bare feet, scurrying back and forth to either side of him as if she might will him not to fall off the dock.

"Libby!" George said. The dog ignored his calls.

"You kids," Dad said. "Come here!"

I tried to catch George's eye, but he had no interest in whatever solidarity we might have formed inside the strangeness of the moment. I looked down at Dad's bare feet, his cast, the spindle of his legs.

"I said come here!" Dad said again. He looked up, his good arm propping him up. He was wearing Mom's glasses.

"How did you get down here?" I said.

"Come next to me," he said.

You're going to get dirty, I thought but didn't say. *Are you okay?* Dirt was smudged on his shirt, stuck to his bare knees and shins.

Dad pointed to the crowd of mangroves in front of the seawall he'd had built. "You see that?" he said. "A great blue heron. She has a baby in there too."

Libby had started yapping again, and George went to pick her up, but she got louder; as George's hands came toward her, she snapped, and he jumped back.

"Libby!" George said. "What the fuck?!"

"She doesn't like to be held when she's outside," Dad said, still horizontal. "Leave her be, George, and come here!"

"How many of those pills did you take?" George asked.

"I want you to see the baby," Dad said.

I sat down next to him, trying to angle my body to be able to see where Dad was pointing, finally lying down next to him to look.

"I had a bunch of those things taken out, you know," Dad said. "It was technically illegal. You can't just plant them back. I googled it. All these guys tried to replant them, but you can't. You have to create the right conditions. The tides. You have to follow this whole process."

George grabbed hold of one of the pilings and lowered himself to sitting on Dad's other side.

"The seeds need to be dry part of the time and wet part of the time. You can't plant them," Dad said. "You just have to let them float."

"Sounds complicated," George said.

I looked back and forth between Dad and the clearing in the mangroves where he'd been pointing.

"I used to see them," Dad said. "The herons." Libby sidled up to Dad, farther from George, and nestled herself between Dad's shoulder and his neck. "They'd scare me sometimes, rustling in the mangroves, breaking branches, when I came out to turn on the sprinklers before work."

He shook his head. I remembered the first time I sat next to him after I'd begun sleeping with Brian. They're the same height, Dad and Brian, except Brian is much larger limbed. I remembered sitting with him on the steps out to the back porch, answering questions about classes, not having told my parents about Brian, wanting to keep him just mine for a few more weeks. I remembered looking at the set of Dad's shoulders, shocked and slightly frightened by how small he was.

"When I was a kid," Dad said, "my dad used to borrow a boat from a friend of his." Our whole lives, he had not ever spoken to us of his dad, not once. I felt myself, and George too, take in one sharp breath. "He would take us out," Dad continued, "in the months right after we got down to Florida, your Aunt Eva and me, and we'd lie out just like this on the flat front."

I looked at George. I thought maybe both of us could see Dad then, like a young George: years still from his growth spurt, moon-faced, anxious, bare belly on the hard, wet fiberglass, burnt face and burnt shoulders, squinting against the sheen of the water's top.

"I thought they were *something*," Dad said. "The way they glided. The way their wings hardly ever flapped."

We watched, but the mangroves stayed still—no more herons. A boat sped through the channel, the wake slapping against the dock.

"Dad?" I said. "Can we help you get up?"

George and I reached for him at the same time, and Libby snapped, and George yelled at her. Dad brushed us away, soothing Libby, rose to sitting and then to standing, awkwardly but with the help only of the closest piling. I pushed his wheelie thing closer toward him, and he angled his cast-clad leg back onto it.

"I should have never taken all those mangroves out," he said.

"We could put them back in," I said.

"Did you listen?" he said. "They can't be planted back."

"We could do the float thing," George said.

"We could?" I said to George.

(One of the texts Fred sent me about wildness, a quote from a *New York Review of Books* article by a guy named David Quammen: "Wildness, as I see it, requires living creatures of many different forms entangled in a system of surging and ebbing interactions, marked by fluctuations that depend on the near-infinite unpredictability of individual behavior as well as the finite predictability of biophysical and biochemical laws.")

"He just said it," George said. "I'll find some on the internet."

"Maybe for my birthday!" Dad said, Libby somehow in his arms again.

"Maybe," I said, staying a couple steps behind him, a couple steps in front of George, as Dad scooted back toward the house.

13

"Dad wants mangrove seeds for his birthday," I said to Jenn, sitting at her island and drinking coffee. I'd come over to help plan Dad's birthday party. All her kids were home.

"I blame Fred," said Jenn.

"I don't think this is Fred."

"Can you find some on the internet?"

Jenn had the baby in her arms and was spooning what must have been four boxes of Annie's mac and cheese into bowls for all the kids. The nanny was upstairs cleaning. School wouldn't start for another week.

Jenn's three oldest took their food and went back upstairs with their phones. She put snap peas next to each of the smaller children's mac and cheese. "Bella," she said to her second youngest, almost four, "try the snap pea."

Bella took a bite of a snap pea and squealed, angry. "I bit my mouth!" she said. "I ate that because of you and now I'm hurt! I don't like you anymore."

Jenn looked at me, then at Bella. "Bella," she said.

"I said I don't like you anymore don't talk to me."

It had been a long time since I'd had a kid that small, and I stared at her. Fred would say this was something having to do with Jenn's parenting, but, really, I was thinking, was this just what four was like?

"If you don't like me, then you don't get to eat my food," Jenn said. She took both the mac and cheese and snap peas and dumped them into the trash. "Go upstairs. Get away from me."

Bella stared at her, shocked. I, too, was shocked; I had never seen Jenn like this. Her third from youngest, Tyler, stared at me, then at her mom, then at me again. "What the hell, Mom?" she said.

"Don't say what the hell to me," Jenn said.

Tyler grabbed Bella, and they both ran upstairs, and Jenn said nothing. She grabbed Tyler's bowl and began to eat what was left of her shells and cheese in big, heaping bites.

"Fuck," she said.

"You okay?" I said.

"What the fuck?" she said.

I shrugged and took Devon from her, tickled the bottoms of her feet to make her giggle.

"Can I watch the iPad?" asked Devon.

Jenn nodded, passed it to her without talking.

Devon curled up on the sunroom couch and let herself be subsumed by screen.

"What do you have in the cart so far?" Jenn said. She still didn't trust that Fred would pull off Dad's birthday dinner and had suggested that we get enough hors d'oeuvres that, if Fred's dinner failed, we'd still have enough food for a main course. I tried to navigate the Publix online-ordering website on Jenn's laptop as we talked.

"Dad likes kid food anyway," Jenn said. "It's possible Fred will make something too weird for him to eat."

"You talk about him like he's a toddler."

Jenn looked at me.

"Fine," I said, and added two platters of chicken fingers to our cart.

Anelise came in, looking accusatorily at her mother. "What did you do to Bella?" she said.

"Anelise," said Jenn.

"You made her cry, you know?"

"She can't be rude like that."

"Neither can you."

"I'm not perfect, Lisey."

"No shit, *Mommy*." Anelise said the last word like it might be the worst word in the whole world.

"I just need a minute," Jenn said. "I'm sorry, okay? I'm in a state because of Grandpa's thing."

"You know you're literally the only person who cares about that stupid party," Anelise said. "You remember, right, that Grandpa's wife—*our grandma, your mom*—just died?"

"You're probably right about the party," Jenn said.

"It's obscene," I said to Jenn as soon as Anelise was back upstairs. "How many kids you have."

"You know you're not out of time, right?" said Jenn, clearly grateful not to have to talk about what either she or Anelise had said.

"Oh, Jenny," I said.

"I'm just saying," Jenn said.

"You sound just like Mom," I said.

"Oh, fuck you," said Jenn. Her face flattened. In fact, her face had frozen and then gotten weird as soon as the word "Mom" had left my mouth.

"You know what's so fucked up, though?" Jenn said. She pulled Devon back onto her lap, held her pudgy foot in her hand like a talisman, like her own comfort toy, as Devon giggled at the pastel characters dancing on her screen. I was, very briefly, deeply envious of all the many feet she'd held like that over the years.

"I think I'm meaner," she said. "Now that she's gone."

I looked at Devon, smiling at the iPad, wondering if we should find her headphones.

"Like, you know, I loved her but I didn't really like her. And now, all that energy I used to spend just being annoyed by her, calling Dad to say how awful she was, telling Adam all about whatever she'd done that day—it's like all that time and energy I spent being angry at her is still there, but now it has nowhere to go."

I watched her face, her eyes and nose were Mom's, her lips and chin looked briefly just like Cass. "You know, I do sometimes wish I had one more," I said, cowardly, redirecting.

"You have time!" Jenn said, taking the bait. "They take care of each other after a while! I cannot believe you let Cass leave you early." No one in our family had approved of boarding school.

"It wasn't my choice," I said.

"Jude, honey, you're her mother."

"Poor thing, huh?" I said. "Stuck with me forevermore."

"Don't do that victim shit with me," Jenn said.

I went back to the computer. "What flavor for the cake icing?" I said. "And what color?"

Jenn put Devon down again and took the computer from me. "I have to look at all of them," she said.

14

"You need a plan, Fred," said David. Fred was naked in his bed. She'd gone running and then swimming and then helped two kids with college essays. She'd gotten texts from Fanny asking if she could go back to the house of the boy who had asked her if she was a feminist, but she'd put her off, said she was all booked up. One of the dads of one of the girls she'd tutored had asked her if she was sure they'd only talk about his kid's essay, and she'd nodded firmly, but he'd stayed listening from a close-by room the whole time. She had to be out of her borrowed house in a week.

She hadn't meant to end up at David's. Too often lately, he'd been trying to talk. Too often she'd been missing talking, eating, being with him all the time.

"I wanted to be married to you," he said. "I wanted us to have a life together. I don't know what this is, but it's not that."

Fred stayed silent for a long time. When they first got together, for years, the recurring nightmare Fred had about David was that he would live down the street from her but not want to be with her anymore. In the dream, he wasn't mean, he wasn't angry, and that was so much worse. He was exactly like he had always been, except he didn't want her anymore.

"Did you know J. Edgar Hoover was gay?" Fred said.

David laughed. "I think so." He knew most things that Fred didn't, read the big nonfiction books, long *New Yorker* articles, that Fred only read the summaries of.

"His dad died of melancholia and a lack of will to live," she said.

"He killed himself."

"J. Edgar hated him for how weak he was."

"Sounds true enough."

Fred had recently switched her listening from novels to non-fiction: more books on Florida, most of Robert Caro. She was now on the book by Beverly Gage on Hoover called *G-Man*. "What if all the ills of the world can be traced back to the repression of small, helpless men?" she said.

"Not a terrible theory."

"Robert Moses and Richard Nixon also had pretty severe issues with their moms."

"LBJ's mom likely loved him too much."

"What if all the ills of the world can be traced back to issues caused by moms?"

She felt the air between them shift. The truth she hadn't told. The facts about her body that she'd kept to herself. She was naked, cross-legged. It was dark, but every inch of him was an inch she could see clearly, an inch she knew and loved.

Talking was a terrible mistake, she thought. She wanted to slip his skin over the top of hers and stay like that forever. She wanted to fold her whole self inside of him, live the rest of her life silent and enveloped, sustained only by his body and its careful steadiness.

She had never not wanted any of this. She imagined she would always want him. It was only that she couldn't bear to be with him after he'd conceded so much to her, after all that lying, after how awful and impossible she was.

"Not everything has to be a fight," he said, still too good at knowing her.

"That's why I'm being nothing for a while."

"That's idiotic, Fred. It makes no sense."

She grabbed his T-shirt, slipped it on, thought of pressing down hard on his shoulders, fucking him again to shut him up.

"You're a person," he said. "You don't get to be nothing. You don't get to be the disembodied voice or whatever Beckett shit." The first year they were together, they'd watched videos of every Beckett play at her request. "There are people in the world who love you. Not in the exact way you wish they'd love you, but that's because they're also people. You need to grow the fuck up and acknowledge that."

One time, a few months after they met, Fred had tried to run away from David. She'd remet him at that bar that night, had gone home with him, and then she'd found her way to him or him to her nearly every night after that. A few weeks in, sex-drunk, laughing more in those first weeks than she maybe had in her whole life, she'd woken up one morning, bleary, hungover, certain that she'd accidentally said she loved him as they fucked. It was a Sunday, before sunrise.

Fred got dressed and put on a coat, shoes, walked north over the bridge then west then north again. David had woken up to her absence and called her. She didn't answer for the first three hours. He called and called. Fred walked and walked. Past Washington Heights, he called a twelfth time, a thirteenth time, and she answered.

"Hey," he said, all easy.

Fred started to cry.

"What's going on?" he said.

"I ran away," she said. She'd just turned twenty-four, had never had a boyfriend. He was twenty-eight and had had so many girl-friends that sometimes his sister joked that you had to date David Doyle in order to get a degree from NYU.

He laughed at her. "You're running away from me?"

His laughter, his ease, made her laugh too. "I guess."

"I'm hungry," he said. "I don't want to eat without you, so come back."

He took her hand now. "I want to show you something," he said. She pulled on her underwear. He led her out into the hall that she hadn't been into since they'd seen the house together almost a year ago. His mom's paintings, the art they'd had up in New York, prints that Fred had bought but never gotten around to framing, all hung on the walls. A big charcoal Barb had done after the last hurricane that Fred had always loved hung in the center of the dining room. David had blown out the east wall of the living room and put in a row of floor-to-ceiling windows, no curtains. The moon shone in from outside. He'd built bookshelves opposite the windows. Their old couch sat next to the bookshelves, a large, overstuffed blue chair. He'd set up one of the guest rooms as an office with a built-in day-bed, more floor-to-ceiling bookshelves, a dark-wood desk.

Fred turned toward him. "I have no imagination," she said. "It's beautiful."

That night, in that house Fred had felt so sure she never wanted, in that bed they'd shared and David had driven down from New York, Fred let David lay her back and push up her shirt. She didn't move, though it was near impossible for Fred not to move. She stayed very still as David lingered over her, her face, her chest, her stomach. He went farther down, placed each hand softly, deftly on her hips. She'd almost never let him do this. Her back arched. She breathed in, arms out, head back. David cupped her ass, pulled her closer to him. She breathed out long, her toes curled in. He fell asleep, and so did Fred.

15

If he'd asked me, I would have told George what a terrible idea it was. I'd gone out driving after leaving Jenn's house. George had gotten into the SUV that Jenn had rented while Dad's car was getting fixed. Dad was settled in his bed with Libby, reruns of *Dancing with the Stars*, a glass of water, and some Vicodin.

George had all that money in his bank account. He would open the bank app on his phone and stare at it. All those zeroes like an accusation.

The idea occurred to him out by the pool, half looking for more herons. He'd googled car repair shops to try to help Maeve. But then he went to Instagram. He got an ad for cars for sale within a five-mile radius. He clicked on one. Thirty minutes later, he was at a dealership.

This was an awful idea, obviously. Like I said, if he'd asked me, I would have told him this. Likely this was why he didn't ask me. Likely, even after, he was glad he'd at least had the high of going to the dealership.

The guy at the dealership, Steve, had also gone to our same high school; he was a couple years older than George, and back when they were in high school, Steve most certainly would not have talked to George. But now George's credit score was near perfect, his bank account so ample and sure. Steve was trained to make George feel powerful, impressive. Steve was trained to ask George what he did and, when George answered, express interest in George's skill and knowledge *w/r/t investments* (a phrase Steve used, saying each letter with so long a pause afterward that he might as well have said the phrase full out).

It was likely that George knew, even as he pulled out of the parking lot with the brand-new Audi Steve had sold him that Maeve would not accept it. That in telling himself he'd bought the car as some grand gesture, he had failed to admit all the ways this was a terrible idea. He'd had to leave Dad's rental at the dealership to bring the car to Maeve's, and now he'd have to ask her, after giving her the car, to give him a ride back.

"No, George," was what Maeve said when she saw the car and made a joke about it and then he told her it was hers. "Absolutely not." They were downstairs in the parking lot of the motel, Tallulah up in the room watching TV. Maeve had spent so much of her grown-up life having to ask people for things, sometimes taking from people she loved and disassociating from the discomfort of it. She didn't want to have to feel grateful, or indebted. It was why she'd left her mother's, why she'd called George the night before instead of anyone she loved. "Absolutely not," she said again, as he stood dumbly holding out the keys. "Absofuckinglutely not," she said, louder, shaking her head. "You Kenners," she said. "What a fucking wreck."

16

George left Dad's rental at the dealership and drove out to the beach in the new car. Once again, those zeroes weren't worth shit. He left his flip-flops in the car and walked out toward the shore break. He walked back up to dry sand and took off his shirt.

"Georgie?" he heard.

It was Fred.

I was there, too, but they didn't see me. I drove out after both of them. I'd seen Fred's car, but I didn't know then that the Audi belonged to George. I walked out on the boardwalk thinking that I'd finally talk to Fred about what she'd done to me, to Cass. I wanted her to make it better, not just what she'd done but Dad and Jenn, George, Mom dead—I'd told Cass I would. I wanted Fred to tell me, to promise somehow that we'd make it to okay.

Here it is, finally: Eight months before, I'd gotten a text from a friend in New York, a link below it: Freddie! The friend was excited. The New Yorker! How great for Fred! Fred had said for years she wanted a story in *The New Yorker*. She would never be a serious writer until she had a story there, she said. And now, here, her whole three names. I wondered briefly why she hadn't told me. I'd thought she was working on her Florida book. Maybe this was, I thought, her Florida book. She had told me she couldn't write about the things she loved too much, that the idea of story had begun to feel corrupted, broken. I thought, by then, that we were something close to friends.

It opened like most of Fred's stories: woman by herself, first person, late thirties, suffering some unknown, unnamed malaise. (Fred had once forwarded me a rejection from *The Yale Review*: *We've just published a few too many middle-age-women-in-crisis stories this year.* Fred had written *LOL* to me in the subject line.) The sentences were simple; I respected this about her. The woman in the story is by herself and gets a phone call. Her niece is in trouble. Her niece is in boarding school and pregnant. Did my body react at the mention of the niece, or was it boarding school? My brain started whirring, shoulders and neck clenched. The niece isn't named, is called *the niece*, the woman, *the woman* the whole time. It's clear the woman has no children of her own. I got queasy, anxious.

The niece needs to terminate her pregnancy, and the woman says immediately she'll help. The woman/writer/first-person narrator borrows a friend's car and drives hours overnight to pick up the niece. She signs her out of school. The niece and woman both seem to forget, once they're in the car, what they've come together for. They talk and laugh, dance and sing along to music with the windows down. In some ways, this was the worst part of the whole story: the ease the two feel in each other's company, how lovingly and well Fred was able to capture something about the texture and the rhythm of my kid when she likes the person that she's with. They stop for diner French fries, milkshakes. Just as it starts to feel a little Lifetime movie, we get crosscuts into the past that aren't clearly delineated as past. You realize slowly.

And now, here, I had to put my phone down. I walked away from it. I walked outside. I went back inside to call Cass, to call Fred, looked to see if I had any emails, missed calls, texts from Brian. My hands began to tremble. I picked the phone back up and sat down.

The memory is of an earlier, different trip for an earlier, different abortion. Again, the character known only as *the woman* drives to Brooklyn this time, to pick up the other woman. They also get French fries. No milkshakes. Too much matching, probably, too treacly, although in real life, Fred and I, we'd also had milkshakes. She'd brought my favorite Haribo gummy cherry candy and dark-chocolate-coated ginger from the Park Slope Food Coop. It becomes clear, in the story, that the other woman, the first abortion, is the sister, the mother of the niece. That when this other, first abortion took place, the woman was much older than the niece. The woman getting the first abortion is referred to as *the mother* the whole time. She is, in case it isn't obvious at this point, a not-even-thinly veiled version of me. The niece is Cass.

Vomit, sweet and rancid, rose up in my throat. Again, I walked outside.

Here, now, let me fill in: I was thirty and had an almost-eight-year-old and a fraying, dying marriage. *Fine, sure, Brian,* maybe it was fraying because I was fraying it, but I, at least, felt dead. Nothing in my whole life had felt like I'd truly chosen it, and I was desperate to make some choices.

How could I have known, then, what a stupid, silly baby I still was. I was a wife and mother, corporate lawyer. And then, I'd had an abscess in my tooth and had to get it removed and was put on antibiotics to kill off the last of the infection in my gums. The drugs had knocked me out. I'd refused Brian's offer to come help me get home. Likely at the oral surgeon's, someone mentioned to me that the antibiotics might negate my birth control, but either I hadn't listened or I hadn't heard. Every day, just as I had since six weeks after Cass was born, I took my birth control.

We had talked about a second baby. Of course Brian wanted one. But I had—oh Cass, baby—I wasn't sure that I'd survive the powerlessness of loving like that twice. None of it, especially the beginning, had felt like choice. Not because I didn't want you but because, once you were born, I couldn't fathom ever wanting anything but you. I didn't think I had it in me to love that obscenely, constantly, obsessively again. Brian and I were having the sort of desperate and sporadic sex that comes when you can feel that all of it might be about to end.

I called Fred. She didn't have a job. She hardly ever seemed to work. I didn't—weak, pathetic, silly baby—I wanted someone to come with me. Just like the mother in the story, I never told Brian or Cass. Fred described the chairs and carpets just exactly as they were that day, the careful sweetness, slicked-back hair and chunky silver earrings of the woman behind the desk, the way one of the women who was young and alone in the chair closest to the door rubbed her hands from thigh to knee to thigh to knee, eyes averted to the floor.

Was the whole thing a story about all the ways that I, the mother in the story, was not ever equipped? Was that the irony? I discovered that I didn't give a fuck. Fred got her *New Yorker* story, and I was the mother who had no right to be a mother. I felt like I might either explode or collapse.

I skimmed it a second time, a third time. And then, with shaky, clammy hands and thumbs, I called my kid.

When the phone began to ring, I realized I had no idea what I would say when she picked up. Maybe she wouldn't ever read the story, I thought, desperate, hopeful. She followed Fred on Twitter, Instagram. Maybe Fred would keep this a secret, not scream, share, tweet, retweet, repost a thousand times until everybody looked and cheered and said how wonderful! How great! But of course Fred wouldn't keep this a secret. She'd put whole paragraphs on

Instagram, and Cass would read it there. Cass had a *New Yorker* subscription sent to her dorm, for which I paid. If she had not already read the story, she would soon enough.

"Cassie," I said, when the call went to voicemail. "Please call me, Cass." I stood there with the phone to my ear, a minute or two, until finally some beep-screech sounded in my ear, and then the phone cut off. I put the phone down. *Cass,* I texted, *please call when you can.* No word bubble, nothing. I picked up the phone again to reread the story a fourth time, and then I changed my mind, grabbed my keys and wallet, and went outside.

I thought of calling Fred and yelling. Maybe I wouldn't use words at all, just scream. For half an hour, three. *Fuck you, fucking Freddy,* I muttered to myself. It was January. I'd not worn a hat or scarf or gloves. I raised the collar of my coat around my neck as I walked over the bridge and through downtown. I got turned around—all those crooked downtown streets—and, indignity on top of indignity, I had to follow the map on my phone to find Broadway again. And then, the phone still in my hand, the story open in my browser, I texted Fred, saw the last message from her a week before, checking in with each other as if we were grown-up people, as if we had freed ourselves from all the bullshit of growing up and become friends.

What the fuck, Fred? I typed, and then I sent it. *What the actual motherfucking fuck?* Within seconds, she had called me. I did not answer. She called again; again I did not answer. She called again the next day and the next day. She emailed, texted. *I fucked up, Jude,* she said. She loved me and was sorry. She was a fucking idiot, she said.

What Fred said later, in one of the many messages she left and that I listened to over and over but to which I did not respond: *Something happens to me. I can't. I don't. It's my fault, and I know that, but when I was writing it I wasn't thinking it was you. I knew it was you, but then it stopped feeling like you and just felt like story. I was in this rush of feeling powerless, of Roe; everything felt so awful, scary, I was in this rush of trying to say or do, to act. I didn't think about*—she stopped, and I heard her thinking on the voicemail—*I know this sounds insane or like some bullshit excuse, but I felt so used to feeling useless, I didn't let myself acknowledge that I might also still be able to do harm.*

What kind of dumbass shit was this?

She sat down and she wrote. She knew it wasn't hers. I've known her my whole life. She thought the fact that her intentions weren't all bad mattered. But I was old enough—I wanted her to understand that she needed to be old enough—to know her intentions didn't matter if and when she hurt my kid. She'd revealed a secret that had only ever lived between us. Another secret that had belonged to Cass—that Cass had deliberately kept from me. Our whole lives, information, secrets, story had functioned first and always as a commodity to trade for love and sustenance, tools wielded back and forth, against us. All these years, Fred had kept this one. And then she'd picked it up, she'd sucked it dry for her own gain.

You could have used your own shit, I said. *Guess you weren't good enough*, I texted, *to make a story about a selfish woman who lies to her husband about her IUD* relatable *enough?*

And Cassie, Fred? I said. *What the actual fuck?*

When she finally talked to me, my daughter—*the niece*, this person I had spent my whole life wanting to love better, the only person toward whom I felt this scary, slavish need to keep her happy and safe—of course when Cass talked to me, it became quickly clear that it was me, not Fred, that she had chosen to be angry with.

Fred's an artist, Cass said. Fred did nothing wrong. *It was fiction, Mother!* In the same breath, the same conversation, she also told me that she understood now that I hadn't ever wanted to be a mother, that I hated all the obligations, the weight, the pressure. That none of this was actually in the story was not something I brought up, if only not to seem as if I might accidentally be defending Fred.

Cassie, I said. *Jesus, Cassie. How could you—* but then there I was, blaming. *Cassie, baby, I love you so much.* I didn't have a defense beyond that.

I watched them now: Fred and George on the beach talking. Taking off their pants and shirts, those bodies filled with so much of what I also had in mine. They walked out to the ocean and swam out.

"What do you do out here?" George asked Fred. They were out in the ocean, past the sandbar. George tried not to think about sharks.

Fred tipped her head back. "I try to float," she said.

Once, before Tess died, Fred had brought her and Hal and Oona down to Florida. Mom and Dad had let them stay at their house and had worked all day, and Tess and Fred and Hal and Oona had the place mostly to themselves. *How awful!* Tess said every morning, sitting outside and looking at the water, drinking coffee. February, 80 degrees and sunny, a breeze off the water. They watched the herons glide by, the water ebb and glint. *I can't fathom how you ever survived this awful place*, Tess said. *Torture*, Fred said. *Indictable*, said Tess. *I'm glad to get to have you here*, said Fred. She'd taken about a thousand furtive pictures of Tess and her kids at the beach. In the ocean, Tess had shown both kids how to float. *Don't overthink it!* Tess said, laughing at Fred. *Water is the kindest element. It's because you trust the world too much*, Fred said, unwilling to stretch her body out the way Tess told her. *Silly me*, said Tess. *I trusted the world, and now I'm almost dead.* Before Fred could respond, Tess put her hands under Fred to float her, the kids swimming up to help. Fred flailed, though, kept sinking, kicking. Oona, Hal, and Tess all laughed. Tess swam up next to Fred, who couldn't quite look at her. *We're alive right now*, Tess said.

"What is this car?" Fred said, once they'd climbed out of the water, grabbed their clothes and keys and phones.

"I bought it for Maeve," George said.

"You did what?"

"Hers broke down."

"So you bought her an Audi?"

"It was a gesture."

"How'd that go?"

"She did not accept."

Fred was quiet.

"I was trying to be nice."

"What'd she say?"

"That she was not taking a fucking car from me."

"An Audi, though, George?"

"It's a good car! The gas is a little touchy, but it's nice."

"Maybe if you got her something with a less touchy gas pedal, she'd have fallen gratefully into your arms?"

They left the Audi at the beach, and Fred drove George out to Busch Wildlife. George convinced her to stop at Chick-fil-A on the way. (*The politics*, said Fred; *the waffle fries*, said George.) Fred wanted him to see the vultures. It was only when they got up close to the cage that they saw Maeve and Tallulah standing there.

———

I had already driven home to cook for Dad, a more proximate attempt at Mom's cooking: steaks, asparagus, potatoes. After dinner, Dad took a Vicodin, and he and Libby went into his room. I did a last wipe of the countertops, dustbusted the sand by the door. The sun was still up, and I stood barefoot in the kitchen, dishwasher whirring, and called Cass.

I asked the questions I had been afraid to ask. Cass waited a long time, but then she talked. Imagine her, now, coming out to Mom and Dad's pool, fully formed just from my calling, from my asking. Teleported, if you will. Watch me walk out to the pool and meet her. Sun on her nose and cheeks, constellated freckles from summer soccer, her long strong solid perfect limbs. We take off our shorts, our shirts, dive in. Without talking, we both dip down to the bottom of the pool and sit. Bubbles from our mouths rise to the top. We play the game that we all used to play when we were kids, that I taught Cass when we came down here all the times that we came down here and we swam together just like this. When we dove down to the floor and told each other secrets, stayed very still, eyes burning from the chlorine, arms flailing to keep our bodies on the ground, watching closely so we might read each other's lips. No one but her and me will ever know the things she said on that phone call, because they don't need to. Because it's mine and hers, not theirs. What it felt like, though, was sitting like that underwater. She talked, and it felt secret, special—a whale conference! I stayed very still and held my breath.

"Fred, Fred, Fred," Tallulah said, running toward her in front of the cage for eagles, also filled with vultures.

"Tallu-lu-lu-lu," said Fred.

"She insisted," Maeve said, smiling at Fred, not looking at George.

Busch Wildlife was close to closing, but Fred and Tallulah led Maeve and George to see the baby alligators, Alligator Fred, the panthers, the big, sleeping, lolling bears.

"It's cool here," George said, looking past Maeve to Fred.

"We love it," said Tallulah, holding Fred's hand, Maeve's hand, grinning at her mother.

"I'm glad I finally got to come," Maeve said.

18

"Jude!" George and Fred whisper-yelled as they came through Dad's front door together.

It was dark, and I was standing alone in the kitchen with a bowl of ice cream.

"Jude!" they said again, as if we were three and eight and ten. "Come play with us."

My whole body felt different, lighter, having talked to Cass. I looked at them both, annoyed but also glad to see them. Dad was asleep. The way the quiet swelled in that big house when no one else was there had always freaked me out.

"Tennis?" George said.

I washed my spoon and ice cream bowl and dried them—the dishwasher was already running—and put them both away.

"Sure," Fred said.

I went upstairs to get a sports bra, shorts. George and Fred found the rackets. I got the can of balls. We walked the six or seven minutes to the courts. George pressed the buttons, let us in. We hit back and forth, but Fred kept missing. I stood on the same side of the net with her as George served and she sprinted and swore. She made contact twice, but both times the ball went out of bounds.

"Freddy," I said, laughing at her when she leapt for a ball and fell elbows and knees first on the clay court. "Maybe that's enough."

"I fucking hate this," she said, wiping blood from her knees. Her scrapes from falling with the meat had reopened. "I hate being so bad at this."

"We're old, Fred," I said. "Making your peace with not having to be good at things is one of the perks of middle age."

I watched her shudder. "God, how awful."

"Oh, Fred," I said. All this time being angry, I'd forgotten, I had not seen as clearly how sad and silly Fred also was.

Fred looked up from her scraped knees and then sat down, a tennis racket's width between us, both our backs against the chain-link fence.

"Jude," she said.

"No more sorries," I said. What I wanted was a reason. I'd wanted, right after it happened, for her to call and tell me she'd had no choice, was broke, this was the only thing that she had left; that she was desperate and had lost a gig and had said this story out loud to her agent who'd transcribed it; that some editor had forced her. I wanted her to tell me that it wasn't her choice, her fault; I wanted her to say how she never would have if not for that. That she had been so angry, filled with fury on behalf of me and Cass as soon as she found out. That it was David's fault, and this was also why she left him: he'd found her journal, thought the story was too good not to share, to sell; he had wanted to exploit us; she'd left him because of this.

Anything at all, I would have taken and held tight to, anything at all to avoid knowing it was her.

But the truth was, I knew already. Cass and I had given it to her. We had offered up our mushy and uncertain bits because we thought we could, because regardless of how much or little we trusted she'd protect them, we needed someone, couldn't hold so tight and close to all of it. And Fred had taken this and turned it into something that was first and only for her. She'd still ruined it.

"I did a wrong thing," Fred said. "I thought . . ." She sighed. "I don't want to make excuses."

We both watched as George walked slowly around the court picking up the balls, stuffing all four in his pockets, serving one after the next, then walking around the court and picking them all up again.

"I thought it mattered that I love you," Fred said. "That I wrote it loving you."

"But writing isn't love," I said.

I watched her watch George, turn toward me. "It is to me," she said.

"But who," I said. "Who is it that you thought you were loving when you took that from us?"

"I thought you'd see I loved you. I do love you. I think I thought that it would be okay somehow because of that."

"We trusted you, Fred," I said. "Your betrayal isn't less of a betrayal because the thing you made was good."

I watched her body twitch and startle. I'd said her art was good, and that still mattered to her. I could have laughed, have hit or hurt her. I could have hugged her. Desperate Freddy. How completely and how doggedly she had always been herself.

19

Happy Birthday, Daddy! Jenn sent the family a group text at six thirty in the morning. We were, Fred and George and I, still up, worn out from the tennis, drinks and French fries after. We'd each had a glass of whiskey, found some frozen French fries Jenn had left behind, tossed them in a bowl with extra salt, passed back and forth as we sat on the dock and watched the sun come up. Two herons flew up out of the mangroves, mother and then baby; they glided a long time close to the water without seeming to move much.

"The fucking birthday party," Fred said. It was her role to say this.

"It won't be that bad," I said; that was mine.

"I didn't get him anything," George said.

"Give him the car!" Fred said, and we all laughed.

At nine, Fred left to run and get ready for the party. At ten, I called Cass to tell her that I loved her, to have her talk to me about soccer, about the classes she was signing up for, about friends.

I texted Molly a picture of the sun coming up over the river. *Hi from Florida*, I said. She texted back, *My yoga instructor said the other day to think, instead of being broken, that we might be broken open to accept greatness in. It made me think of you.* I laughed down at the phone's screen, texted back, *Thanks!* Another picture of the rising sun.

Dad didn't want to go. The mangrove seeds had shipped but not arrived.

"I fucking hate bringing the fucking printout instead of a gift," Jenn said.

She had me pick up the cake and the chicken fingers, the sandwich wheel, the crudités with dip, the Publix cheese. Dad rode with George, Libby on his lap. We hadn't, any of us, had a drink in hours by the time we got to Fred's. Jenn was early, with a tablecloth and lots of tut-tutting about the cleanliness of the bathrooms and the kitchen floor. She had brought her own cleaning supplies and, for a minute, seeing her from behind on hands and knees, hair pulled back, I thought that she was Mom.

"A party!" she said when she saw me.

"A party," I said back. I helped her clean the other bathroom.

Fred was cooking. She'd grilled thick portobello mushrooms with caramelized onions, served on warmly toasted brioche buns; rice and lentils cooked with curry, garlic, poblano and green peppers; a salad of diced cucumbers, tomatoes, and red onions, with a yogurt-lemon-butter dressing dolloped over top. George stood at the bar a long time, purportedly trying to figure out what to make us all for drinks. He'd settled Dad outside with Libby.

"Let's just leave her," I'd said back at Dad's house.

"It's my birthday," Dad said. "She's my favorite child now." He walked around the backyard looking at the defunct fruit trees, the still-hearty palms. Libby circled his feet, yipping, licking at his toes when he stopped to inspect a cragged and dried-out bush.

"What's he doing out there?" George said.

"Assessing the house's value?" Jenn said.

"Maybe he can help me with the plants," said Fred.

Jenn forgot the candles. (*What the fuck is wrong with me?* she said.)

"I'll go get candles!" Fred said.

"Good," Jenn said, taste-testing the lemon-butter-yogurt dressing. "This isn't bad."

Fred's car was blocked in by Jenn's and George's cars.

"Just take mine!" said George.

"You mean Maeve's?" said Fred.

George laughed.

Fred took the keys from George, her bag, her phone. She didn't look at that damned screen that showed what was in her rearview: it was too fancy, unnecessary. Her Prius didn't have one of those screens. And so, but so, as she backed out, Libby must have gone under the car. Fred didn't look. She didn't see the dog and backed out, felt a bump, maybe a crack.

We heard Fred yell. We all ran out.

Libby was caught under the wheel well, the car George bought for Maeve stopped halfway out into the street. Fred leapt out of the car and crawled beneath it. Slow and careful, she dislodged Libby's hip and leg, and Libby yipped and mewled, and Fred whispered to her. The concrete scraped Fred's bare feet and legs.

I'm so sorry, Fred kept saying. She handed Libby to George, and Libby twitched, her back legs bent like legs should never bend. So obviously in pain.

"Call 911!" said George.

"Georgie," Jenn said, coming toward him, both eyes on the dog.

Libby yelped again.

"Where's the nearest vet?" George said.

"Oh god, Libby," Dad said.

It was a Sunday. I grabbed my phone and googled. "There's a twenty-four-hour place on Kanner Highway," I said.

Fred stood close to George, desperate, staring. Dad stood frozen, shaking slightly. George opened the car door.

"I don't think . . ." said Jenn, looking down at Libby.

I called the number. Got a voicemail. *We are a family business. Have gone up north to escape the heat until after Labor Day.*

"You can't just fucking close down the emergency vet because you're hot!" George said.

I googled again, called three more places. None of them were open.

Libby kept twitching, legs still bent.

Jenn grabbed hold of Dad.

"George," Dad said, looking down at Libby.

"Fuck," George said.

"Georgie," Fred said, coming closer to him.

I thought briefly: Mom would know what to do.

"Let's take her to the hospital," George said.

I came toward him, shook my head. Those years with Brian, riding horses, I'd seen more than one animal put down. "She's not going to be okay," I said.

Libby quivered, jerked, and spasmed. Dad winced. George stared at all of us, like how could we not help her.

"I have that gun," Fred said, not looking at George.

Libby moaned like none of us had heard a dog moan, more human than animal, desperate, afraid, and we all looked at her, and Jenn said, "You have *what?*"

Fred ran into the house. We all walked slowly, shakily, Dad's hand on George's shoulder, around to the backyard, Jenn still close to him.

Dad looked at me. "Why does she have a gun?" he said.

I shook my head again. I didn't know.

Fred came back out, gun in her hand. Libby moaned again, and Fred cried more, and George looked back and forth between Dad and Libby's awkward, crooked legs.

"We can't help her, George," said Jenn.

"Put her down," I said to George.

"What the fuck?" George said.

"I'm so, so sorry," Fred said again to George.

Both of them, plus Dad, plus Jenn: all of them looked at me.

George set Libby down.

"Jude," Fred said.

I hardly remember the gun in my hand, but I took it from Fred. I straightened my arms out. I pulled the trigger gently, light and springy underneath my finger, and then one hard pull, the quick kickback; the gun went off; Libby was dead.

Dad grabbed George.

Fred stared at me.

"You fucking shot the dog," Jenn said.

I laughed, which was not the right response, but, really, what would have been the right response? "I fucking shot the dog," I said. I sat down on the chair next to Libby, put down the gun, and took a sip of George's drink.

At least twice, I saw Fred look up, no doubt for those vultures. She finally had some carrion. She let it stay a thought, unspoken, thank god. George wanted to bury Libby then and there, but Fred was out of the house at the end of the week.

"This is not something we need to figure out right now," Dad said. He'd stopped shaking, walked a lap around the pool, come back, his face sad and wet, now staying close to George.

George looked confused, flattened like that basketball Mom had flattened in the driveway with her van, and I grabbed his arm and knocked my head against his chest. "I'm so sorry, George. We couldn't leave her like that," I said.

Jenn found bleach and cleaned the red-brown splotches of blood out of the pool deck.

––––––

We didn't want to stay. Our nerves were jangled, frayed. Jenn and Fred wrapped Libby up and put her in the freezer (*We've been through fourteen hamsters*, Jenn said, *this is what you do*). While she was in there, Jenn grabbed the vodka from the freezer drawer. Dad requested the last bit of mint chip ice cream, his cake all melty, the letters smudgy, a few tiny splats of blood across the top.

"Let's go swimming," George said, wiping his eyes.

Fred looked defensive and then sorry, then relieved. "Okay," she said.

"We don't have towels," Jenn said.

"Jenn, shut up," Fred and I both said.

20

"You kids," Dad said, tears in his eyes but not wanting to show us, after Jenn drove all of us the six minutes to the ocean—George in the front seat for perhaps the first time ever; Dad between Fred and me in back. George and I helped Dad out of the car, Fred behind us still *so sorry*, Jenn rubbing her back. Dad let George wrap an arm around his waist as he hobbled up the boardwalk stairs and down onto the sand. George lay his own shirt in front of Dad for a not-sandy space to rest his cast.

"Did I ever tell you about the time the car I was in flipped?" Dad said.

We had all heard the story, but we let Dad tell it.

When he was in high school, he told us, as he had before, Dad had driven with friends the few minutes to the beach to surf and drink after work. Dad did cleanup, sometimes checkout, at the local grocery store. Most often he was responsible and careful, home early with food from work for his mom and sister, cleaning up after the cats and dogs, keeping the kitchen and the bathrooms clean. But that night, Dad was with three friends, two cases of Coors Light. They got very drunk after two hours surfing the disappointing Florida waves. None of them had eaten; all of them were wasted.

On the drive home, the car flipped. Dad was in the backseat. His friend swerved, caught the curb, the car bumped hard, then flew. No seat belts. Windows open and cool late evening breeze still off the ocean air. Dad felt himself give over to it, thought probably he'd die.

The car popped up, flipped, crashed down. Dad and each of his friends climbed out the open windows, all of them unscathed. They touched themselves, brushing arms and legs, chins and heads, in shock. *You good? What the fuck? You okay?* No phones. No cops. No other cars. Dad's friend's car was destroyed.

They walked home along the empty road, deep ditches filled with cakey mud. Each kid peeled off as they came upon their various parents' houses' streets. Dad had come into his mom's house no longer drunk, had looked in on his sister and his mom in the bed they shared, crawled into his own, and gone to sleep.

Jenn and I shared a quick glance; we hadn't heard that story since our own kids had become old enough to drive.

"You know, though," Dad said. We all looked at him. "For a long time, when you kids were little, and with your mom sometimes after you all left, I felt like maybe that car never really landed, like I was still up there floating somehow. In a matter of time, I was going to come crashing down. But that was fine, because you kids, your mom, this life we've had—it's felt like something I could not have fathomed fifty years ago, some dream I could not possibly have hoped to dream."

"I fucked up and I'm sorry," Fred said, coming up behind me. I looked around for George, but he was a hundred yards away, holding Dad up while Jenn tied an extra plastic bag around his cast.

"Do not ever," I said, but I didn't finish. I thought of that day, more than thirty years ago now: *We aren't* ever *coming back*; her tiny body tumbling down that bridge, the awful rawness of her scratches. Jenn had found the hydrogen peroxide, cotton balls, a tube of Neosporin, gone off again in search of George. Fred had sat down naked in the bathtub, and she had winced and shrieked as I had cleaned and wiped her cuts. I thought of walking home with her, her bouncing backpack, the rain pouring, the pedals of our bikes scratching at our calves, talking, laughing, soaking wet, eating both those Snickers bars, the stick and chew of caramel, melted chocolate on our fingers and our lips.

I didn't want to make her promise because I wanted still to love her.

"I won't," she said.

It felt close enough to true.

A whale conference! I thought, as Fred and I silently took off our clothes and went into the ocean. Fred crawled out farthest, and Dad stood a long time, just before the shore break, holding tight to George's shoulder. Jenn fastened a third plastic bag around his shoulder sling.

I couldn't look straight at him. I thought for the first long, conscious time about Mom. Our mom. My mom. Deborah Kenner. The way she wanted so much, tried so hard. *Judy, Judy, Judy*, she said on the phone the day I called to tell her I was leaving Brian. She was up two days later, in her suit and heels, telling each New York lawyer we met with that they best get me everything I asked for. *I don't want to fight him*, I said. *It's my job to protect you*, she said. And then, that time, lots of other times, she had.

"Hey Dad!" Fred said. "Come swimming."

Cast wrapped in plastic, collarbone still fractured: "He can't swim like this," George said.

"We could float him," Fred said.

"You would drown me," Dad said.

"Maybe," Fred said. "But maybe, if we don't, it could be fun?"

Dad looked at all of us, one after the other. "You kids . . ." he said.

"Come on, Dad," said George.

George made the first move: picked him up. Jenn walked behind them, making cautious, worried sounds as he got deeper in.

"Careful, Georgie," Fred said.

Dad looked tiny, his limbs gangly.

"Lean your head back," Fred said. She came up on the other side of Dad and nodded toward me to come closer once George had him deep enough that the water lolled up to his chest. *We're alive right now*, I heard Fred whisper to herself. George straightened his arms so Dad was flat before him.

Fred reached underneath Dad. "Come help, Jude," she said.

"You kids," Dad said again. "I've got this."

He straightened his limbs out, put his head back. We all stood back, held still.

THE END (added upon the request of Luli Strong who helped their mom with the ending)

ACKNOWLEDGMENTS

TK

ABOUT THE AUTHOR

TK